DEATH OF A WEDDING CAKE BAKER

A bell jingled as Hayley entered the bakery, but no one came out to greet her.

"Lisa?"

There was no answer.

"Lisa, it's me, Hayley. I've come to apologize."

Still no answer.

She scooted around the glass case full of tasty cakes and pies and cupcakes and poked her head through the door to the kitchen area that was divided by a bright print pink and white curtain.

"Lisa, are you here?"

There was a nagging feeling in the pit of her stomach and a little voice in her head that kept screaming to just get out of there and send her a conciliatory email. But Hayley Powell was never one to listen to any voices in her head. She just plowed ahead anyway.

As she entered the kitchen area, she suddenly knew why that little voice in her head had been screaming so loud.

Lisa was facedown, dead on the floor, her face buried in a smashed three-tier wedding cake, with a pair of small bride and groom figurines staring down at her from the drooping, melting top tier . . .

DEATH of a WEDDING CAKE BAKER

A Hayley Powell
Food and Cocktails Mystery

LEE HOLLIS

KENSINGTON BOOKS
KENSINGTON PUBLISHING CORP.
www.kensingtonbooks.com

Chapter 1

"I'd like to propose a toast," Hayley Powell announced, raising her fizzy glass of champagne.

The twelve other women in the room obediently lifted their flutes, all beaming and excited and aflutter. Hayley stood in the middle of a pile of discarded gift wrapping paper that littered the floor just in front of a mountain of wedding shower gifts that were piled high on top of an oak end table in the living room of this well-appointed, tastefully decorated, otherwise neat and tidy, immaculately kept home.

"To my BFF, Liddy Crawford, let me speak for everyone when I say our hearts are full of love for you today as you soon begin this new and exciting journey. As most of us already know and can attest to, marriage isn't always an easy road, but it can be the most rewarding trip of your life. As a famous writer once said, and forgive me, I can't for the life of me remember who exactly said it, but I'm sure it was someone famous, always remember,

'A successful marriage requires falling in love many times, always with the same person.' Here's to you, Liddy, and a long and bright future with Sonny!"

There were a lot of "ooohs" and "aaahs" before the roomful of women cheered and happily gulped down their champagne.

Not bad, Hayley thought.

The quote seemed to work.

She would probably regurgitate it when she gave the matron of honor toast that would be required at the actual wedding reception in a few weeks.

If only she could remember who had said it so she could give proper credit.

It was a woman.

Of that she was certain.

A journalist from the 1950s, or sometime around then.

Mary something?

No, it wasn't a common name.

It was something more exotic.

It didn't really matter.

Whoever said it was long dead and could hardly object to Hayley borrowing the quote for her own speech.

"What a lovely toast," Celeste, a very regal, proper, fashion-conscious, impeccably made-up older woman said, smiling at Hayley. Celeste was the mother of the bride and the host of today's wedding shower.

Mona Barnes, the third member of Hayley's close-knit trio, including herself and the bride-to-be, polished off the rest of her champagne and reached out for one of the bottles with some remaining bubbly to refill her glass. Mona, who mostly wore sweatshirts and blue jeans in her daily life, had made a halfhearted attempt to dress up for this frilly affair, at Hayley's urging. Although her slacks were unironed and her off-the-rack embroidered paisley top was a bit ill fitting, Hayley was proud of her for trying.

"Say, Liddy, what'd you have to do to get Sonny to go along with this whole circus?" Mona joked as she upended the bottle of champagne and emptied the rest of it into her flute. "Drug him?"

Celeste stiffened, appalled by the joke, but the bride, now used to Mona's peculiar sense of humor, took it all in stride.

"Yes, Mona, I have enough Ambien to keep Sonny sedated until well after the honeymoon," Liddy said.

Mona chuckled.

Hayley had to admit to herself that she had been somewhat surprised when Liddy posted photos of herself on Instagram and Facebook flashing an expensive-looking engagement ring while on a Hawaiian getaway with her boyfriend, the much-younger Sonny Lipton, a local lawyer in Bar Harbor. How on earth did she ever rope him into proposing? Frankly, not a lot of people thought their volatile relationship would last. A few mean-spirited gossips in town were quick to blame the free-flowing, potent mai tais at the all-inclusive Maui resort to explain why Sonny decided to pop the question. But Liddy insisted it was all

Sonny's idea, and she was quick to point out that the proposal involved rose petals on the bed, an expensive bottle of Dom Pérignon on ice, and a twenty-four-carat diamond ring at the bottom of her champagne glass. The entire evening was swoon-worthy, to say the least. And she had the pictures on her iPhone and on all of her social media accounts to prove it.

Still, there were a lot of skeptics who doubted Sonny possessed the kind of imagination to plan such a perfect proposal. Of course, that said, no one dared to publicly dispute Liddy's colorful version of events after the happy couple arrived home.

Although Sonny wanted a long and leisurely engagement, Liddy's mother was having none of it. Before the engagement was even announced on the happy couple's newly posted Facebook wedding page, Celeste was already pressuring them to set a date. Sonny, true to form, dragged his heels for a month or so before finally caving in, and a date in June was quickly set. Now, with only a few weeks to go before the big day, there were a lot of wedding details still to be worked out.

As matron of honor, Hayley was already overwhelmed with her own responsibilities of helping the bride plan the event, so the time crunch was only adding to her stress. But at least today she could enjoy a little bubbly and relish some diverting girl time with her close friends at Celeste's beautifully decorated seaside home in Hulls Cove, situated just outside of town.

The shower had been moving along swimmingly,

the gift-giving portion of the afternoon had been raucous and fun, Hayley's toast had luckily gone over well, and the bride-to-be looked radiant and happy. There had been one uncomfortable incident where Celeste caught Liddy's adopted black Lab dog, Poppyseed, or Poppy for short, chewing on her brand-new Oriental rug she had bought in a spice and textiles market on a recent trip to Istanbul, but overall, the gathering was on the verge of going down as a major success.

But that was before Celeste swallowed one glass of champagne too many, slammed her flute down on the coffee table, and slurred, "I still can't believe you refused to invite your cousin Lisa to your wedding shower!"

Hayley knew from the sour look on Liddy's face that the perfectly lovely afternoon was about to take a sharp turn toward Disaster Alley.

"I told you, Mother, I only wanted friends who love and support me at my shower, and we all know that Lisa despises me," Liddy said evenly. "And frankly, I can't stand *her*, so why should either of us pretend otherwise?"

"Because she's your cousin, she's part of the family, and she should be here!" Celeste spit out, nearly clocking the cheek of the young receptionist at the real estate office where Liddy worked with some flying saliva.

"I don't want to have this discussion right now, if that's okay with you, all right, Mother?"

"Fine," Celeste said, scowling as she grabbed the bottle of champagne from Mona and tried pouring some into her own glass before finally realizing it was empty.

She cast the bottle aside. "But I did promise her that she would be baking the wedding cake."

All the guests suddenly froze, and there was a staggeringly awkward silence.

Lisa Crawford, Liddy's first cousin from her father's side, owned a bakery in town. Although Lisa had a reputation for being difficult and ill-tempered, no one could dispute her talent as a master baker. She had honed her skills at dozens of restaurants and bakeries in Boston for years before finally moving back to Bar Harbor to open up her own shop. After one of her three-tier cakes had been prominently featured on a Food Network show called *Ridiculous Cakes*, and after she advertised that fact with a big window display, her business started booming, especially with tourists who loved the fact that they were frequenting a bakery that was, in their minds, famous for being on TV.

So Lisa's bakery, which was called Cake Walk, was a natural choice for many special events in Bar Harbor, such as weddings, birthdays, Super Bowl parties—you name it. However, Liddy had made it abundantly clear after her engagement became public that she would *not* be hiring Lisa to bake her wedding cake. The only problem was, Celeste rarely listened to a word Liddy had to say.

"Mother, how could you do that? I told you a dozen times I don't want that crude, awful ogre Lisa involved with my wedding in any capacity."

"Well, that's just nonsense. She's your cousin," Celeste said, glancing around the room for support.

She didn't get any.

All of the wedding shower guests sat frozen, as if petrified in suspended animation, like those poor residents of Pompeii after Mount Vesuvius blew up and covered everything in lava.

"I don't care that she's my cousin. She's mean and spiteful and she's not baking my cake," Liddy said, determined to stand up to her mother and not let her get her way this one time.

But as strong-willed and bullheaded as Liddy was, the undisputable fact was that she inherited those traits from her domineering mother.

And let's face it, Celeste was a force to be reckoned with, and one not easily defeated.

"I see," Celeste said quietly. "If you feel that way . . ."

"I do," Liddy quickly added.

"Then perhaps I should reconsider paying for the wedding."

Checkmate.

Hayley knew Liddy was cash-poor ever since a recent downturn in the local real estate market and too many weekend shopping sprees to New York. She was drowning in credit card debt and hadn't sold a house in months.

Celeste had magnanimously swooped in and insisted upon covering all expenses for the wedding, since it was, after all, traditionally the family of the bride's responsibility. If it were up to Sonny, they would just elope to Vegas, but neither mother nor daughter ever wanted to see that scenario unfold, so Liddy quickly accepted Celeste's kind and generous offer.

Celeste, sensing an opportunity for controlling her daughter's big day, whipped out her checkbook while promising the wedding would be a first-class affair. However, it was dangerously naive on Liddy's part to ever assume Celeste's generosity would not come with strings attached.

And those strings were finally coming into focus.

Liddy refused to acquiesce and humiliate herself in front of her wedding shower guests.

But Hayley knew the argument was over.

Celeste was going to get her way.

And like it or not, "that crude, awful ogre Lisa"—Liddy's words, not Hayley's—was going to design and bake Liddy Crawford's wedding cake.

Chapter 2

Hayley stood in the fitting room, mouth agape, as she stared at herself in front of the full-length mirror, marveling at just how horrendously ugly the matron of honor dress that was hanging off her was. When the store clerk first arrived carrying the dress on a hanger, Hayley had to bite her tongue, especially since Liddy seemed to like it. As Hayley took the dress from the clerk and headed into the fitting room to try it on, she just stared at the over-the-top design, aghast at the Pepto-Bismol pink color, the puffy sleeves, the frilly ruffles, and the smattering of tacky bows. It had to be the ugliest dress she had ever seen. And here she was trying it on for size. Her only hope was that it wouldn't look as bad when she wore it, but unfortunately, it looked even worse. Mona, whom Hayley could hear mumbling to herself in the next room, was given a similar dress as a bridesmaid, except in purple. Hayley didn't have to wait long to hear Mona's reaction to her own dress.

"Oh, no friggin' way am I wearing this! I look like Little Bo Peep!" Mona barked.

"Well, at least come out so I can see for myself, Mona," Liddy sighed.

Hayley heard the door to the adjoining fitting room fly open and bang against the wall as Mona shuffled out to model the bridesmaid dress.

"Oh, Mona, I think you look adorable," Liddy said.

"It's very flattering," the clerk echoed, singularly focused on just making a quick sale and commission.

"What are you talking about? You can see all my back fat!" Mona cried.

"Hayley, how does yours look?" Liddy asked, ignoring Mona.

"Uh . . . I'm really not sure . . ." Hayley said, attempting a bit of diplomacy before opening the door to the fitting room and stepping out.

Hayley could see Mona aggressively trying to adjust the dress so it fit her better, but having no success. Mona was right. She did look like Little Bo Peep, and so did Hayley.

Except in pink.

"I think they're lovely," Liddy said with a bright smile.

"Of course that's what you would say," Mona growled. "You're afraid we might upstage you by looking prettier than you at the wedding!"

"Mona, I'm afraid of many things, but trust me, I do not fear *you* upstaging me at my own wedding," Liddy said confidently.

"I would really like to look at a few more dresses if

you don't mind, Liddy," Hayley offered in a calm tone. "Maybe something a little more . . . understated?"

"Fine. I certainly don't want to force you to wear anything you're not comfortable in," Liddy huffed.

The clerk took her cue. "Let me see what else we have in the back."

She scurried off.

Mona didn't even bother going back inside the dressing room. She just shook off the dress right then and there and stood in front of them wearing just a bra and the ratty blue jeans she hadn't bothered taking off before slipping into the dress. "I'm rethinking this whole bridesmaid business, Liddy. Can't you find someone else to do this?"

"Absolutely not, Mona! You and Hayley are my best friends! You need to march down that aisle and stand beside me and show your support when I get married! I never ask you to do anything for me, and by God, this time, for once in your life, you are going to just suck it up and do it, do you hear me?"

Mona was taken aback, then nodded, surprisingly docile. After a long pause, she couldn't resist quietly asking, "Okay, but couldn't I do all that in a sweatshirt? I mean, not a ratty old sweatshirt with a dirty joke on the front like the ones I usually wear, but a nice, clean one I can pick up at Walmart?"

"Talk to her, Hayley," Liddy said.

"Mona, just be patient. We'll find dresses we're not embarrassed to wear, I promise," Hayley said.

"What do you mean, *embarrassed* to wear? You look so pretty in pink," Liddy said.

"Honestly, I don't feel pretty," Hayley confessed. "I feel like one of Cinderella's ugly stepsisters."

From behind her, Hayley heard the door to the dress shop open. "Oh, Hayley, you look absolutely enchanting in that dress, like a fairy princess!"

Hayley recognized the voice.

She spun around to see Sabrina Merryweather bounding toward them, looking stylish in a sleek black pantsuit, her brown hair tied back in a ponytail.

Sabrina was formerly the county coroner and a classmate of Hayley's from high school. They were never especially close back in the day, and once Sabrina founded her own clique, she froze Hayley out and treated her as persona non grata, like a true mean girl. Their friendship never quite recovered. But eventually, a decade and a half past those painful high school years, they did manage to reconnect and establish a professional working relationship as adults when Hayley gained a reputation as a local crime solver and relied on Sabrina's medical expertise in the course of her amateur sleuth investigations. But then Sabrina abruptly quit her position and moved out of town, and the two of them ultimately lost touch again.

So it was a surprise to see her blow so unexpectedly into the dress shop.

"Please tell me that's the dress you're going to wear as the maid of honor at the wedding!" Sabrina cooed.

"*Matron* of honor," Hayley corrected her.

"Oh, that's right. I forgot you were married once," Sabrina said, pretending not to be bitchy, but coming off as totally bitchy.

"Hayley hates the dress," Liddy said.

"I didn't say I hated it. I just think it's a bit much," Hayley lied.

"I think it's perfect!" Sabrina argued.

Of course she did.

Hayley knew the game she was playing. If the dress made Hayley look hideous, then Sabrina would insist it was the perfect choice.

"What is she doing here?" Mona asked loud enough for Sabrina to hear after retrieving her sweatshirt from the fitting room and shimmying into it.

"Sabrina's my second bridesmaid," Liddy whispered, almost as if she hoped Hayley wouldn't hear her.

But Hayley heard every word and couldn't help but blurt out, "What?"

"Every bride needs a maid of honor, excuse me, matron of honor, and at least two bridesmaids," Liddy said. "Sabrina has generously agreed to be one of my bridesmaids. Isn't that sweet of her?"

Hayley and, most shockingly, Mona were both rendered speechless.

The clerk returned with an unexpectedly tasteful cream-colored, sleeveless dress that Hayley actually liked, but before she could reach out and take it to try on, Sabrina snatched it out of the clerk's hand.

"Oh, this is gorgeous! I'll try this one on!"

And then she sashayed into Hayley's fitting room and slammed the door shut.

"I am so over this," Mona snarled before pounding out of the shop.

Hayley marched over to Liddy and murmured in her ear so Sabrina could not hear her, "Sabrina Merryweather? Really?"

"I know," Liddy whispered. "It's an unexpected choice."

"Unexpected?" Hayley said, a bit too loud.

Liddy gestured with her hands for Hayley to lower her voice. "Look, I'm aware I've spent years despising her with every fiber of my being. But let's face it, Hayley, other than you and Mona, I don't have a lot of close friends, and my mother insisted I have two bridesmaids, which is what she had at her own wedding. I'm already on thin ice with her for not wanting Lisa to bake the cake. So when Sabrina saw on Facebook that I was getting married and reached out to me to offer her congratulations, I thought that was so sweet, and I was honestly touched by the gesture. We started sending messages back and forth, and she seemed so interested in the wedding, and the next thing I knew, I was asking her to be a bridesmaid."

Hayley understood the pressure Liddy was under.

As much as Liddy might fall under the category of a bridezilla, Celeste was perfectly suited for the role of overbearing, controlling mother of the bridezilla. The best course of action was to just appease her as much as was humanly possible.

But Sabrina Merryweather?

Hayley seriously wanted to give her the benefit of the doubt. Maybe Sabrina had mellowed now that she was older and no longer in a position of power. Besides, Hayley's job as matron of honor was to make sure the bride remained calm and was not subjected to any undue stress.

So she vowed to herself at that moment to make this unexpected arrangement work.

Sabrina was now going to be a part of the wedding party.

For better or for worse.

Sabrina sailed out of the fitting room, looking ravishing in the cream-colored number that accentuated every curve of her well-rounded, toned body. "What do you think? I think it could work. It's very understated. The last thing in the world I would want to do is outshine the maid of honor— wait, sorry, *matron* of honor."

Hayley stared at her glumly. "You look beautiful."

That was going to be her dress, and now it belonged to Sabrina, and she looked stunning wearing it.

And Hayley, in her pink frilly assemblage, felt as if she had just walked off the pages of a Mother Goose nursery rhyme. There were other dresses in the store, but Hayley's heart sank because she knew this was the one the bride-to-be wanted her to wear. She was stuck with it.

Chapter 3

When Hayley arrived at her brother Randy's bar Drinks Like a Fish after the dress fitting, she found her *Island Times* coworker and current boyfriend Bruce Linney sitting on top of a stool, drinking a beer, engaged in a very intense discussion with Randy, who stood behind the bar, nodding. On the other side of Bruce, Randy's husband, police chief Sergio Alvares, was out of uniform and off duty, enjoying a straight bourbon. They all appeared to be in a jocular mood.

Sergio spotted Hayley coming through the door first and gave her a wink as she sidled up next to Bruce to steal a sweet peck on the cheek.

Bruce turned and smiled at her. "Oh, good, you're here. I've been telling these guys you'd agree with me."

"About what?" Hayley asked, nodding to Randy, who was trained to fetch Hayley her usual happy hour cocktail, a Jack and Coke, so off he went.

"How long Liddy's marriage is going to last. Now

Randy says it'll be over in two years, and personally I think he's being *way* too optimistic, right? I mean, you've known Liddy since you two were kids. I say the whole thing blows up in six months, nine months maximum. You're on my side, right?"

Hayley's mouth dropped open. She couldn't believe what she was hearing. "Are you serious?"

"Of course I'm serious. I got twenty bucks riding on this," Bruce said matter-of-factly, taking a generous chug of his draft beer.

"You guys are betting on how long Liddy's marriage is going to last?" Hayley asked incredulously.

Sergio leaned forward and smiled. "Liddy hates to admit when she's wrong, so I think she will hang in there and try to make it work as long as she can. You know, try to make it through at least their first wedding anniversary to make a point. But after that, I see the whole thing sliding right into divorce court, so I'm betting a year and a half tops."

"This is unbelievable. I've never heard anything so cynical in my life," Hayley said as Randy returned with her drink and slid it across the bar in front of her.

"Well, how long do *you* think it's going to last?" Randy asked.

"I'm hoping forever—like the vow says, till death do them part!" Hayley declared.

They all laughed.

"No, honey, be serious, really, how long do you give the marriage?" Bruce asked.

Michelle, Randy's bartender and manager, sailed past them on her way to the kitchen. "I say they crash and burn on the honeymoon."

More laughter.

Except from Hayley.

She took a deep breath and tried to remain calm. "I am not going to participate in this discussion. I think you're all being incredibly callous and insensitive. Liddy is one of my best friends. She has finally found the happiness she so richly deserves, and here you all are treating the whole thing like some joke."

"Don't be mad, Hayley, we're just having a little fun. Everyone in town's doing it," Randy said.

"I'm not," Hayley said, pushing the untouched Jack and Coke back over to Randy. "I don't want this anymore. I'm going home."

And then she stormed out the door, jumped into her Kia Sportage, and roared away.

Hayley seethed with anger the whole drive home.

She knew in her gut Liddy and Sonny's marriage would surely have its challenges, given their age difference, but having observed their on-again, off-again romance over the last couple of years, Hayley clearly saw the genuine affection the couple shared for each other. In her mind, their marriage had just as many chances of working as anyone else's. It bothered her that anyone, especially those closest to her, like her boyfriend and her brother and her brother-in-law, not to mention Michelle the bartender, was belittling this pivotal, joyous event that meant so much to Liddy. If poor Liddy ever heard what they were saying at the bar, how derisive they were being, she would be hurt and devastated.

When Hayley pulled into the driveway, she saw

her children, Gemma and Dustin, in the kitchen window, having an intense conversation. Both were adults and living on their own now, Gemma in New York City and Dustin at a visual arts school in California, but she was thrilled when both of them had agreed to come home to Maine for the summer wedding.

Hayley was still steaming when she slammed through the back door, but as her dog, Leroy, happily raced to greet her and her kids welcomed her with big smiles, she felt the tension in her stiff neck finally start to melt away.

"What smells so good?" Hayley asked.

"I'm making chili-rubbed steak tacos," Gemma said. "I hope you're hungry. Is Bruce going to join us for dinner?"

"Not if I can help it," Hayley found herself saying.

"Uh-oh, trouble in paradise?" Dustin asked.

"No, he just ticked me off when I went to meet him for a drink after the dress fitting. Can you believe he said—?"

"By the way, Uncle Randy called just before you got home," Gemma said as she mashed some avocados in a mixing bowl with a fork to make guacamole.

"What did *he* have to say?" Hayley asked, folding her arms.

"He said he was sorry, and you were right to be mad at him for only giving Liddy and Sonny's marriage a year and a half before it falls apart," Gemma said absentmindedly as she concentrated on preparing the perfect guacamole for her tacos.

"I can't believe he said that," Dustin remarked, shaking his head.

Hayley beamed with pride. At least her kids understood how cruel and hard-hearted people—her own flesh and blood—could be!

Dustin chuckled. "A whole year and a half? Wow, what was he thinking? We all know it'll be over in a few months."

"Six," Gemma said, chopping cilantro. "I say six months."

"Whoa, that's way too long! How much do you want to bet?" Dustin asked.

Hayley threw her hands up. "My God, am I the only optimistic person left in this whole town?"

Her children stared at her blankly, and Hayley finally gave up and marched out of the room, refusing to backslide in her belief that this improbable marriage could work, and praying Liddy and Sonny would have the mettle and resolve and love to prove her right.

But deep down inside, Hayley wrestled with a nagging fear that, in the end, she might be the one who was proven dead wrong, that the skeptics would prevail, and the marriage would be a disaster from the start, maybe before any rings were exchanged, before the bride and groom even had a chance to say their "I do's."

She had no idea at the time just how prophetic her feelings would turn out to be.

Chapter 4

Hayley quietly picked at her prosciutto-wrapped chicken Florentine with lemon butter sauce and glanced at Bruce, who was busily cutting into his grilled filet mignon of Black Angus beef while Liddy and Sonny, both ignoring their Maine lobster pies, argued at the table at the Bar Harbor Inn's restaurant, the Reading Room. This was only the second double date Hayley and Bruce had been on with the couple since they had announced their engagement, and also the second time the evening had dissolved into a barrage of incessant bickering.

"I just thought you'd be more involved," Liddy snapped before picking up her glass of chardonnay and taking a healthy swig.

"Of course I'm involved! I'm the guy you're marrying," Sonny growled, both embarrassed and annoyed that they were having this conversation in front of Hayley and Bruce.

"You haven't expressed any interest in planning

the details," Liddy said. "You've left everything for me to decide."

"That's because you're a type A control freak," Sonny muttered before catching himself and quickly adding, "which is what I love most about you."

"Have you even bothered to be fitted for your tux yet?" Liddy asked.

Sonny sighed. "I have an appointment next week."

"And will you come with me and Hayley to pick out the cake at that stupid, awful ogre Lisa's bakery tomorrow?"

"I can't, honey," Sonny said. "I have to be in court."

"You're always in court!" Liddy wailed.

"I'm a lawyer! That's what we do! We go to court! Look, sweetheart, we shouldn't be doing this in front of Hayley and Bruce," Sonny said.

"It's nothing we haven't seen before," Bruce laughed.

Hayley shot Bruce a look stern enough that he shut up and went back to cutting his steak.

"We're supposed to be having a good time tonight, not arguing about the wedding. Can we put a pin in this for now and discuss it later?"

"You're always putting a pin in it, Sonny, and we *never* discuss it later," Liddy groaned.

Liddy did have a point. Most grooms would do anything to get out of participating in the wedding preparations, leaving all the decisions to the bride and her mother, but Sonny's utter lack of interest from the very beginning had sent up a red flag in Hayley's mind. Sonny wasn't even going through the motions of pretending to care about the invitations, the flowers, the menu, the dress, the cake, or anything, and Hayley feared he might be coming down with a case of cold feet. They were all barreling full steam ahead toward the big day, and it was getting harder for everyone, especially the bride-to-be, to ignore the groom's obvious lack of enthusiasm.

Sonny tried changing the subject. "How's your steak, Bruce?"

"Delicious," Bruce said with his mouth full.

"Bruce, if you were the one getting married, wouldn't you at least want to know about *some* of the wedding details?" Liddy asked.

Bruce gave a noncommittal shrug. "Maybe, I don't know. I've never come close to getting married."

Liddy, unsatisfied with Bruce's answer, turned back to Sonny. "I went to the wedding website today, and not one member of your family has RSVP'd for the ceremony or reception."

Sonny shrugged.

"Doesn't that strike you as odd?" Liddy said, looking around the table, hoping to garner some support from Hayley and Bruce.

She didn't get any response, so she turned to the young, cheery waitress, who was refilling Liddy's wineglass with an open bottle she had picked up from the ice bucket next to the table.

"What about you? Don't you think it's odd?"

The waitress clutched the bottle of chardonnay, eyes wide open, like a deer caught in headlights, suddenly nervous about being dragged into any customer drama. "A little."

Then she dropped the bottle back into the ice bucket and scurried away.

"See, even the waitress agrees with me," Liddy said.

Sonny finally dug into his lobster pie, and everyone ate in silence for a few moments, except for their clinking silverware.

"It's just very odd," Liddy said, feeling the need to reiterate her point.

Sonny set his fork down. "Listen, I've told you a dozen times I'm not that close to my family. In fact, I'm barely on speaking terms with any of them, so it really shouldn't come as a surprise to you that I didn't invite them to the wedding."

"You didn't invite them?" Liddy gasped. "But I gave you a stack of invitations that were addressed and stamped! You said you would mail them!"

"I don't see any reason why those people should be a part of my wedding day when they've been miserable to me my whole life."

"You *lied* to me," Liddy whispered.

"I didn't lie to you. I changed my mind."

"And you didn't tell me!"

"That's not lying," Sonny mumbled.

"I think it is."

"What do you think is in this demi-glace?" Bruce interjected as he chewed on a piece of his steak.

"I don't know, but you have to try this Parmesan basil risotto," Hayley said, scooping some onto her fork and feeding Bruce.

"Man, you're right," Bruce said after swallowing. "De-lish."

Liddy and Sonny got the hint and stopped quarreling.

The happy couple valiantly attempted some small talk about the weather, and implored Hayley and Bruce to spill any good gossip they had heard at the *Island Times*, but mostly there was an uneasy awkwardness that permeated the rest of the meal.

When the jittery waitress arrived to clear the plates and asked if anyone was interested in seeing a dessert menu, Hayley and Bruce quickly interjected.

"None for me, thank you," Hayley said.

"No, just the check, please," Bruce almost begged as he handed the waitress his credit card without even waiting to see how much the bill was.

"You don't have to pay for us," Liddy said.

"No, I want to, this is my treat," Bruce said, anxious for this whole evening to come to a merciful end.

"Thanks, Bruce," Sonny said.

"Yes, thank you," Liddy said.

They both knew not to casually suggest they all stop by Randy's bar for a quick nightcap, because it was painfully obvious Hayley and Bruce just wanted to get out of there and go home.

"This was fun," Hayley lied.

Another long, awkward silence.

As the waitress returned with the bill and Bruce's card and he frantically added a tip and scribbled his signature, Hayley glanced over at Liddy, who was trying with all her might to maintain a calm and pleasant demeanor.

But Hayley had known Liddy for far too long not to know she was dying inside. She was obviously shaken by the news that Sonny had decided not to include any of his family in their wedding day. And although it was perfectly reasonable to accept that Sonny was estranged from his relatives and had every right not to invite them, Hayley had a strong suspicion that there was more to the story than he was willing to share.

She just hoped that whatever it was wouldn't spoil Liddy's promising future as Mrs. Sonny Lipton.

Chapter 5

"You're a scheming, amoral traitor and you should be ashamed of yourself!" Lisa Crawford bellowed as Hayley, Liddy, and Celeste entered the Cake Walk bakery. The three of them nearly collided with one another in the doorway as they all suddenly stopped at the sound of vehement shouting.

Standing next to Lisa behind the counter was the object of her verbal abuse, Helen Fennow, a petite, wispy young woman with long brown hair and a perplexed look on her pretty, heart-shaped face. She was wearing a pink T-shirt with the Cake Walk logo and blue jeans. Helen had been Lisa's loyal baking assistant for the last five years. However, as of this morning, that had all apparently changed.

"Lisa, I've been up front with you for months that I was thinking about striking out on my own . . ." Helen stammered.

"Is this a bad time?" Celeste asked.

Lisa ignored her. Her round, plain face was a deep, scarlet red and there were traces of white flour in her curly, short hair as she pushed her way up close to Helen's face, pointing a pudgy finger at the tip of Helen's cute button nose. "I never thought you were serious! Let's face it, you've always been lazy, and I never saw a hint of actual motivation, so why on earth would I believe you? I trained you, nurtured you, taught you everything you know . . . This is such a betrayal!"

"I think there's enough room in town for two successful bakeries, don't you?" Helen asked hopefully.

"You think so? Well, I don't, Helen. And I promise you, I will make it my personal mission to see that your sad little experiment of opening your own place will lose so much money you'll be tied up in bankruptcy court for years!"

"We can come back another time when it's more convenient," Celeste whispered, starting to back out of the store.

But Hayley and Liddy didn't move.

They were too riveted to the cake war showdown.

Lisa was so incensed and focused on poor Helen, she either didn't hear them or was willfully ignoring them.

Helen was now shaking as Lisa angrily and threateningly invaded her personal space.

"Lisa, if you would just calm down, we can talk about this and maybe not ruin our friendship."

"*Friendship?* That was off the table the second you decided to stab me in the back!"

"You know that's not true . . ." Helen said quietly, backing away from Lisa's bulky frame until she found herself up against an open window, ready to jump through it if the situation escalated any further.

Luckily they were on the ground floor.

But Lisa finally turned her back on Helen and marched around the counter to where a trayful of freshly baked cupcakes was waiting to be set out in the glass case for her customers to buy. "I'm done with you. Get out of my shop."

"Lisa, please . . ." Helen pleaded.

"I said get out of here!" Lisa screamed, picking up one of the cupcakes and hurling it at Helen, who managed to duck in time. The cupcake landed on the window behind her with a splat.

Helen was so stunned she just stood frozen in place, unable to move.

Lisa snatched another cupcake and fired it at her, but her aim was widely off this time, and it hit the wall. Chunks of vanilla frosting flew in all different directions, a few bits winding up in Liddy's hair before she could move out of the way.

"Go! I never want to see your sniveling, conniving face in here ever again, do you hear me?" Lisa snarled as she grabbed another cupcake and raised it above her head, threatening to attempt to nail her again.

Helen nodded, speechless, then scurried past Hayley, Liddy, and Celeste in a flood of tears and disappeared out the door.

Lisa set down the cupcake on the counter, took a deep breath, and exhaled. Then she lifted up the bottom half of her stained white apron and fanned her face, trying to calm herself down.

Hayley, Liddy, and Celeste still stood awkwardly in the doorway, none fully committed to coming all the way inside the shop yet.

When Lisa got herself nearly back down to a resting heart rate, she was finally able to become aware of her surroundings again, and that's when she noticed she had some waiting customers.

"Aunt Celeste, what are you doing here?" Lisa asked with a half smile, as if Hayley and Liddy were not even present.

"Uh, didn't we have an appointment today?" Celeste asked, suddenly worried she had confused the date and time.

"Maybe. I rarely write anything down. Don't just stand there. Come in," Lisa barked, annoyed they were all still crowded by the door, blocking potential customers from entering.

Celeste pushed Hayley and Liddy ahead of her and closed the door behind her as Lisa discarded her apron and walked back around the glass counter to greet them, feeling no need to even mention the loud screaming fit they had all just witnessed.

"So what can I do for you today?" Lisa asked.

Celeste stared at her blankly. "We're here to talk about Liddy's wedding cake. You agreed to design it."

"The wedding cake," Lisa said, a light bulb appearing to go off in her head. "Is that still happening?"

"Yes, it is!" Liddy snapped.

"Okay, congratulations," Lisa remarked, nodding,

a surprised look on her face. "Good for you, Liddy. I guess there's hope for everyone."

Liddy looked as if she was going to lunge at Lisa, but Hayley quickly grabbed Liddy by the hand and squeezed it tight, keeping her firmly in place.

"So what were you thinking?" Lisa asked, already bored.

"I sent you an email with my ideas. Didn't you get it?" Liddy asked.

"Maybe it went to my junk folder. Who knows? I rarely read my email anyway," Lisa said.

"I see," Liddy said tightly, tossing her mother an irritated look that said, *This is all your fault.*

Hayley jumped in. "Liddy loves angel food cake, and she's always wanted something classic, a traditional three-tier—"

"Yes, perhaps with a sweet buttercream frosting and maybe with a frilled, smooth finish to give it a polished look," Celeste said.

"And definitely sprinkles of vanilla bean or a textured piping!" Liddy added before gasping excitedly as another thought popped into her head. "What about a delicate adornment of sugar ruffles?"

Lisa took this all in, churning it over in her mind. There was an unbearable silence as they watched her nod and think, playing the role of creative genius, coming up with just the right idea before speaking.

"Pistachios," Lisa whispered.

"What was that?" Celeste asked.

"I think she said 'pistachios,'" Hayley offered.

"A Sicilian pistachio cake with lemon syrup and

white chocolate ganache," Lisa said, arms up, hands out, trying to get them to picture it in their minds.

"I'm allergic to nuts," Liddy said.

"The wedding cake should be about the guests enjoying it, not the bride and groom," Lisa said, shaking her head at Liddy as if she had just said the most stupid, ridiculous thing in the world.

"The wedding cake should absolutely be about the bride and groom! Especially since we'll both be feeding each other a piece at the reception."

"Do couples still do that? It's so old-fashioned," Lisa sneered.

"But that's what I want, an old-fashioned wedding!" Liddy roared. "With an old-fashioned wedding cake!"

"Darling, what does it matter? Your dress will probably be so tight you won't even be able to eat the cake!" Celeste said, trying to defuse the tension.

Liddy's nostrils flared. "Is it too much to ask for a wedding cake with no pistachios? I'd really like to make it through my wedding day without going into anaphylactic shock!"

Lisa sighed. "Fine. No pistachios. I did do this fabulous peanut butter pumpkin wedding cake for a couple from Millinocket, which went over really big—"

"*All* nuts! I'm allergic to *all* nuts!" Liddy screamed.

"Liddy, for the love of God, calm down. I'm just spitballing ideas, that's all," Lisa said, almost enjoying how much she had upset her high-strung cousin. "Seriously, if you are this stressed out about the wedding, are you sure you're ready for an entire *marriage*?"

Liddy seemed to be resisting the urge to attack, especially since Hayley was still gripping her hand with all her might.

"Yes, Lisa," Liddy seethed. "I'm ready. I just need a cake that's not going to kill me. Do you think you can help with that?"

"That's what I'm here for." Lisa shrugged as if she was simply an innocent party to Liddy's wildly erratic mood swings.

They spent a better part of the next hour throwing around more thoughts, with Liddy continually circling back around to her initial idea of a three-tier angel food cake with buttercream frosting. But Lisa resisted, feeling it wasn't creatively inspired enough to showcase her talent, oblivious to the fact that Liddy's wedding day was actually about Liddy and not about Lisa's talents as a baker.

Finally, Hayley ended the meeting by explaining that she had to get to the office and file a column. Lisa promised to make a few different samples for them and told them to come by the bakery again in a few days to try them.

Once they were out the front door and hustling down the sidewalk, Liddy tried one more time to appeal to her mother's reasoning.

"She's already causing trouble, Mother. I think we should cut our losses and find someone else to make the cake. You heard Helen Fennow. She's opening her own shop, and she's just as skillful a baker as that stupid, awful ogre Lisa!"

But Celeste stood firm. "Lisa is your cousin, she's family, and we are not going to fire family. And stop calling her mean names."

Liddy whined a bit more, but she knew in her heart it was a losing battle.

As long as her mother was springing for the wedding, including the cake, Liddy was never going to be in any sort of power position.

Celeste rocketed ahead of them, not wanting to discuss the matter any further.

"You can always just elope," Hayley suggested softly.

"Sonny would love that," Liddy said. "But I've dreamed of this day my entire life, and come hell or high water, it's going to be perfect!"

Hayley didn't need a crystal ball to know that with the way things were going, a perfect wedding was not going to be a safe prediction.

But what she didn't know, or couldn't know, was just how bad things were about to get.

Island Food & Cocktails
BY HAYLEY POWELL

Recently I attended my best friend Liddy's wedding shower, where the champagne was flowing and the beautifully decorated tables were piled high with delicious sweet treats and finger sandwiches. Of course, I had to try one of everything, and in the case of the bride-to-be's grandmother Dolly's walnut-filled horns, more than one. Truth be told, when the shower was over and I noticed a few horns left on a plate, I surreptitiously wrapped them in a napkin and stuffed them in my purse to munch on later that evening. I didn't think Liddy would mind since she was allergic to nuts, after all. Dolly also knew about her granddaughter's nut allergy, but still made her horns for the shower because in her words, "A bride-to-be shouldn't be scarfing down sweets before the wedding anyway!"

I hadn't been home more than twenty minutes when I remembered the horns in my purse and decided it was time for a snack, along with one of my favorite indulgences—a chocolate white Russian. As I gorged on my stash, I replayed the lovely afternoon over again in my mind, remembering how Liddy's mother Celeste had gone all out with the fancy food, opulent decorations, and flowers, which, unfortunately, was the exact opposite of how my own mother handled my one and only wedding over twenty years ago!

Back then, my ex-husband, Danny, and I were hopelessly in love, planning our future together, swept up in all the romance, our hopes and dreams. Yes, I know what you cynics are thinking, but we were just kids! Anyway, we decided we would get married by the end of the summer in my mother's beautiful, lush backyard garden with its white trellis and sea of flowers, with all of our friends and family in attendance. And as a bonus, it would be a lot cheaper than a large church wedding and having to rent a reception hall. Romantic and practical! Mom would be so proud.

But sadly, she wasn't. When Danny and I sat her down and presented her with our plan, expecting joyous tears and shouts of happiness, we got one word when we were finished.

"No."

And then she got up and calmly walked right out of the room.

Danny and I were shell-shocked. This was not at all what we were expecting. Maybe she just needed time for all of it to sink in, so I sent my fiancé home, assuring him I was certain Mom would come around later that evening once she thought about it.

But she didn't.

That was mid-June, and after a couple of weeks of begging, pleading, crying, desperately trying to convince her just how much in love we were, and how right this was for us, she still stubbornly refused to give us her blessing.

Or her backyard.

She threw all the usual arguments at us. We were too young. We needed to get our lives together first. We should wait at least a couple of years and then see.

I fought back, explaining how I knew with every fiber of my being that Danny was the one, and that I wanted to be with him forever, till death do us part.

Okay, I can hear you cynics laughing, so try to keep it down until I get through my story.

By August, Danny and I forged ahead with our wedding plans, which included booking a justice of the peace, accepting my BFF Mona's kind offer to supply lobsters for the reception, recruiting my other BFF, Liddy, to be in charge of the cake, Danny reserving a couple of kegs of beer, and all the invited guests volunteering to bring covered dishes.

The only thing we still lacked was a location.

I secretly prayed my mother would have a last-minute change of heart.

But she didn't.

She never even discussed the wedding, and when Danny would occasionally stop by the house, desperately trying to charm her with compliments— like how she could be my sister—my mother would just shake her head and mutter under her breath, "Well, I see the apple doesn't fall far from the tree."

That was my first clue that something else was going on here.

With only two days left before the big day, it looked like my own mother was actually going to blow off her only daughter's wedding.

Danny's uncle Otis and aunt Tori finally came to our rescue. They kindly offered to let us get married in their smaller, but well-kept, backyard in Tremont. We gratefully accepted. Tori could not hide her surprise that Danny was getting hitched. He had always been a bit of a Don Juan, just like his uncle Otis back in the day, before Otis grew a long, scraggly beard and adopted a rather unkempt appearance.

That's when it hit me.

I raced home and found my mother's high school yearbook on a shelf in the living room. I remembered reading something years ago, and asking my mother about it, but she brushed me off and said it was nothing.

I found the page I was looking for. Next to his picture, a boy had written, "I love you with all my heart, Sheila, and I know we will be together for-ever and ever. What we have is more special than what anyone else could ever have. Love always, O."

The boy looked eerily familiar.

A fresh-faced, scrubbed-clean kid who years later would turn into a crotchety, long-bearded, dirt-smudged back-sider.

O.

Otis.

The mystery of my mother's strange behavior was finally solved. Otis had eventually broken her heart, and she was simply trying to prevent the same fate befalling her daughter.

I left the book open and out on the coffee table and went to bed.

My mother never mentioned the yearbook the next morning, but I knew she had seen it, because over breakfast she casually said, "If you and Danny are going to have a wedding in my backyard, we had better start getting it ready."

I jumped up to call Danny and deliver the good news, but first stopped, leaned down, and gave my mother a warm kiss on the cheek, whispering in her ear, "Thank you."

I never found out exactly what had finally changed her mind, but I presumed she had seen the yearbook. Perhaps it brought back a few happy memories from her youth, and maybe she thought, "It may not have worked out for us, but Hayley and Danny are not me and Otis. They should have the chance to write their own destiny." Or maybe she just thought, "If I don't let her get married in my backyard, I'm never going to hear the end of it."

I didn't care in the end which version was the truth. The fact was, I had my mother's blessing.

The day of our wedding finally arrived, and everything went off without a hitch. It was perfect. I just wish the marriage had been. As it turned out, I should have listened to my mother.

But on that day, life was so full of promise. And I remember Mom decided it was a good time to bury the hatchet with Otis (at least it wasn't in him), since they were going to become a part of the same family. I watched them laughing and talking, recalling shared memories from their younger days, as they happily shared a dance, cheek to cheek, on our perfect wedding day.

CHOCOLATE WHITE RUSSIAN

Ice
½ ounce chocolate syrup
1 ounce vodka
1 ounce Kahlúa
2 ounces heavy cream

Fill a rocks glass with ice. Drizzle your chocolate syrup over the ice.

Add your vodka, Kahlúa, and heavy cream and stir.

Sip and fully enjoy this heavenly cocktail. If you're anything like me, I tend to go over the top and enjoy mine with a small plate of assorted chocolates on the side. Cheers!

GRANDMA DOLLY'S WALNUT-FILLED HORNS

DOUGH
One 8-ounce package softened cream cheese
1¼ cups real butter, softened
2 egg yolks
1 entire egg
1 teaspoon vanilla
3½ cups flour

In a stand mixer, add your cream cheese, butter, egg yolks, and one entire egg and mix until well combined.

Add your vanilla and mix in.

With the mixer on low, slowly add in your flour until well combined.

Using a small scoop or spoon, scoop and roll your dough into 2-ounce balls about the size of walnuts and place on parchment paper–lined cookie sheets two inches apart. When finished rolling the balls, place them in the refrigerator and chill for two hours.

While they are chilling, prepare your filling.

FILLING
3 cups ground walnuts
3 egg whites, partially beaten
1½ cups sugar
2 teaspoons vanilla

In a stand mixer or bowl, mix together all of the above ingredients.

Preheat your oven to 350°F.

When your dough is chilled, remove from fridge. Take a ball and, with a rolling pin, roll flat. Add a tablespoon of filling in the middle of the circle. Fold over one side and seal with your finger to make a half moon or horn shape, then place back on parchment-lined baking sheet. Continue to do the same with the rest of the balls.

Bake for 15 minutes or until a nice golden brown. Remove from oven and enjoy!

Chapter 6

Hayley gawked at Sabrina, who sat on her couch across from her with a handful of brochures, certain she had not heard right. "I'm sorry, where did you say?"

"Napa Valley—wine country, in California," Sabrina answered, a bright, enthusiastic smile on her face.

"You want to go all the way across the country for Liddy's bachelorette party?" Hayley asked.

"Liddy loves wine, and I thought we could do a whole tour of the vineyards. Plus I found the perfect place where we can stay. It's a lovely B and B with its own spa in Calistoga for only five hundred a night," Sabrina cooed, excitedly flipping through one of her brochures.

"How much?" Hayley gasped.

"Five hundred. But that's for the whole suite, which the three of us would split."

"Plus airfare, plus the car rental, plus meals," Hayley said, quickly adding everything up in her head.

Mona, who sat in the recliner adjacent to Hayley,

mumbled something unintelligible under her breath, but Hayley assumed it was not a ringing endorsement for Sabrina's self-described "out-of-the-box idea" for Liddy's bachelorette party.

Sabrina noticed the utter lack of enthusiasm and grimaced. "Well, if it's too expensive, we can just do something else. I also found a vacation package for four days, three nights, in Las Vegas, a suite at the Bellagio, tickets to the latest Cirque du Soleil show, airfare included, for only fifteen hundred a person."

Hayley gulped.

Mona snickered. She knew Sabrina was fighting a losing battle. There was no way they would ever pull the trigger on one of these costly excursions.

Sabrina sighed and, disappointed, set the Vegas brochure down on the coffee table. "Or we could find another option."

She riffled through the stack of brochures, stopping at one. She stared at it longingly and sighed. "So I guess the five-day cruise to the Bahamas is out of the question."

"Good guess," Mona barked, folding her arms and throwing an annoyed look Hayley's way.

Did they really have to sit here and indulge Sabrina like this?

Neither Hayley nor Mona could still quite grasp the concept that Sabrina Merryweather, whom Liddy had spent years trash talking, was now a vital and integral player in the wedding party.

"Okay then, maybe one of you has an idea. Mona?"

Sabrina asked tentatively, almost afraid to hear the answer.

"Well, as a matter of fact, I do," Mona said, nodding. "I say we pick up a keg of beer and some lobster rolls and have the whole party in my backyard."

Hayley perked up at Mona's suggestion.

She felt terrible that her financial situation was too tight to be able to afford one of Sabrina's staggeringly expensive packaged tours. After all, if she had the money, she wouldn't think twice about throwing Liddy a first-class bachelorette party in some exciting destination, but unfortunately that wasn't her current reality. And although Sabrina was gung ho about the wine tours and the Vegas shows and Caribbean cruises, she wasn't exactly offering to spring for the cost of everyone. Ever since she quit her job as Hancock County's coroner, she had not been bringing home a steady paycheck.

No, the more Hayley thought about it, the more Mona's low-key party with close friends, and maybe a potluck theme with everyone bringing their own dishes, might be the best way to go.

And although Liddy Crawford had rarified tastes when it came to shopping and dining and decorating, unlike Sabrina, she was also the type of woman who could appreciate and enjoy a laid-back afternoon in Mona's backyard with a bunch of her favorite girlfriends, pounding down a keg of beer, gorging on Mona's locally famous lobster rolls, and just hanging out telling stories and sharing laughs.

Sabrina stared at Hayley, waiting patiently to hear her opinion.

"I think Mona's idea sounds fun!" Hayley finally said.

Sabrina frowned, not a professional when it came to hiding her feelings, knew she was outvoted and gracefully backed down. "Let's go with beer and lobster rolls in Mona's backyard, then."

Dustin suddenly blew into the room, a ball of pent-up energy. "Mom, I need your credit card!"

"What for?" Hayley asked, startled.

"I need to put a down payment on the photography studio I'm renting tomorrow. I'll pay you back just as soon as Liddy writes me a check."

Celeste was in the process of hiring one of the top still photographers in the state to be in charge of Liddy's wedding photos, but Liddy had insisted that they hire Dustin to take the picture of her and Sonny for the wedding announcement photo for the local newspapers and magazines. Liddy knew Dustin was passionate about photography, in addition to video game design and filmmaking, and she wanted to encourage him by giving him his first paid gig. She endured a few protestations from Celeste, but given the fact that she was already being forced to use Lisa to make the cake, her mother finally realized it was probably in her best interest to give Liddy at least one win in the wedding planning to keep her happy.

Dustin was over the moon and was taking the assignment very seriously. He did not want to disappoint the bride-to-be. For a boy who rarely lifted a finger to clean his room, he certainly was on top of every detail of the photo shoot.

Hayley was so grateful to Liddy for making such a grand gesture and building her son's artistic confidence in such a dramatic way, it just made it all the more painful for her to have to downsize and skimp on the bachelorette party. Liddy deserved the best, and if Hayley had the means, she would not hesitate to whisk her BFF off to Paris or London or Madrid, instead of Mona's backyard.

"My bag's on the kitchen table. I want you to put the card right back when you're done," Hayley warned.

"I will!" Dustin yelled as he shot out of the room.

It was nice seeing him so excited.

Sabrina kept quiet for the rest of the meeting in Hayley's living room as she and Mona went over the guest list for the bachelorette party.

Hayley sensed that Sabrina had suddenly lost interest because they had shot down her extravagant ideas. Hayley assumed she was pouting and willfully ignored her until they were done discussing the details.

Finally, she glanced over at Sabrina and asked flatly, "Are you sure you're okay with all this?"

Sabrina nodded, a tight smile on her face.

But she clearly wasn't.

She was obviously hoping to be more of a strong voice, a deciding influence in the proceedings. But in hindsight, she should have been relieved her ideas were quickly discarded, because at the end of the day, Sabrina Merryweather could claim no responsibility for the major disaster looming ahead.

Chapter 7

"Sonny, where the hell are you? You were supposed to be here almost an hour ago!" Liddy screamed into her cell phone as Hayley and Dustin hovered around her at the small photography studio they had rented, which was located just behind a gas station on lower Main Street.

Hayley nervously checked her watch, fearing they would be charged an extra hour of studio time if Sonny didn't show up soon. Liddy had arrived early, in a lovely Lela Rose illusion-yoke half-sleeve sheath dress, with her makeup and hair camera-ready for the photo shoot. She had been afraid that Sonny, who would be rushing over directly from his office, would arrive disheveled and sweaty, with armpit stains and his suit hopelessly wrinkled. The last thing she expected was for him not to show up at all.

"Did you try his office?" Hayley asked.

"Yes, right after I got his voice mail the first time.

His secretary said he left at ten minutes to three. He should have been here by now!"

Hayley could hear the panic rising in Liddy's voice as she contemplated any number of bad-news scenarios that might explain Sonny's mysterious absence.

Dustin went back to check the lights he had set up in the space for a third time just to keep himself busy while they waited. He tried to remain upbeat, but there was unmistakable disappointment on his face as he began to realize that his first professional photography gig was on the verge of being canceled.

"Let's think," Hayley said. "Where could he have gone?"

"I called his house, and there was no answer. He sometimes works out at the YMCA, but nobody at the reception desk today has seen him. It's as if he's just vanished into thin air!" Liddy wailed.

Hayley took matters into her own hands and texted Police Chief Sergio to see if there had been any accidents reported. He quickly responded that it had been quiet all afternoon, with no reports of any kind.

When Hayley relayed the good news to Liddy and Dustin, Liddy didn't seem at all relieved or reassured.

"If he had been in an accident and was laid up in the hospital, at least that's an excuse I could live with!" she growled.

After a few more minutes of agonizing and worrying, a text popped up on Hayley's phone.

It was from her brother.

Sergio called and said you were trying to find Sonny.

Hayley quickly texted back. *Yes! Have you seen him?*

After an interminable wait of a few seconds, Randy replied, *I'm looking right at him. He's here at the bar having his third scotch.*

Hayley took a deep breath. She was not anxious to share this news with Liddy, but after steeling herself, she turned to Liddy, who stood, arms folded, stewing, while watching Dustin fuss with the lights.

"I found him."

"Where is he?" Liddy asked, whirling around and dropping her arms.

"Drinks Like a Fish," Hayley muttered.

Liddy's face instantly turned a deep beet red as the rage boiled up inside her. She turned to Dustin and said in a controlled, steady voice, "I'm sorry, Dustin, but we are going to have to reschedule. But don't you worry, I will reimburse you for the studio and of course pay you for your time today."

"No worries," Dustin said, eyeing her warily, fearing she was about to explode.

But Liddy remained outwardly calm, although her flushed face told an entirely different story. She turned to Hayley. "I'm going to head over to the bar now. Would you like to come with me?"

"Yes," Hayley lied.

She so didn't want to be there when Liddy ripped Sonny's face off.

But she could see Liddy needed her by her side, and it was her job as a best friend and matron of honor to be there for moral support.

"I'll drive," Hayley offered, mostly because there was no way she wanted Liddy behind the wheel in her frazzled state.

After giving Dustin a quick peck on the cheek, Hayley left him to pack up the lights and equipment, and then led Liddy outside to her car.

They drove to Randy's bar on Cottage Street.

Liddy didn't say a word the entire trip. She just stared out the window, with a grim, stoic look. Hayley found a parking spot right out front, and they spotted Sonny through the large picture window, slouched over the bar, staring into an empty glass as Randy refilled it with another scotch straight up. Hayley could almost see the steam coming out of Liddy's ears as she got out of the car and marched inside.

Sonny was raising his glass to down his fourth scotch as Liddy snatched it from his grasp. "Cut him off, Randy. He's had enough."

Sonny, startled, turned to Liddy. There was a flicker of agitation, but then he quickly covered it with a smile. "Hey, darling, fancy meeting you here."

Liddy's whole body stiffened and her face got three shades redder as her mouth dropped open in utter disbelief.

Randy, who stood behind the bar watching, whispered, "Oh no, she's going to blow."

"*Fancy meeting you here*? That's all you have to say to me?" Liddy asked, clutching the glass of scotch so tightly Hayley feared it might crack in her grip and spill all over the floor. "What the hell is going on here, Sonny?"

Sonny gave her a puzzled look. "What do you mean?"

"Why are you here?" Liddy shrieked.

"I got finished with my meetings early and decided to swing by here and get a drink. Did I do something wrong?"

"You were supposed to meet me at the photography studio to have our wedding announcement photo taken!"

Sonny stared at her blankly before it finally began to sink in why she was so angry. "Was that *today*?"

"Yes! I emailed you this morning to remind you!"

"I've been really busy preparing for a case going to trial next week. I guess I forgot to check my emails this morning. I'm sorry, darling, can we do it another day?"

"Why bother? It's obvious you have no interest in marrying me!"

Two women, bank tellers at the First National, ambled in just in time to hear Liddy's dramatic pronouncement. They stood behind Hayley, not sure whether to turn around and leave or try to slip past Liddy and find a table. They chose to just hover by the door and watch.

Sonny, like a scolded puppy, slid off his stool and looked down at the floor. "Come on, Liddy, you know that's not true."

"How do I know? Every action you've taken, every word you've uttered, has suggested otherwise. From the moment you proposed to me, there has been a shocking lack of effort on your part to help with the details, or even muster the slightest amount of excitement or enthusiasm. This isn't some shotgun marriage, Sonny! You do have the right to pull out! It will hurt like hell, but I will get over it! I just need to know now, before my mother spends another dime on this wedding . . . Is this something you want? Do you want to marry me, Sonny? Or are you just going along to keep me happy? I need to know, Sonny! I need to know right now!"

Sonny stumbled forward, a bit tipsy from the multiple scotches, and grabbed Liddy by the shoulders. "Of course I want to marry you! I love you! I'm just exhausted. Work has been overwhelming lately! I have a lot on my mind! And when I get tired, I sometimes become forgetful. The photo shoot completely slipped my mind! I feel terrible." He turned to Hayley. "Tell Dustin I will pay him double to make up for wasting his time today."

"You don't have to do that, Sonny . . ." Hayley said.

"I insist," he said, before turning back to Liddy and pulling her into a hug. "As for you, I'm not going anywhere. You're stuck with me, and like it or not, I'm going to be at that altar in a snappy tux, and come hell or high water, I'm going to marry you, Liddy Crawford."

Liddy wanted to stay mad at him, but she couldn't.

Sonny was a charmer, and he was laying it on thick.

And it was working.

Liddy melted in Sonny's warm embrace.

All appeared to be forgiven.

For now.

Hayley, however, wasn't buying it.

She suspected there was a lot more on Sonny Lipton's mind than just a taxing workload, and whatever was preoccupying him would eventually leak out before or, God forbid, after the wedding.

She could only hope that Liddy was ready to handle whatever might come her way.

Chapter 8

"She's a backstabbing liar who can't be trusted! How dare you take *her* word over mine!" Lisa shouted at Chief Alvares, who stood in front of her bakery counter as Hayley and Liddy entered the Cake Walk shop.

"I'm not taking anyone's side. I'm just here to ask you a few questions," Sergio said patiently as Lisa threw off her apron and scooted out from behind the counter.

Sergio stepped back, afraid she might be on the attack.

"I had nothing to do with whatever she's accusing me of!" Lisa shrieked, like a wild animal with rabies that had been cornered and was aggressively lashing out.

"She's saying you planted mice and rotten food in the back of her shop and then called the health department to report an anonymous tip, knowing she would fail their inspection and they would shut her down."

Hayley suddenly realized they were talking about Lisa's rival.

"I would never do anything that malicious and underhanded! What kind of person do you think I am?" Lisa wailed.

The kind of person who would do exactly that, Hayley thought to herself, turning to Liddy, who was obviously thinking the same thing.

"I don't even know where that ridiculous Helen's new bakery is even located!"

Lisa was lying. Hayley knew it, because she had seen Lisa driving by Helen's bakery just yesterday and gawking to see if any of her loyal customers were being turncoat traitors by patronizing her former employee's new business. Hayley happened to be one of those traitors, since Helen's bakery was closer to her house, and she had begun getting into the habit of swinging in to pick up a bagel on her way to work. When Hayley had spotted Lisa's car passing by, she had quickly ducked down below the large picture window that faced the street to avoid being spotted.

"I don't even want to know! How did she open a new bakery so fast anyway? She must have been secretly plotting to stab me in the back for months while she was working for me!"

Sergio sighed. "If we can get back to what happened at Helen's—"

"It wasn't me! I can't imagine where that sniveling, jealous Helen Fennow gets her crazy ideas! If you ask me, I think she planted those mice and that spoiled meat and called the health department herself just to get me into trouble!"

"Meat? I just said 'food.' I never mentioned meat," Sergio said, eyes boring into Lisa, who flinched slightly, but quickly regained her composure.

"Meat, vegetables, whatever, I was just guessing . . ."

"It was rotten meat, so that was a remarkably good guess," Sergio said.

"Listen, I've lost enough business to that scheming two-faced witch. I don't need you scaring off my foot traffic by hanging around here giving the impression that the shop is a target of the police. So if you don't have enough evidence to arrest me, then I suggest you leave right now and not come back here until you do!" Lisa screeched in his face.

Sergio glared at her, clearly resisting the urge to snap some handcuffs on her wrists on the spot and drag her down to the station. But he kept his cool and said in a friendly tone, "I'll be in touch."

And then he turned on his heel and walked out of the shop, nodding his head to Hayley and Liddy as he passed by them. "Ladies."

"Chief," Liddy said, smiling.

Once he was gone, Lisa finally noticed Hayley and Liddy and frowned. "What are you two doing here?"

"We had an appointment. *You* called *me* just this morning and told me you had a cake you wanted me to taste!" Liddy sighed, exasperated.

"Right," Lisa said with a vague, distant look. "I don't have a calendar. I'm not some anal-retentive idiot who keeps track of those kinds of details. I'm an artist and more right-brained."

Hayley bit her tongue. She desperately wanted to point out to Lisa that people who used the old left-brain, right-brain excuse to cover their forget-fulness were usually just not using either side of their brain.

"Well, if this is a bad time—" Hayley said.

Lisa interrupted her. "No, it's fine. I need something to get my mind off the police harassment lawsuit I'm about to file against your brother-in-law!"

Hayley knew Lisa would never carry out that threat, because the risk would be too great. It just might expose her for what she really was—guilty.

Lisa scurried into the kitchen in the back of the bakery and returned with two small plates with a healthy piece of chocolate cake and a tiny silver dessert fork perched next to it on each one. She handed one to Liddy and the other to Hayley. "I thought about everything you said at our consultation, and I came up with this. You wanted something traditional and basic, with a little flare, last night, when I was *not* sabotaging that Betty-dict Arnold's stupid bakery, I came up with the perfect cake for your wedding. A chocolate walnut cake with a cocoa glaze. Understated, clean, simple."

Liddy stared at her piece of cake. Hers was decorated more elaborately than Hayley's, with a chocolate rose sprinkled with bits of walnut fashioned on top—a piece befitting the bride-to-be.

Lisa stared at them expectantly, waiting for them

to taste her delicious cake, but Liddy reached over and dropped her plate on the bakery counter, refusing to take a bite. "You didn't listen to a word I said."

"Yes, I did!" Lisa yelled defensively. "You wanted a traditional wedding cake!"

"I'm allergic to nuts! How many times do I have to tell you?"

"You need to get over that. Your guests are going to love this cake!"

"This cake is not traditional! White frosting is traditional! Maybe some edible roses! That's traditional! A chocolate walnut cake with a cocoa glaze is *not* traditional!" Liddy screamed, losing it.

"I never should have taken this job. I knew working with you was going to be a nightmare," Lisa growled.

Liddy had heard enough.

She marched forward until she was inches from Lisa's face.

Hayley thought about grabbing Liddy and hustling her out of the shop before the two cousins started to tear each other's hair out, but she hung back as Liddy pointed a crooked finger in Lisa's angry face.

"You are a despicable, infuriating human being with no manners or people skills who should not be running a business where you have to deal with the public!" Liddy shrieked.

Lisa stood her ground, not backing down, refusing to be intimidated by Liddy in the least. In fact, when Liddy was finished berating her, Lisa broke out into a devilish smile, almost as if she had enjoyed her cousin's insulting tirade.

"What do you have to say for yourself?" Liddy demanded to know.

"I have nothing to say to someone with no taste or class," Lisa sneered.

"You're fired!" Liddy screamed, and then she whipped around and barged out of the bakery, leaving Hayley behind, her mouth agape.

"What about you? Are you going to just stand there? At least try my chocolate walnut cake and tell me if you like it!" Lisa asked.

Hayley looked at the piece of cake she was holding, and then scooted over and gingerly set it down on the counter next to Liddy's. "I better not. I really should go."

And then she chased Liddy out of the shop.

Hayley had to run to catch up to Liddy, who was keeping a vigorous pace and was already halfway down the street.

"I cannot believe I share the same genes as that woman! How can we both be part of the same family?"

"Well, you do have a few things in common . . ." Hayley offered.

"Like what?" Liddy snapped.

"You're both really stubborn . . ."

"Not helpful, Hayley!"

"Sorry," Hayley muttered under her breath. "But you just fired Lisa, and your mother said . . ."

"I don't care about my mother! If she refuses to

pay for my wedding because I don't want that stupid, awful ogre Lisa involved, then so be it! Sonny and I will get married in my living room with just a few of our closest friends. I'm sure Sonny would prefer a much smaller, more low-key ceremony anyway!"

"That sounds lovely, actually," Hayley said, trying her best to be supportive.

"And *you* can bake the cake!"

"I'm sorry, what?"

"You write a food column every day, half of which are about you baking cakes and pies and assorted desserts. I assume your recipes are all kitchen-tested, so how hard would it be for you to bake my wedding cake?"

"Liddy, I'm not sure I should—"

"Why not?"

"I just don't want to get in the middle of a family squabble. I mean, you firing Lisa and hiring me just doesn't look good . . ."

"You're my best friend, and I want you to bake my wedding cake. There's nothing controversial about that. And the best part is, you'll design and make the cake I want! Angel food cake with butter-cream frosting!"

There was no squirming out of this one.

Liddy had made her decision, and for the sake of their friendship, Hayley knew she had no further choice in the matter. After all, Liddy's wedding day was supposed to be about her, not the wedding cake baker, and it was Hayley's responsibility to make sure her big day was a happy one.

"Okay, I'll do it," Hayley said, however reluctantly.

In hindsight, she should have chosen to put her own happiness first and refuse Liddy's request, because there was no doubt in her mind she was going to rue this day—the day she crossed the very mean and spiteful Lisa Crawford.

Chapter 9

Not even two hours after Liddy had drafted Hayley into baking her wedding cake, it was as if a small explosion erupted inside the building of the *Island Times* when Lisa Crawford blew through the doors, wild with fury.

Most of the reporters fortunately were out of the office covering stories, and Sal, the paper's intrepid editor and Hayley's boss, was at a dentist appointment, so they were all mercifully safe from the verbal shrapnel Lisa was spewing.

Hayley, however, was on the phone with a subscriber from California, who was complaining that she had missed an issue and was droning on about how it might be the fault of her mail carrier, who was forever losing her mail before it made its way to her mailbox. Hayley, trying to keep a paying customer happy, offered to stuff a copy of the missing back issue into a large manila envelope and send it her way immediately.

She couldn't hear the grateful customer thanking

her profusely for being so kind, because Lisa was standing in front of her desk screaming at the top of her lungs.

Hayley held the phone to one ear while plugging the other with her finger so she could hear what the caller was saying.

"Is everything all right there?" the concerned caller asked, suddenly aware of the yelling in the background.

"Yes, I will get that issue out to you right away," Hayley said.

The customer spoke, but Hayley couldn't make out what she had said.

"What?" Hayley asked.

"I said thank you!" the caller screamed.

"You're very welcome, have a nice day!" Hayley said, hanging up the phone and finally turning her attention to Lisa, who was now pounding on Hayley's desk with her fist.

"I knew you couldn't be trusted! Just like that crooked and hypocritical Helen Fennow! I have to say, I'm surprised at you, Hayley, I thought you had more scruples!"

Hayley sighed deeply. "Is this about the wedding cake, Lisa?"

"You're damn right it is! I called Celeste and she told me everything! How dare you swoop in and steal my client! When did you become such a conniving backstabber! I used to like you! Have you been hanging out with Helen lately?"

"I didn't steal anything from you, Lisa," Hayley said calmly. "You refused to do what Liddy wanted, so she decided to make a change. And for what it's worth, I don't want anything to do with baking Liddy's wedding cake, but she insisted."

"That's richer than my chocolate walnut cake—which was delicious, by the way, *and* the perfect choice for Liddy's wedding, if she wasn't so mule-headed!"

"It's not the cake she wants. End of story." Hayley sighed.

Lisa sized her up derisively. "You've always fancied yourself a master chef, haven't you? Ever since Sal Moretti was dumb enough to let you write the *Times*'s food column! It's been torture for everybody in town having to put up with your cutesy stories about how much you like food and your idiotic anecdotes about your stupid family! I mean, who cares about that crap?"

Hayley bristled.

She could handle some well-directed criticism, and had been given plenty in the Letters to the Editor column, but this was a full-frontal attack, especially on her family, and she was not going to just sit there and take it.

Hayley stood up from her desk. "That's enough, Lisa. If you want to meet later and have it out, fine, but this is not the appropriate place to do this. This is a business—"

"You think I care about causing a scene at this muckraking rag you call a newspaper? Please, there is nothing legitimate about this dump! Everything you people print is fake news! The best use I have for it is lining the bottom of my cat's litter box!"

"I really think you should leave now—"

Lisa boiled over with rage and picked up Hayley's desktop computer off her desk, yanking free the attached cords, hoisted it above her head, and hurled it across the room, where it smashed against a wall and crashed to the floor, the flying cords nearly whipping Hayley in the face.

Hayley gasped, shocked as she stared down at the busted computer.

Even Lisa was taken aback for a second, stunned by her own unbridled rage. But she quickly recovered and turned her attention back to Hayley.

"I'm not going to let you get away with this," Lisa growled.

Suddenly Bruce raced into the front office from the back bull pen. "What the hell is going on out here?"

Hayley had completely forgotten Bruce was back in his office, typing up a column with the door closed.

Hayley calmly held up a hand to Bruce. "Everything's fine. Lisa was just leaving."

"This isn't over, Hayley," Lisa snarled. "Not by a long shot! I'm going to make sure you regret this for the rest of your life!"

"Lisa, if you don't get out of here right now, I'm calling the police," Bruce said, his eyes drawn to the shattered computer on the floor.

Fists clenched, Lisa, who appeared to be on the verge of lunging at Hayley and physically attacking her, suddenly realized she was outnumbered and thankfully retreated, backing out of the door to the *Island Times*, her angry, threatening eyes still locked onto Hayley until the door slammed and she was finally gone.

Hayley dropped back down in her chair, her whole body shaking.

Bruce scooted around the desk, leaned down, and put a comforting arm around Hayley's shoulders. "Are you okay?"

"I knew she had a volatile personality, but I had no idea . . ." Hayley's voice trailed off.

"She vandalized office property. We have every right to call the police station and report it."

Hayley shook her head. "No. The IT guy is coming tomorrow to install a new computer. This one was heading to the scrap heap anyway. And besides, I don't want to set Lisa Crawford off any more than I already have."

It took Hayley most of the afternoon to calm down her nerves.

She debated whether or not she should call Liddy and tell her what had happened, but she decided against it. Liddy had enough on her mind already with all the wedding preparations. She didn't need one more thing to worry about. But Hayley knew she had to do something. She didn't need an enemy plotting against her. Especially one as unstable and unpredictable as Lisa Crawford.

She had to at least try to make peace before the situation worsened to the point where Lisa might carry out her threat and show up at Hayley's house one night. She might just wake up to find Lisa standing over her bed brandishing a baseball bat, which was exactly the nightmare scenario that was currently running through Hayley's jittery mind.

Chapter 10

When five o'clock rolled around and it was finally quitting time for the day, Hayley gathered up her tote bag and was halfway out the door when Bruce bounded out from the back bull pen.

"Want to go to Drinks Like a Fish and wind down from the day a bit?"

She stopped in the doorway and spun around. "I'll meet you there."

"Got an errand?"

"Yes, just something I need to take care of first," Hayley said.

She was being purposefully vague, and Bruce picked up on it immediately.

"Want me to go with you?" Bruce asked.

"No, that's all right. You go on to the bar, and I'll be there in a half hour."

Bruce folded his arms, suddenly suspicious. "Honestly, I don't mind."

Hayley sighed. "No, Bruce, I should handle this myself."

A light bulb went off in his head.

"You are not going over to the Cake Walk bakery, are you?"

"No! What makes you say that?"

She was a terrible liar.

At least when it came to Bruce.

He had become remarkably good at reading her face, and it bugged her, because the idea that he knew her so well was a bit unsettling. Even her ex-husband Danny had never been so clear-eyed when it came to picking up on what was really going on in her mind at all times.

However, Bruce Linney, much to her dismay, had become a master.

It gave her goose bumps that he knew her so well.

She didn't know whether to be happy or terrified, but she had to admit, it sort of warmed her heart too.

"Hayley, why on earth would you go over there? That horrible woman almost physically assaulted you earlier today! If I hadn't been here—"

"Yes, Bruce, you're my knight in shining armor, rescuing me from the evil witch, that's your story and you're sticking to it, but I have to at least try to repair this rift between me and Lisa, because she's Liddy's family, and she may still come to the wedding, and I don't want there to be any tension . . ."

"It's way too late! There's already tension! She thinks you stole her gig as Liddy's wedding cake baker. Everyone in town knows that Lisa is bullheaded and completely unreasonable, and there's no chance she'll ever forgive you. Honestly, I think you should just stay out of it and keep your distance."

"I can't. I have to at least try . . ."

Bruce shook his head. She could tell what he was thinking—that she was just as bullheaded and unreasonable as Lisa—but he wisely kept his mouth shut.

"Well, I will not allow you to go over there alone."

Hayley's mouth dropped open.

"You won't *allow* me?" she scoffed.

Bruce immediately tried walking back the comment. "I mean, you do whatever you want, you're a strong, independent woman and it's not my job to try and control you or anything like that, but—"

"I'll meet you at the bar, Bruce," Hayley said, knowing he had boxed himself into a corner.

"Right," he said, spinning on his heel and skulking back to his office.

Hayley hurried down the sidewalk to where her car was parked. It was chilly for a late-June afternoon, and the skies were cloudy and gray. She wished she had brought a sweater to work with her today, but she had forgotten to check the weather report on the way out the door that morning.

She jumped into her car, turning on the heat to warm herself up, and drove across town to the Cake Walk bakery. When she pulled up in front, the shop looked empty, although the cardboard sign that said "Open" was still in the window. She took a deep breath, mentally preparing herself for what might be an all-out verbal assault once she got inside. She got out of the car, slammed the door shut, marched up to the front entrance, and walked inside.

A bell jingled as she entered, but no one came out to greet her.

"Lisa?"

There was no answer.

"Lisa, it's me, Hayley. I've come to apologize."

Still no answer.

She scooted around the glass case full of tasty cakes and pies and cupcakes and poked her head through the door to the kitchen area that was set apart from the front of the store by a bright print pink and white curtain.

"Lisa, are you here?"

There was a nagging feeling in the pit of her stomach and a little voice in her head that kept screaming to just get out of there and send her a conciliatory email. But Hayley Powell was never one to listen to any voices in her head. She just plowed ahead anyway.

As she entered the kitchen area, she suddenly knew why that little voice in her head had been screaming so loud.

Lisa was facedown, dead on the floor, her face buried in a smashed three-tier wedding cake, with a pair of small bride and groom figurines staring down at her from the drooping, melting top tier.

Island Food & Cocktails
BY HAYLEY POWELL

With all the hoopla surrounding Liddy's upcoming nuptials, I've become a little nostalgic for all the past wedding receptions I've attended over the years. The one that has stood out the most in my memory, however, was my buddy Mona's. It was a rather simple affair in her parents' backyard. As I recall, because Mona's lobster business had yet to take off and she had very little cash on hand for any kind of elaborate wedding celebration, Mona requested potluck. So instead of gifts, everyone brought their favorite dish. As I was just discovering my joy of cooking at that time, I chose an easy yet delicious appetizer, my pimento cheese deviled eggs. After the guests greedily gobbled them up on that day years ago, every potluck dinner I have been invited to ever since always comes with a special request—"Bring your pimento cheese deviled eggs!"

What made Mona's wedding reception so memorable, however, was *not* the food!

Mona met her husband, Dennis, the summer before when he came to Bar Harbor to work for a buddy at his windowpane company. They were first introduced at a mutual friend's keg party, hit it off immediately, and soon began dating. One year to the day after they met, Mona and Dennis planned to get married. Mona was never overly sentimental. When Dennis proposed, instead of weeping with joy, she just shrugged and said, "Looks like I'm never getting rid of you, so we might as well make it legal."

The wedding would be the first time the families of the bride and the groom would meet, but no drama was expected, since both sides were very fond of their future son- and daughter in-law, respectively. Everything was falling perfectly into place, which is exactly how Mona prefers things. No fuss, no mess.

Neither the bride nor the groom expected all their uncles, aunts, and cousins to RSVP, but sure enough, they all did. It was going to be a crowded affair. In fact, on the big day there were upward of sixty to seventy people crammed into Mona's small backyard. It would be years until she could afford to expand the property with the profits from her lobstering business.

Not one to drag things out, Mona kept the ceremony down to five minutes, and even interrupted the minister to hurry things along when he tried injecting a poem about true love he had personally composed for the occasion. Mona knew her cousins had short attention spans, especially when a buffet table with trays of lobster rolls and two kegs of beer were in their eye line.

Once the minister was sternly encouraged to

wrap things up, and the party finally got under way, Liddy and I circled the crowd making sure everyone had heaping plates of steamed mussels, coleslaw, potato salad, and plenty of lobster rolls, not to mention my pimento cheese deviled eggs.

That's about the time I noticed the two families were staying firmly planted on opposite sides of the backyard, as if they were intentionally avoiding each other. In fact, they were grimacing and pointing and whispering among themselves, obviously disturbed about something. Mona and Dennis were too busy gazing into each other's eyes between plastic cups of beer to notice the dividing line right down the middle of the backyard keeping the families apart. Actually, Dennis gazed and Mona just kept telling him to stop acting so stupid. I didn't think much about the families keeping their distance, because I simply assumed they were unfamiliar with one another, and sometimes it takes time to break the ice, especially with naturally shy people.

Well, as I came to find out, that certainly wasn't the case, because just as I served my last deviled egg, suddenly Dennis's uncle Joe abruptly stood up, raised his glass, and yelled at the top of his lungs that he wanted to make a toast. Dennis and Mona looked at each other nervously, because Uncle Joe's tone wasn't exactly warm and celebratory.

"Here's to Dennis and Mona, may you have a life full of love and happiness . . . and I pray to

God that Mona doesn't inherit her aunt Betty's trollop ways and leave my beloved nephew heartbroken!"

There was a stunned silence, followed by complete pandemonium as both families sprang from their seats and began shouting and arguing with one another. Mona's grandfather Cliff tried to race over to Joe in his electric wheelchair and attack him, but Mona's father managed to grab the hand brake and stop him. Aunt Betty was in tears, and Mona's mother desperately tried comforting her. Joe's wife, Esther, spit out her lobster roll and began pointing her finger at Betty as if she had a scarlet A embroidered on her kelly green cashmere sweater from J. C. Penney. Finally, Betty's enraged husband, Al, managed to reach Joe, and the two began pounding on each other as they fell to the ground and rolled around until they knocked over the buffet table and were covered with steamed mussels.

Mona finally got up on a chair, her wedding dress covered in grass strains from trying to break up the fight, and let out an earsplitting whistle, which finally got everyone to stop fighting.

"What the hell is this all about?" she wailed. "You've ruined my wedding day!"

Finally, as always, the truth came tumbling out. Apparently, back when Joe was a sophomore at the University of Maine at Farmington, he met Al, a freshman, when they played on the university basketball team together. The two young men became best friends and fraternity brothers. Joe met Betty at a fraternity party one night after a big game, and they fell for each other fast and hard. The three of them, Joe, Betty, and Al, all became besties and were inseparable all through college. When Joe graduated, he asked Betty to marry him. Of course Betty was ecstatic. The wedding was planned for the following summer, and Joe asked Al to be his best man.

Well, apparently a lot can happen in a year. While Joe was off in Skowhegan on a construction job, it got harder for him to visit Betty on the weekends, because the project was on a strict deadline. Betty and Al grew closer, and although they tried to keep things platonic, they couldn't help but fall in love. Betty desperately tried to tamp down her feelings for Al before her wedding to Joe, but to no avail. She finally had to confess to Joe that she was in love with Al. Joe was understandably hurt and angry and never saw or spoke to either of them ever again—that is, until Mona's wedding day.

It was a lovely and sad story, but Mona was having none of it. She told all three of them in no uncertain terms that if they wanted her and Dennis to stay in their lives, they had better mend fences, and fast. It took all afternoon, but by the time the second keg of beer was tapped, both sides had decided to let bygones be bygones, much like my mother and my husband's uncle Otis on my own wedding day. I guess weddings have a tendency to bring people together.

Just in case you were wondering, Uncle Joe, who had stubbornly stayed single over the years,

met Betty's cousin Nancy that day when they both
went for the last lobster roll, and by November,
they were married. By February, Joe and Nancy
were on a Caribbean cruise as a foursome with
Al and Betty.

Life is full of surprises.

PIMENTO CHEESE DEVILED EGGS

1 dozen large hard-boiled eggs, peeled
2 ounces finely shredded sharp cheddar cheese
1 cup real mayonnaise
½ teaspoon paprika, plus extra for garnish
½ teaspoon garlic powder
Salt and pepper to taste
2 ounces diced pimentos, rinsed and patted dry

Cut your eggs in half lengthwise and remove the
yolks. Place the yolks in a medium bowl and set
your whites aside on a plate.

Mash your egg yolks with a fork, then add your
pimentos, cheddar cheese, mayonnaise, paprika,
garlic powder, and salt and pepper.

Stir your mixture until it's all well-incorporated.
Taste and add a little more salt and pepper if
needed.

Fill your eggs with the mixture and refrigerate
until needed. Right before serving, sprinkle a
little more paprika on the eggs. Serve and watch
them quickly disappear.

BEER COCKTAIL

We enjoyed kegs of beer at Mona's wedding, but for Liddy's reception, along with her favorite fruity cocktails, we thought those who prefer beer might appreciate a twist.

Ice
1 ounce rum
1 lemon or lime (your preference), juiced
1 orange, juiced
1 ounce simple syrup
4 ounces of your favorite beer

Fill a tall glass with ice and add your rum, lemon or lime juice, orange juice, and simple syrup, and top with the beer. Serve it up to your friends and enjoy!

Chapter 11

Hayley heard sirens fast approaching as she stood over Lisa's prone body, shaking. She noticed that the cake Lisa had fallen into and knocked to the floor with a splat was an angel food cake with buttercream frosting, the exact cake Liddy had requested for her wedding, the same cake Lisa had adamantly refused to make. What had caused her to suddenly change her mind, especially after Liddy had so unceremoniously fired her? Was this some kind of last-minute bid to win back her job as the official wedding cake baker?

As the sirens got closer and she heard tires squealing to a stop just outside the bakery, Hayley also noticed Lisa was still clutching her cell phone in her right hand, as if she had been trying to make a call right before she collapsed. Next to her was a glass plate that was cracked in the middle and a silver fork with smeared frosting on it, indicating she might have been eating the cake when she died.

The doors to the shop flew open, and Sergio, accompanied by Officer Donnie, his tall, lanky, not-so-wet-behind-the-ears-but-still-borderline-incompetent patrolman, burst inside, radios crackling, batons drawn, just in case. Hayley sighed with relief and stepped aside, still breathless from her grisly discovery, to allow the police to take over the scene.

Sergio did a sweep of the area where Hayley had found Lisa's corpse, surveying every inch and corner of the kitchen before kneeling down and inspecting the body.

Officer Donnie hung back, and Hayley noticed he appeared slightly nauseous, his nose crinkled up, as he stared down at the body.

Minutes before the cops had arrived, Hayley texted Liddy to update her on what was going on, but never heard back. She knew Liddy detested her repugnant cousin, but couldn't believe she would have zero interest in learning she had just died. In fact, Hayley wondered to herself if anyone in town would be broken up over Lisa's untimely and tragic death. She hardly had any friends, and most people in Bar Harbor would cross the street if they saw her approaching to avoid having to talk to her. Her reputation as moody and vindictive far preceded her.

"I can't believe you got here so quickly after I called nine-one-one," Hayley remarked to Sergio, who stood back up and studied the smashed wedding cake spread out all over the floor.

"Lisa managed to dial nine-one-one herself in her final moments, but apparently died before the operator was able to get any information out of her."

Hayley couldn't see any signs of foul play at first glance, but Sergio was the professional, so she refrained from drawing any of her own conclusions before hearing what he had to say. As she patiently waited for him to announce his own determinations, she was surprised when he never got around to it. He muttered a few asides to Officer Donnie, but they were too low for Hayley to make out what he was saying.

She understood that although Sergio was married to her brother, she couldn't automatically assume he would draw her into any investigation. Usually she had to horn her way in on her own without an invitation, which could make family dinners somewhat tense at times.

Officer Donnie was by the door when it slammed open again and Liddy and her mother Celeste scuttled into the shop with pale faces and stunned expressions, still grappling with the unexpected and disturbing news. Donnie swiftly blocked them from entering any farther with his rail-thin body, his skinny arms outstretched and his big bony hands raised.

"That's far enough, ladies," Officer Donnie said.

"Oh, please, Donnie, out of the way before I take one breath and blow that scrawny body of yours halfway to Hulls Cove," Liddy yelled.

"Let them through, Donnie. I'd like to have a word with them," Sergio said.

Donnie scowled and then dutifully took a step to his left, allowing Liddy and Celeste to pass. As they entered the kitchen area and their eyes fell upon

Lisa lying facedown on the floor, both mother and daughter gasped.

"Oh, dear! Poor Lisa! What on earth happened?" Celeste wailed as Liddy put a comforting arm around her distraught mother.

"Isn't it clear, Mother? She died! Do you know how it happened?" Liddy asked, staring at the body, trying to muster up some emotion, anything to show the slightest bit of grief, but failing that, she just gave up and acted as if she was simply in the shop to buy a box of fudge brownies.

"I was hoping you could help me with that," Sergio said. "On the surface, there do not appear to be any suspicious signs to suggest anything other than natural causes."

"Frankly, I'm surprised, since pretty much everyone in town wanted to see Lisa dead," Liddy cracked.

"Liddy, please!" Celeste cried.

"It's true," Liddy said, shrugging.

"Lisa was a member of our family! Show some respect," Celeste moaned as her eyes welled up with tears and she reached into her purse for a tissue.

Hayley gingerly stepped forward and gently placed a hand on Celeste's arm. "Celeste, did Lisa have any health problems that you knew about?"

"Oh, Lord, yes! High blood pressure, high cholesterol, type two diabetes, you name it!"

"I never saw her touch a vegetable ever! It was all sweets all the time! No wonder she was a walking time bomb when it came to her health!" Liddy noted.

"Liddy!" Celeste squealed.

"I'm only stating the facts for the police, Mother, not judging her," Liddy lied, judgment clearly written all over her face. "You just have to look at her family history to understand what happened."

After glaring at Liddy for a few seconds, Celeste turned back to Hayley and Sergio. "Lisa's father, my brother Stan, suffered from heart disease, God rest his soul. He died of a massive coronary two weeks after his sixty-third birthday."

"Yes, but Lisa was in her early forties; that strikes me as a little young to have a massive heart attack," Sergio noted.

"That's true," Hayley said. "But Liddy is right. I remember in grade school, all the kids coveted Lisa's *Melrose Place* lunch box because it was always stuffed with Twinkies and Devil Dogs and Mars bars. We were all so jealous!"

"A heart attack . . . how awful . . . the poor dear," Celeste whispered, shaking her head, still in a state of shock.

"It looks like she was eating one of her wedding cakes at the time she died," Sergio said, circling the body once more.

Hayley scooted up behind Liddy and spoke quietly in her ear. "Angel food cake with buttercream frosting."

Liddy suddenly noticed the obliterated cake surrounding Lisa's prone body. When Sergio's back was turned, she quickly knelt down and examined the cake closely. Her eyes widened. "You're right, Hayley. But why? She was so insistent about not making the cake I really wanted for my wedding. What suddenly made her change her mind?"

Hayley shrugged. "Who knows? Maybe she felt bad about not baking you the cake you really wanted for your wedding, so she decided to surprise you."

Liddy laughed. "That doesn't sound like stupid, awful ogre Lisa at all!"

"Stop speaking ill of your cousin, Liddy!" Celeste warned. "This is such a horrible tragedy, beyond comprehension."

"You're damn right it is." Liddy nodded. "Leave it to Lisa to decide to die right before my wedding and completely steal focus!"

Hayley prayed that Lisa's death was not ruled a homicide, because given Liddy's callous and flippant reaction and painfully obvious ill will toward the victim, the blushing bride-to-be would undoubtedly be the first suspect brought in for questioning.

Chapter 12

Hayley had just removed the dinner plates from the dining room table and was rinsing them off in the sink when she felt Bruce's arms slide around her waist from behind. He pulled her in close to his chest as he softly kissed the side of her neck.

"We haven't even had dessert yet," Hayley said, dropping the dishes in the sink and shutting off the faucet.

"I'm having mine right now," Bruce said, spinning her around to face him, locking his fingers over the small of her back.

"You are such a dork," Hayley said, laughing.

Bruce leaned down and kissed her gently on the mouth.

Damn, he was a good kisser.

She tried not to swoon as he unlocked his fingers and cupped the back of her head with his hand, kissing her with more passion and urgency.

Then, his lips slowly pulled away and he was

nibbling on her ear a bit before whispering, "Let's go upstairs."

Before she could even respond, he took her by the hand and led her out of the kitchen, down the hallway, and up the stairs.

About halfway to the second floor, the front doorbell rang.

Hayley stopped suddenly and turned around.

"Ignore it," Bruce pleaded.

She debated with herself.

Gemma and Dustin were both out with friends from high school.

It could be Liddy or Mona or the gas meter reader or a Girl Scout selling cookies.

"Come on, if it's an emergency, they'll call or come back," Bruce said, taking one last shot.

But Hayley couldn't help herself.

She bounded back down the stairs and swung open the door.

It was Sabrina Merryweather.

"Thank God I caught you at home!" Sabrina cried as she pushed her way inside, spotting Bruce staring glumly down at her from halfway up the staircase. "Oh, hi, Bruce. I hope I'm not interrupting."

Bruce opened his mouth to say something— probably something rude—so Hayley jumped in before he had the chance. "Can I get you some coffee?"

"Yes, thank you. Dash of cream and maybe a spoonful of sweetener," Sabrina said as she wandered into the living room and shook off her lightweight pale blue wrap and plopped herself down on the couch.

Hayley scooted into the kitchen, where she had already put the coffeepot on, expecting to have some with the cherry pie she had baked for her and Bruce's dessert, which was still cooling on a rack on top of the stove. She grabbed three mugs from the cupboard.

"How about a piece of homemade cherry pie?"

"Yummy!"

Bruce pounded back down the stairs, making no secret of his annoyance. He stalked into the kitchen, muttering under his breath, "She's got fifteen minutes, and then I'm kicking her out."

Hayley shot Bruce a look to let him know he was talking loud enough for Sabrina to hear him, but he didn't seem to care much.

By the time Hayley served the pie and coffee, leaving Bruce sulking in the kitchen, Sabrina was off and running as to why she had shown up at Hayley's house unannounced.

"Well, as you know, I still keep in contact with a few of my old work colleagues at the county coroner's office. We were a close-knit bunch there for a while, always going out for cocktails after work. Like you do, Hayley—no judgment, by the way. Anyway, they've all missed me terribly ever since I decided to quit a few years back."

Hayley heard Bruce loudly clearing his throat and then covering with a fake cough, barking, "Ten minutes!"

He was making sure Hayley knew she was on a

timer, and the clock was ticking toward Sabrina's forced departure.

"Yes, it's nice you all still keep in touch," Hayley said, smiling.

"They *adore* me! Anyway, I stopped by there today just to say hello and to let them know I'm back in town, but it was quite busy, so I didn't stay long. I did, however, get the chance to catch up with Celia, one of my former lab assistants. She only had a few minutes to talk because they were swamped working on Lisa Crawford's autopsy."

Hayley quickly set her pie plate down on the coffee table and leaned forward, curious.

Bruce was suddenly quiet in the kitchen.

Sabrina stopped to cut a generous piece of pie with her fork and shove it in her mouth. There was an interminable wait for her to chew and swallow until she spoke again.

Hayley tapped her foot impatiently.

Bruce appeared from around the corner and sat down on the armrest of the recliner where Hayley was seated. He wasn't about to miss hearing this.

Mercifully, Sabrina finally swallowed her large chunk of cherry pie.

"So delicious. Anyway . . ." she said.

But then she decided she needed to wash the pie down, so she set her pie plate on the coffee table and picked up her coffee mug. She took a long, leisurely sip.

Bruce audibly sighed, and Hayley poked him in the rib cage with her finger. He sat up straight on the armrest, his eyes fixed on Sabrina, who was now taking her second sip of coffee.

Bruce placed a hand down on top of Hayley's knee to stop her from tapping her foot. Both of them needed to take lessons on how to be more patient.

After wiping the sides of her mouth with a cloth napkin, Sabrina finally continued. "Celia gave me a sneak peek, and you are never going to believe this . . ."

Sabrina eyed the pie and reached for it again, stabbing at the last piece on her plate and stuffing it in her mouth. She was too elegant to speak with her mouth full of pie, so they were in for another wait.

Hayley glanced at Bruce, who had a weird frozen smile on his face, trying not to give away the fact that his head was about to explode because he was so vexed by how long this was taking.

Finally, with no more pie left on her plate, Sabrina once more dabbed at the sides of her mouth with the cloth napkin and dropped it in her lap.

"I had trouble believing it myself," Sabrina said, reaching down and picking up her coffee mug again. She peered into it, noticing it was empty. "I could use a spot more coffee, if you don't mind."

"Sabrina!" Bruce blurted out, startling Hayley and Sabrina and himself.

"Bruce, calm down," Hayley scolded.

"Just tell us what was in the report," Bruce begged.

Sabrina glared at Bruce, silently admonishing him for his impoliteness, but then, deciding she had

drawn out the suspense long enough, she dropped
the bombshell. "Lisa was murdered."

Hayley gasped.

In a way, she had been expecting this. But hearing it out loud gave her suspicions a disturbing
resonance.

"Dr. Alden, my replacement—sweet man, but
nowhere near as skilled as I was—found traces of a
rare fast-acting poison in her system, a toxin closely
related to ricin, but this one works much faster. He
suspects someone planted the poison in one of
Lisa's cake ingredients and she ate it."

"Was it in the angel food cake with buttercream
frosting? That's the cake Liddy wanted her to make
for her wedding," Hayley said.

"They're testing all of the baked goods in Lisa's
shop to see which, if any, had traces of the poison,"
Sabrina said. "Now, the report is not going to be
released to the public for another day or two, so
please do not share this information with *anyone*."

"Of course not," Hayley said. "We won't say a
word, right, Bruce?"

She turned to notice Bruce only half listening.
"Huh?"

"Sabrina does not want us sharing any of what she
told us," Hayley said firmly, locking eyes onto him.

Bruce shrugged. "Yeah, sure."

She could tell he was lying.

After Sabrina chowed down on a second piece of
cherry pie and two more cups of coffee, droning on
and on about her upcoming vacation to Bali and

how she feared her bridesmaid gown would be too tight after gorging on too many lobsters from Mona's shop, she finally left.

Hayley turned to Bruce, who stood at the foot of the stairs hoping they might pick up where they left off. "Promise me that none of what you just heard is going to appear in your column tomorrow."

Bruce hemmed and hawed and made some noises about waiting until the report was released, but Hayley knew he would not be able to stop himself. Because in his heart, Bruce was a reporter. And good, effective reporters are all about getting the scoop first.

By the time the latest edition of the *Island Times* hit the newsstands and was posted online, the headline of Bruce's crime column was "Coroner rules Crawford Death a Homicide."

Hayley felt obligated, out of respect to Sabrina, to give Bruce a proper dressing-down, which she did in his office when the paper first landed on her desk. But she knew his apology was halfhearted, and on some level, she didn't blame him. Sabrina had also probably known Bruce wouldn't keep his promise. She had never prefaced her big news with an "off the record" warning.

By mid-afternoon it didn't even matter, because the report was released, along with a new addendum Sabrina had been unaware of at the time she broke the news to Hayley and Bruce—the poison was *only* found in the angel food cake with buttercream frosting. The rest of Lisa's cakes and cookies and assorted pastries that were in her shop had all tested negative, which meant the killer had deliberately added the poison to the cake directly, or to one of the ingredients, right before Lisa made that specific cake, the last cake she would ever bake.

Chapter 13

"I don't understand what you're trying to say to me," Liddy said matter-of-factly as she sat on her porch in a wicker chair, slowly sipping a glass of lemonade.

Liddy's black Lab, Poppyseed, slept soundly at her feet.

Hayley and Gemma, who were sitting opposite her on a porch swing, rocking back and forth, exchanged a quick glance.

Hayley cleared her throat and tried to delicately explain again. "Gemma and I have been talking, and we both think, very strongly in fact, that you should choose another kind of cake for your wedding."

"But I've been very clear from the beginning. I want the angel food cake with buttercream frosting. It's the whole reason I fired Lisa and hired you."

"Yes, we know," Gemma jumped in. "But given what's happened . . ."

"What?" Liddy said, perplexed.

"Well, your cousin Lisa was found dead in her shop

poisoned by a piece of cake, which just happened to be angel food cake with buttercream frosting."

"So?" Liddy said, still not quite getting it.

Hayley leaned forward. "Let's just say it might appear to be a little insensitive, and perhaps even a bit ghoulish, if you serve that exact same cake."

"It's all anybody will be able to think about at the reception," Gemma added.

Liddy rolled this over in her mind. "I see. So you think that even in death, from all the way down there in hell, Lisa will manage to ruin my wedding?"

Hayley and Gemma exchanged another look. They were getting through to Liddy, but not in the way they had imagined.

They both shrugged and nodded.

"Yes," Hayley said.

"But that's only if you choose to go with the angel food cake," Gemma said, pulling out a bridal magazine and opening it to an earmarked page before setting it down on the wicker coffee table with a glass top. "However . . ."

Liddy peered at the photo of a beautiful three-tier traditional wedding cake.

"Mom and I talked it over, and we both would recommend something completely different, like this one we found that we could easily make. Classic design, chocolate fudge filling, white frosting, sugar roses, the works . . ."

Liddy forced a smile. "It is lovely."

"We just don't want anything overshadowing your big day, and right now, Lisa's murder is definitely on everyone's mind."

"Okay, let's go with this one," Liddy said, taking another sip of her lemonade, trying hard to hide her disappointment.

It was the right thing to do.

And Liddy knew it.

"There's one more thing," Gemma piped in. "I know you hired Mom to bake the cake, and I'm not sure she mentioned this to you yet, but I've enrolled in a culinary school in New York City."

"Mention it? It's all Hayley ever talks about. She's so proud of you," Liddy said.

"Well, I was wondering if you would mind if we designed and baked the cake together as a team?" Gemma asked warily.

"Mind? Of course not! I would be honored!" Liddy exclaimed. "Mother and daughter cake bakers! It sounds like a brand-new show on the Food Network!"

"Thank you, Liddy," Gemma said excitedly. "I'm going to text Conner right away and tell him I have my first professional catering job!"

Gemma scooted into Liddy's house, banging the screen door shut behind her.

Hayley watched her go, a cheerful smile on her face.

"She's still seeing that actor?" Liddy asked.

"Yes. They're living together. I'm not exactly thrilled about that part, but she seems happy."

Suddenly their conversation was abruptly interrupted by a fire-engine red Cadillac ATS swerving into Liddy's driveway, kicking up enough pebbles and dust that Hayley had to wave a hand in front of her face to keep from choking.

Poppyseed, startled awake, sprang up on all fours, and panicked, galloped down off the porch and around the side of the house to find cover.

The driver's side door flew open and Liddy's mother Celeste jumped out. She was in a frenzied state as she stomped up the porch steps.

"I just came from Roberto's salon!" she cried.

"Congratulations, Mother. He did a nice job as usual."

"You like it?" Celeste asked, patting her coiffured and curled hairstyle. "I was afraid he cut it too short, but the shampoo girl insisted it makes me look ten years younger."

"Is that why you raced over here? For a second opinion?" Liddy sighed.

"Of course not! I know I have a beautiful head of hair. It's not thinning like Gladys Hawkins. That poor woman needs to invest in some wigs. No, I was under the dryer with my eyes closed and Gladys, who was under the dryer to my left, thought I had fallen asleep, which of course I would *never* do in public!"

Liddy turned to Hayley. "Because she snores really loud."

"I do not!" Celeste gasped before collecting herself and continuing. "Anyway, Gladys turned to Cathy Jenkins, who was to *her* left and said she believed that *you* were the one who poisoned your poor cousin Lisa because you didn't want her baking your wedding cake!"

"Well, what did you say to them?" Liddy asked.

"Nothing," Celeste said.

"You didn't defend your own daughter?"

"What could I have said?" Celeste said, throwing up her hands.

"I don't know, Mother, maybe you could have said 'My daughter Liddy does not have a violent bone in her body! She is absolutely incapable of committing such an unspeakable act and I am appalled that you would even think so!' You could have started with something like that!"

Celeste nodded. "Yes, I suppose, but people are going to believe what they want to believe."

"That's not the point! You're my mother! You should stick up for me!"

"Yes, yes, I know, but . . ."

"But *what*?"

"It just appears very suspicious! You despising Lisa, you firing her for refusing to bake an angel food cake, and then her suddenly dying after eating one that had been mysteriously poisoned . . ."

Liddy raised an eyebrow. "So?"

"So it just raises a lot of questions . . ." Celeste whispered.

Liddy stared at Celeste, her mouth open in shock. "Mother, are you saying there is a small part of you that thinks I may have done it?"

Celeste was lost in thought but quickly snapped out of it. "No! Of course not, dear. You're my daughter. And if you were tried and convicted of the crime, I would come visit you in prison once a month, except in July, when I'm planning on renting that

gorgeous villa in Italy. I have to do it. It's one less
item on my bucket list before I die."

"Mother!"

"What?"

"You're already picturing me in prison! That
doesn't exactly bolster your argument that you believe me!"

"I *believe* you!" Celeste wailed.

Hayley noticed that Celeste's wide eyes told a
completely different story. Liddy's mother was not
one hundred percent convinced that her daughter
was innocent, and at the moment, she was just
saying what Liddy wanted to hear in order to keep
the peace.

"Now, enough talk about all that nasty business,"
Celeste said, desperate to change the subject. "We
need to send out the cards announcing the postponement."

"What postponement?" Liddy asked.

"The wedding. Obviously we need to push back
the date a few months out of respect for Lisa. After
the burial, then we can send out a reminder so people
don't forget the new date."

"I'm not postponing the wedding, Mother,"
Liddy said quietly.

"Liddy, we can't proceed as if nothing has happened. She's your cousin!"

"If I wait too long, I'm afraid Sonny might never
go through with it!"

"Surely he will understand," Celeste pleaded.

"Absolutely not! The invitations have already
gone out! Everyone has RSVP'd! The wheels are in

motion! I'm not going to throw my whole wedding into disarray just because of stupid, awful ogre Lisa . . . may she rest in peace . . ."

Celeste opened her mouth to press her point further, but clearly knew she was never going to win this one, so she just flung her arms up in the air and stalked inside Liddy's house. "Whatever! I need a drink! Do you have any scotch?"

"You know where to find it," Liddy sighed. Then she turned to Hayley expectantly. "I'm not a monster for wanting my wedding to continue as planned, am I?"

Hayley desperately wanted to suggest she follow her mother's advice and postpone. If people were already speculating about Liddy's involvement in Lisa's murder, the gossip would only intensify over the next couple of weeks as they barreled toward the big day. But she knew her best friend. And once Liddy Crawford was committed, she was a brick wall, and there was nothing that would be able to break through to her. So in this moment, this one time, Hayley chose the path of least resistance.

"Of course not," Hayley said. "You need to do what you think is right."

It wasn't exactly a ringing endorsement of her plan.

But it was the best Hayley could do.

The wedding was on!

Chapter 14

The following day, when Liddy called Hayley mid-morning in a state of hysteria, she knew her friend desperately needed her and would have to take an extra-long lunch hour. While showing an opulent million-dollar shorefront property listing to some prospective buyers from Connecticut, Liddy had received an ominous text from Sonny asking her to come to his office on Cottage Street as quickly as she could manage. Liddy's instincts screamed that this was it, this was the moment Sonny was going to pull out of the wedding and break off the engagement.

Hayley tried reasoning with her, that he would most likely not choose the middle of the workday to do something like this, but in Liddy's heightened state, with so much drama already consuming her wedding plans, reasoning with her was just about the most useless option Hayley could have chosen.

Liddy insisted Hayley accompany her to Sonny's law office for moral support. Hayley had tried to explain that if Sonny's intention was to call off the wedding, it would be exceedingly awkward with Hayley sitting there next to her. But Liddy was determined to have Hayley's hand within reach to squeeze if her worst fears were confirmed. Unable to talk her way out of it, Hayley finally agreed to meet her at Sonny's office at one thirty.

Sal was a bit perturbed by Hayley requesting an extra hour for lunch today, especially since it was busy and there were a lot of details to attend to before putting tomorrow's issue of the *Island Times* to bed, but he begrudgingly relented after she promised to stay an extra hour past quitting time to ensure her inbox was empty when she left.

And so, after a quick lunch at Drinks Like a Fish, she hurried down the street to Sonny Lipton's law office, situated on the second floor above an insurance company next door to the local post office, and found herself sitting next to Liddy opposite Sonny's big mahogany desk, which Liddy had bought for him last Christmas, nervously waiting to hear what Sonny had to say that was so important they had to interrupt their workday.

Sonny sat behind his desk, his shirtsleeves rolled up, his tie loosened, his face drawn from too many hours at the office, shuffling papers. Hayley wondered if he was pretending to skim through these mysterious papers in order to avoid eye contact before dropping the big bomb.

Hayley glanced over at Liddy, whose body was tense, a tight smile on her face, her left hand gripping Hayley's right hand tightly.

Sonny finally looked up from his papers and folded his hands. His expression was serious, if not grave. "I probably should've given you a heads-up as to why I called you here this afternoon, Liddy . . ." He then looked at Hayley, feeling the need to include her in the conversation since she was sitting right in front of him. "And Hayley . . ."

Liddy clenched Hayley's hand tighter until it hurt, causing her to wince.

"But I wasn't sure how to prepare you, so I thought it was probably best to get you over here and just come out with it . . ."

"Sonny, please, don't do this! We can work out whatever problems we have! I'm sorry if I did anything to upset you, just give me another chance!" Liddy wailed, tears running down her cheeks.

Sonny sat back in his chair, surprised by her outburst. "What?"

"Don't call off the wedding! I love you, and I know you love me!"

"Pumpkin, calling off the wedding is the furthest thing from my mind. This is about Lisa."

Hayley suddenly sat up in her chair. "Lisa?"

"Yes," Sonny said as he jumped up and ran around his desk. He leaned down and put a reassuring arm around Liddy's shoulders while kissing her softly on the forehead. "Nothing's going to keep me from marrying my girl, understand?"

Liddy nodded, reaching into her purse for a handkerchief to wipe away the wet tears on her cheeks. "I'm sorry, I thought that's why you wanted to see me," she sniffed. "I don't know if you noticed, but I've been very high-strung and emotional lately."

Both Hayley and Sonny wisely chose to keep their mouths shut. After a moment of silence, Hayley cleared her throat.

"What about Lisa?" Hayley asked, more than a bit curious.

Sonny gently rubbed Liddy on the top of her head with the palm of his hand before returning to his chair behind the desk. Liddy instinctively reached up to pat down her hair, fearing he may have mussed her hairstyle.

Like mother, like daughter.

"Several years ago I helped Lisa prepare her last will and testament," Sonny said, back to being all businesslike.

"You did?" Liddy asked, surprised. "Why didn't you tell me?"

"Attorney-client privilege," Sonny said. "I can't discuss any matters regarding a client, not even with a judge."

"Well, that doesn't seem fair," Liddy said, huffing as she stuffed the handkerchief back into her purse.

"Anyway, since both of Lisa's parents have passed on and she was an only child, she . . . well, she named you, Liddy, as her executor and sole heir."

There was another long pause in the room.

Finally, unable to stand the silence anymore, Hayley spoke. "Excuse me?"

"The estate is not insignificant. She owns the property where her shop resides, and her business has been in the black for a while now, accumulating a healthy fortune with very little overhead."

"How much, exactly?" Hayley couldn't resist asking.

"Enough to pay for the wedding, the honeymoon, and maybe a second vacation home somewhere for the two of us."

"But Lisa *hated* me!" Liddy shouted.

"That's not the impression I got when she came in here to discuss the details of her will," Sonny said solemnly. "You and Celeste were her family—pretty much her only family, here in town, anyway."

Liddy dropped her purse on the floor. The contents scattered all over the room, but she didn't make a move to pick anything up. She just sat there with a bewildered look on her face, processing what she had just heard.

Hayley didn't know whether to congratulate her or offer her condolences, so she kept mum and just allowed Liddy to keep squeezing her hand. But then, suddenly, Liddy released her grip and brought both hands to her mouth. "Oh my God, how could I have mistreated my dear cousin so badly?"

Hayley raised an eyebrow.

Dear cousin?

Liddy despised Lisa.

"I fired her! The poor woman just wanted to flex her creative muscles and come up with something original and inspired for my wedding, and I forced her into a box, insisting she bake exactly what I wanted! I'm a terrible person!"

"Aw, Pumpkin, don't beat yourself up. It's your wedding. It's not unreasonable for you to have an opinion about the wedding cake!"

Liddy looked up at the heavens. "I'm so sorry, Lisa!"

Hayley suppressed a chuckle. This rewriting of history, with Liddy now pretending Lisa was some kind of saint heading straight to heaven when on more than one occasion Liddy had remarked Lisa was undoubtedly bound for the depths of hell, was almost too much to hear, even from Liddy.

But with a windfall of money coming Liddy's way, Hayley knew Lisa from here on in would be known as Liddy's favorite cousin, even though everyone knew she was Liddy's *only* cousin.

After hearing a few more details, specifically when the estate would be closed and the money wired into Liddy's bank account, and how soon she could put the Cake Walk property on the market, Sonny suggested they discuss funeral arrangements.

"Well, Lisa was such a frugal person, I don't think she would want us to spend a lot of money on an expensive coffin and too many flowers . . ." Liddy said, trying her best to at least appear sensitive to her beloved late cousin's wishes.

"You don't have to worry about any of that. Lisa stipulated that she wants to be cremated."

A wave of relief washed over Liddy. "That's great! Simple, clean, and cheap!"

Hayley shot her a look.

"I mean, isn't that just like Lisa?" Liddy followed

up, finding it more difficult to contain the glee rising up inside her as the news of her impending unexpected fortune began sinking in and taking hold. "She was always so practical, never wanting any kind of fuss made."

"Plus, if we did plan a memorial, it would be tough getting anyone to show up," Sonny added, before catching himself. "I'm sorry, sometimes I say things I'm thinking and don't even realize it."

"That's okay, Sonny, we all grieve in our own way," Liddy said, mustering a somber tone, although Hayley could tell Liddy was seconds away from leaping out of her chair and dancing around the room.

"There's one more thing," Sonny said, glancing down at the papers in front of him.

Liddy took a deep breath as if expecting to hear this whole shocking reading of Lisa's will had been a massive prank and she was about to be hit with cold water in the face. "Yes?"

"As executor, it is your responsibility to clear out Lisa's belongings at her bakery and at her apartment and donate everything to Goodwill, per her instructions."

Liddy heaved a big sigh of relief.

She was still getting the money.

"That's easy, Hayley can help me with that. Right, Hayley?"

"Of course," Hayley said, still amused by how hard it was for both Liddy and Sonny to suppress their unadulterated giddiness.

"Well, I guess that's it, then," Sonny said with a

twinkle in his eyes. "Again, I'm so sorry, Pumpkin, I know how hard this is on you."

"Thank you, sweetie. Knowing you are here for me, that you love me and want to spend the rest of your life with me, well, that certainly helps alleviate the pain and grief."

"Oh, Lord . . ." Hayley blurted out, unable to keep silent anymore, dramatically rolling her eyes at the unabashed fakeness of the moment.

The happy couple chose to ignore her.

Hayley agreed to meet Liddy at Lisa's apartment the following Saturday to pack up her belongings. They would deal with the bakery at another time since the police still had yellow police tape wrapped around the perimeter. Liddy wanted to clean out the entire place before lunch because she had a meeting with the florist at one to discuss the arrangements at the reception.

While Liddy plowed through the apartment, tossing assorted knickknacks and cookbooks and potted plants into cardboard boxes, Hayley sat down at a small desk in Lisa's bedroom and went through her personal paperwork, unrelated to her business. She happened upon a jumble of words and letters scribbled on a Post-it note and discovered it was the password to Lisa's home computer, which sat atop the scuffed wooden desk. She clicked through Lisa's files, mostly recipes she had found online, before scrolling down her email. What surprised Hayley was how few personal emails were in her account. It was mostly junk mail, work orders, and receipts, or testimonials from customers who had bought her cakes and cookies and wanted her to know how much they had enjoyed them. She did find a few emails from Celeste, promising to make sure Liddy hired her to bake the wedding cake and keeping her informed of her progress. Farther down she noticed an email from lobsterstud34. She clicked on it and read it.

Bitch, if you don't wise up and take care of business, I'll see to it you never bake another cake.

In the sender box, next to lobsterstud34, in parentheses, was the name Timmy Blanchard, automatically put there from the Contacts app. Hayley knew Timmy Blanchard. He had dated Lisa for a couple of years, until recently, but like most of Lisa's relationships, romantic or otherwise, it had ended badly.

Liddy walked into the room carrying a box. "Hayley, stop snooping on Lisa's computer and help me. We haven't even started on the bedroom closet yet, although I can't imagine there are a lot of clothes in there. Lisa's wardrobe was basically jeans and T-shirts. Honestly, she made Mona look like one of America's Next Top Models."

"Lisa got an email a few days ago, right before she died, from Timmy Blanchard."

"That loser? God, I thought she dumped him!"

"She did, but they were apparently still in contact. I don't like the violent tone of his message."

This got Liddy's attention.

She scurried over and peered over Hayley's shoulder.

"That's a death threat," Liddy gasped.

"It's disturbing."

"So what do we do?"

"Didn't he once haul traps for Mona?"

"Yes, but that was like years ago."

"I vaguely remember he left suddenly—one day he was there and the next he was gone. I think we should go talk to Mona and find out if he was fired or if he quit and why."

Liddy agreed.

Neither one had to verbalize what they really wanted to know.

If Timmy Blanchard might be capable of murder.

Chapter 15

An audible gasp escaped Hayley's lips as she stepped out of her car in the driveway of Mona's lobster shop. Liddy was still struggling to free herself from the seat belt on the passenger's side and had yet to notice the young man, probably in his early twenties, stunningly gorgeous, shirtless and sweaty, wearing just a pair of tan shorts, who was loading traps into the back of Mona's red, dented pickup truck. When Liddy finally got out of the car and followed Hayley's gaze, curious to know what she was so fixated upon, she nearly smashed her fingers when slamming the door shut because she too was suddenly distracted by the young man flexing his muscles as he lifted a heavy trap.

"Oh . . . my . . . God . . ." she whispered.

They both stood there for a moment, taking in this perfect vision of youthful masculinity. He was just over six feet, with a beatific face, lean frame but with nicely contoured muscles, smooth chest, and strong, sturdy legs dusted with light blond hair.

There was a tattoo of the American flag on his left bicep. Both Hayley and Liddy sighed, loud enough to garner the young man's attention. He politely nodded at them and then went back to work.

Sabrina bounded out of the shop, followed by Mona carrying a Styrofoam cooler.

She excitedly waved at Hayley and Liddy. "Hi, girls!"

Sabrina's high-pitched squeal snapped them out of the R-rated fantasies that were currently playing out in both of their minds.

Sabrina pressed a button on her remote to pop open the trunk of her Ford Mustang convertible, which was parked next to Hayley's far less glamorous Kia.

"Just put the lobsters in there, Mona," Sabrina ordered before spinning around to Hayley and Liddy. "I'm having a family cookout with my relatives at my rental this afternoon and I'm serving fresh lobsters from Mona's shop."

Mona set the cooler in the trunk and banged the lid shut.

Sabrina's eyes glazed over as she glanced at the young man loading the traps. "Isn't he dreamy? That's Mona's new assistant, AJ."

"What a stud!" Liddy cooed.

"You think so?" Mona asked, scrunching up her nose, not convinced. "I guess he's all right."

"He's splendid, Mona, and you know it! Stop being so coy," Sabrina teased.

"He's strong and he works cheap. That's all I care about," Mona growled, although she too could not stop staring at the physical beauty of her newest employee.

"I've got to get going," Sabrina said, pressing another button on her remote to unlock the doors. "I still have to get to the Shop 'n Save to pick up the corn on the cob, and I haven't even thought about what to serve for dessert yet! I had planned to pick something up at Lisa's bakery, but, well . . . that's not going to happen now . . ."

There was an awkward silence before Sabrina realized how callous she sounded, so she quickly dropped the subject by turning and waving at the young man who had just finished loading the traps and was clapping the back of the truck closed. "Bye, AJ!"

"Goodbye, Mrs. Merryweather," he grunted.

"It's Ms. Merryweather! I'm not married. Let's be clear about that. And you can call me Sabrina!"

He looked at her funny, then shrugged. "Okay."

Mona had heard enough of Sabrina's shameless flirting. She called out to AJ, "Drive those traps down to the pier and load them up on my boat so they're ready for when I head out in the morning."

"Yes, ma'am," he said, fishing the keys to the truck from a pocket in his shorts.

"Then you can call it a day. I'll see you tomorrow at the pier. Boat's leaving at five A.M., so don't be late."

"I'll be there, ma'am," he said, and then he got in the truck and backed out of the driveway as Hayley, Liddy, and Sabrina all watched with rapt attention until he drove off and disappeared around the bend toward town.

"'Ma'am'? Not only is he magnificent to look at, he's polite too!" Sabrina gushed. "See you girls later!"

Sabrina hopped in her Mustang and peeled away.

"I'll bet anything she's following him to the pier hoping to get her hooks into him," Liddy cracked.

"You really think so?" Hayley asked.

"Sure. It's exactly what I would do if I wasn't about to get married."

"Enough about AJ! He's half your age!" Mona barked. "What brings you two here?"

"Timmy Blanchard," Hayley said.

"What about him?" Mona asked, a distasteful look on her face.

"We found an email he wrote to Lisa right before she died, and it wasn't exactly a love letter. In fact, it was rather menacing."

Mona shook her head. "I don't doubt it. Timmy's a miserable hothead. When he worked for me, he would spout off all the time about this guy looking at him the wrong way or that guy disrespecting him. He was always picking a fight with somebody. I was the only one he didn't dare tangle with, because the little bugger knew I would eat him alive."

"Why did he leave?" Hayley asked.

"Because I fired him. He was lazy and unreliable and I didn't like his attitude. He only worked for me for a few weeks, but that was enough for me to know I didn't like him."

"He was dating Lisa at the time he worked for you, is that right?" Liddy asked.

"Yup. I overheard him a couple of times talking to her on his phone when he was supposed to be working behind the counter taking orders from customers. He was constantly screaming and yelling at her about something. Believe me, it was *not* a healthy relationship."

Hayley gulped. "Do you think he might be capable of—?"

Mona interrupted her before she could even finish. "Yup. It wouldn't surprise me at all if it turned out he was the one who spiked the cake that killed Lisa."

Chapter 16

When Hayley and Liddy pulled up in front of Lisa's shop, they saw that the police had finally removed the yellow tape from around its perimeter. It was now safe to rummage through Lisa's office for any important documents related to the business that they would need in order to execute her wishes as stated in her last will and testament. Liddy had obtained the key to the bakery from Lisa's house, but waited until she was given the all clear by Sergio before showing up and possibly disturbing the crime scene. Again, she recruited Hayley for emotional support. Plus, if they had to clear out or clean up the place, she certainly wasn't prepared to do that on her own. Her housekeeper was on vacation in Fort Lauderdale, so that pretty much left Hayley.

Liddy slipped the key into the lock on the front door and turned it. She tried to push the door open, but it wouldn't budge.

"That's strange," Liddy said.

"Maybe it's stuck. Here, let me try," Hayley said.

Liddy stepped back, and Hayley pressed her right shoulder against the door and thrust her body against it, but to no avail. That's when she noticed the thick steel lock in the small crack between the door and the doorjamb.

"It's been bolted shut from the inside," Hayley said.

Liddy withdrew the key. "Well, that doesn't make any sense."

"Maybe one of the investigating officers locked the door from the inside and left out the back. Come on," Hayley said, heading around the side of the building.

As she rounded the corner, she stopped cold. "Liddy, look . . ."

One of the windows on the side of the building had been smashed. Shards of glass were scattered all over the ground.

Liddy gasped.

Hayley cautiously approached the window, ducking just underneath it before taking a deep breath and slowly raising her head up to peek inside. She couldn't see anything, just a glass case full of dried-out bakery goods, but she heard someone in the back office foraging through drawers and closets.

Hayley waved at Liddy to follow her, and they continued around to the back door. Liddy handed her the key, and as quietly as she could, Hayley inserted it into the lock, turning it until it disengaged and the door slowly creaked open. Whoever had broken into the bakery must have climbed through the window and bolted the front door from the inside to make certain no one came in to surprise him or her, but had forgotten all about the back door.

Hayley crept inside with Liddy close behind her. Liddy gripped Hayley's arm so tightly it hurt. When they rounded the corner and had a full view of Lisa's office, they caught sight of Timmy Blanchard rifling through Lisa's expensive-looking mahogany desk.

"Hold it right there, Timmy!" Liddy barked, as if she was armed and sporting a police badge, which was not the case. In Hayley's mind, it had been a dumb move to call attention to themselves when they weren't sure if Timmy was packing and in a dangerous frame of mind.

Timmy popped his head up and spun around, a slight look of relief washing over his face when he realized it wasn't the cops. "Jesus, you two nearly gave me a heart attack!"

"What the hell are you doing here, Timmy?" Liddy demanded to know.

Timmy dropped a file stuffed with paperwork on the desk. "That's none of your business."

"It is most certainly my business, because Lisa made me executor and principal heir of her will, so this is technically *my* property now," Liddy huffed.

"I find that hard to believe," Timmy scoffed, scratching the three-day scruff on his face.

"Frankly, so do I, but she did," Liddy said. "Isn't that right, Hayley?"

Hayley whipped out her cell phone. "I'm calling the police to report a breaking and entering."

"Wait! Hold on!" Timmy begged, suddenly panicked. "Don't do that! I wasn't here to steal anything. I just came over here to pick something up that was mine to take, I swear on my life!"

Hayley kept her finger hovering over the 9 button on her phone, ready to dial 911 at any moment, but she was not going to complete the call just yet. Not until she heard what Timmy had to say. "Go on . . ."

"Lisa had a cash flow problem recently and had to borrow some money from me . . ."

"That doesn't sound remotely plausible. Lisa was worth a fortune," Liddy argued.

"Yes, on paper, but she sometimes came up short when she needed to buy baking ingredients, and so she just happened to catch me on a day when we weren't fighting, and I was feeling generous, so I wrote her a check for three hundred dollars."

Hayley shook her head, disgusted. "So you smashed a window and were combing her office for any money she might have had lying around because she's no longer alive to pay you back?"

"No! Lisa called me the day before she died to tell me she had an envelope for me with the money she had borrowed, plus interest. She said I could stop by anytime to pick it up, but I was busy that day and told her I would swing by the next day. Unfortunately, by then, she was dead and the police wouldn't let anyone near this place. So I waited until things died down."

"That's still breaking and entering," Hayley reminded him.

"I just came here to get what's rightfully mine! Honest!" he whined.

"Did you find the envelope?" Liddy asked.

"Not yet. Hey, would you two mind helping me look?"

"Yes, we would mind, Timmy! You have ten seconds to get out of here before I call the police!" Hayley warned.

"Please, ladies, I'm dead broke and could really use the cash," he pleaded. "I lost a lot last week playing the slots in Bangor."

"If we come across the envelope with your name on it, we'll make sure you get it!" Hayley said.

"There should be three hundred and thirty bucks in it—that includes the ten percent interest!" Timmy said, smiling.

"Out!" Hayley screamed.

Timmy nodded and slowly moved away from the desk, his hands up in the air. But before he could reach the back door, Liddy stopped him. "Wait! Was it you, Timmy? Did you kill Lisa?"

Timmy froze in his tracks. "What? Me? No, of course I didn't! We may have had our problems, but I would never do anything so drastic! Why would I do that?"

"Maybe a crime of passion?" Liddy suggested.

"Maybe you never got over Lisa breaking up with you."

"I broke up with her, not the other way around!" Timmy wailed.

"It's no secret that you two had a number of screaming matches on the phone and in person all the time," Hayley said. "I bet if we ask Chief Alvares, he could drum up one or two reports of being called out to Lisa's house during one of your knock-down, drag-out slugfests!"

"Once! It happened once! But I didn't kill her! We barely saw each other anymore, and when we did, everything was cool between us. We were better as friends than we were as a couple, and we both knew it! Like I already told you, I even lent her money when she needed it!"

Timmy, his eyes wide with worry at the suggestion that he'd had anything to do with Lisa's murder, lowered his hands and continued, in a quiet, calm voice. "Listen, ladies, I read all the details in Bruce Linney's column about the murder. He said Lisa was poisoned by some very rare, hard-to-get poison. Look at me. Where would I get my hands on anything like that?"

The kid had a point.

But Liddy was still not convinced. "You better hope you had nothing to do with my beloved cousin's murder, because if I find out otherwise, I will hunt you down like an animal and shoot you between the eyes without giving it a second thought! And that's a promise!"

Timmy stared at Liddy, his mouth agape, paralyzed with shock. Not because Liddy was threatening to snuff out his life, but because she had just called Lisa her "beloved cousin."

It was obvious to Hayley, based on Timmy's dumb-founded expression, that Lisa's not-too-bright, ill-tempered ex-boyfriend may be a jerk, but he didn't have much of a motive to kill Lisa. Now Liddy on the other hand, who was at the moment in real time busy rewriting history when it came to her fractured relationship with her now "beloved" cousin, had cause to worry because so far she was the only one with a solid, indisputable motive to commit murder.

Island Food & Cocktails
BY HAYLEY POWELL

I was rummaging through my refrigerator for something to snack on a few days ago when I spied a plastic-wrapped bowl of leftover Roma tomatoes from the previous weekend when I made a big pot of my homemade spaghetti sauce. I grabbed those tomatoes, because I suddenly had a eureka moment—I had a taste for bruschetta. I even had a baguette on the counter that was still soft and fresh and some goat cheese chilling in the fridge.

You can make bruschetta with just about anything, but I had my own special recipe, one I hadn't served in quite a while. Not since I made it for a friend's wedding reception a few years back, and let me tell you, it was divine!

I'll never forget that wedding. It all started when my BFF Liddy's real estate firm's business was booming, and she decided she needed some extra help. Well, much to everyone's shock, she wound up hiring a young, newly licensed realtor, who was, in the words of my brother Randy, "runway ready," which meant she looked like a supermodel!

All of our friends were downright flabbergasted when Liddy so kindly took this knockout under her wing and generously became her mentor in the Bar Harbor real estate world.

Now don't get me wrong, Liddy has always been the utmost professional. She runs a tight ship and is a definite stickler for following all real estate and office protocol. However, as we all know, she can be a bit competitive (sorry, Liddy, I love you, but you know it's true), and she was never one to go out of her way to give another person a slight edge against her, especially if it threatened to kick her out of her number one spot of Top Downeast Real Estate Seller of the Year!

And the fact that the new girl in her office was a twenty-five-year-old, drop-dead gorgeous, blue-eyed blonde named Megan was even more stupefying! I could hardly believe how beautiful this young woman was when Liddy brought her to lunch for me to meet soon after she started working at the office. And the two got along like long lost twins, smiling at each other and giggling at each other's jokes. And just to make things even more puzzling, I noticed Megan wasn't wearing a wedding ring! She was single too! Liddy made a point of never fraternizing with young, pretty, single women. She considered all of them predators invading her territory in a town that wasn't exactly flush with single, eligible bachelors. (This was long before that fateful day when Liddy met the man of her dreams, Sonny Lipton.)

While gabbing over a plate of fried clams at my

brother's bar, Drinks Like a Fish, I was dying to
ask Liddy what her game was. There had to be
some ulterior motive for her to cultivate such an
unlikely alliance. When Megan stood up to go to
the ladies' room and had to stop to fend off the
advances of a lovesick lobsterman by the bar, I had
my chance.

"What is going on here, Liddy? This is not like
you at all!"

"Patience, Hayley, patience," Liddy said, raising
her eyes from the menu and smiling sweetly.

After Megan returned to the table, we finished
placing our orders with the waitress and were
chatting among ourselves when a well-dressed
young man stopped by our table to say hello to
Liddy. She introduced him as Todd, a loan officer
at Bar Harbor Banking and Trust. We all politely
said hello and went back to our conversation. He
just stood there, a little reluctant to leave, but soon
moved on since none of us was paying any more
attention to him. Not a minute later, two more
handsome young men whom I recognized from
when they came by the newspaper office recently
to place ads for their new summer scooter rental
business also stopped by to casually say hello to
me, and I introduced them to Liddy and Megan.

The pair lingered longer than was comfortable,
but finally got the hint to move on when we downright ignored them. Then yet another young man
stopped by to say hello, and that's when the light
bulb finally went off in my head!

I had it all figured out. Liddy had befriended the
stunning and quite honestly funny and charming

Megan for a reason. Liddy knew every man in
town would be sniffing around for an introduction,
and having Megan in close proximity to herself
would just mean Liddy could also benefit from
being around lots of young, studly, available men
too! And it worked like a charm. Liddy enjoyed all
the attention and later called our time with Megan
our "Twenties Do-Over Summer"!

As it turned out, Megan was really a fun, caring,
and smart girl, and the three of us enjoyed going
out together on the weekends for cocktails at all the
local hot spots, and like clockwork, Megan would
attract men like bees to honey. Even though I knew
they weren't there to impress me, I enjoyed all the
free cocktails the men would buy for us while
vying for Megan's undivided attention.

Liddy was another story. She would flirt shamelessly with all of these young men, some nearly
half her age, to the point where I was slightly
embarrassed by her behavior. But Megan would
just laugh it off, because she truly adored Liddy
and considered her a dear friend.

Unfortunately all good things must come to an
end, and much to Liddy's dismay, by the fall of
that year Megan had met a bright, good-looking
young man who worked at First National Bank
and was on the fast track to a VP position. Liddy
made noises about Megan being too young to
settle down and still needing time to play the field,
but it soon became obvious, even to Liddy, that
Megan had met her soul mate, and so a wedding
date was set.

Luckily, Megan's fiancé was a cool guy and secure enough in his relationship with Megan that he had no problem with her still going out for cocktails with me and Liddy, knowing the men at the bar would fawn over her and, by osmosis, us too. So Liddy managed to hold on to a little bit of glory. That is, until Megan's fiancé finally got the VP promotion, but at another branch of the bank, in Bangor. Megan applied for a job at Bangor Real Estate Agency to be closer to her groom-to-be, and though distraught at losing her best Realtor and close pal, Liddy magnanimously wrote a glowing letter of recommendation.

As they hugged goodbye on Megan's last day as Liddy's employee, I saw Liddy actually tearing up. She really did love the girl. Before they parted, Megan whispered something in Liddy's ear, and as she wiped away her tears, she lit up with a big smile on her face.

As Megan got in the car and drove away, I had to ask Liddy what she had said. Liddy turned to me, and with a big grin on her face, said, "Megan's mom lives in California and won't be around to help with the wedding, so she wants me to help her plan everything, which means lots of trips to Bangor, where there are lots of bars and restaurants and single men—way more than here in little ole Bar Harbor!"

I just had to shake my head and laugh as Liddy's imagination exploded with all kinds of possibilities.

By the way, Megan's wedding was absolutely

beautiful, and since Megan's husband is from a large Italian family, that meant the reception was filled with scrumptious Italian flavors, including my homemade bruschetta, as well as this yummy, simple cocktail, which started the festivities off with a bang!

LIMONCELLO PROSECCO COCKTAIL

1 ounce Limoncello
1 chilled bottle of Prosecco

Pour Limoncello into a champagne glass. Top off with chilled Prosecco and hand the cocktails out to your guests. Make a toast and enjoy!

TOMATO, BASIL, AND GOAT CHEESE BRUSCHETTA

2 cups Roma tomatoes, chopped
2 cloves fresh garlic, finely minced (more, if you love garlic like I do)
1 tablespoon extra virgin olive oil
1 tablespoon balsamic vinegar
½ cup chopped fresh basil
Kosher salt and ground pepper to taste
1 baguette
1 whole clove garlic, sliced in half
¼ cup to ½ cup crumbled goat cheese (use the amount you desire to your taste)

In a mixing bowl, add your chopped tomatoes, minced garlic, olive oil, balsamic vinegar, basil, and salt and pepper. Mix all together and set aside. If you would like, you can make this a few hours in advance to allow time for the flavors to mix together.

Preheat your oven to 375°F. Slice your baguette and place slices on a cookie sheet. Place in oven for ten minutes or until lightly browned and toasted. Remove from oven and rub your garlic halves on all of the slices. Sprinkle your goat cheese crumbles on the warm baguettes and then spoon your tomato mixture on top. *Buon appetito!*

Chapter 17

"The strawberry scone looks delicious. I'll take one of those," Bruce said, pointing his finger at the last one sitting invitingly on a plate inside the glass case. Bruce's eyes scanned the other baked goods on display. "And the blueberry muffin . . . and the banana walnut bread."

Hayley sighed. "We just came from lunch."

"I had a salad. I'm going to be starving by four o'clock," Bruce reasoned.

Helen Fennow smiled as she picked up a pair of metal tongs and withdrew the scone from the display case and carefully placed it in a brown paper sack with her bakery's logo on the side, which was a half-eaten cookie with the name of her bakery, The Cookie Crumble, below it.

Hayley sighed again. "Yes, but we didn't come here to—"

"And one of those peanut butter cookies . . . Wait, make it two . . ."

He glanced at Hayley. "You want one?"

Hayley shrugged. "Sure."

"Make it three—no, four . . . what the hell, just make it a half dozen."

Helen happily nodded and got to work fulfilling the suddenly large order by pulling a bigger bag with handles out from underneath the counter.

Hayley refrained from commenting any further on Bruce's sudden sweets binge, even though his doctor had warned him about his rising glucose numbers, which were teetering dangerously close to pre-diabetes levels. She had already lectured him at lunch, forcing him to order a salad, which hadn't sat well with him at all.

She was also still sore about his impulsive, ham-fisted decision to break the story of how Lisa Crawford was poisoned despite Sabrina's direct request that they keep mum about the revelation until after the coroner had had the opportunity to release his final autopsy report. Hayley knew deep down that Bruce was a reporter first, and a reporter never ignores a scoop. That was just part of the package, and she had come to accept it. And as a small consolation, she hadn't heard one word from Sabrina about ignoring her condition of not revealing the information, which made Hayley feel a little bit better about breaking her confidence.

In fact, a small part of her suspected that Sabrina knew Bruce would never keep his word about not sharing it, because on some level Sabrina actually wanted to get the news out there somehow. At least that's what Hayley hoped. In any event, Hayley was inclined to forgive Bruce and let the whole matter go. His utter lack of healthy food choices, however, not so much.

While at lunch, Bruce had eagerly tried to change the subject of his eating habits by discussing possible suspects in the Lisa Crawford murder. One name that kept coming up was that of Helen Fennow, Lisa's former assistant. If Lisa had done any of what she was accused of, planting rotten food and mice in Helen's brand-new bakery, then that would certainly be a motive for Helen to commit murder.

Helen finished filling the bag with her baked goods and rang up the order on the register.

Hayley noticed that the glass display case was at this point nearly empty, in desperate need of some restocking. "Looks like you've been busy today."

"I had a line out the door this morning. I'm going to have to hire extra help. This week's been crazy, and every day seems to get even crazier than the last. Business has been booming ever since I became the only game in town!"

The moment she said it, Helen obviously regretted it. She instantly wiped the big grin off her face and struggled to adopt a more reflective and somber tone. "I just meant that there's been a small silver lining in the midst of this horrible tragedy. I'm so sorry, I didn't mean to be callous."

"Of course not," Bruce said softly, attempting to put her at ease.

"Lisa was very good to me; she taught me everything I know. We were the closest of friends until . . . until I decided to break out on my own."

"And then she turned on you," Hayley said.

"Yes, and with such a stunning viciousness. I was so taken aback. I didn't expect her to go to the lengths she did to hurt me."

"By trying to wreck your new business?" Bruce asked.

"Yes. She didn't know I had installed a security camera the day before she broke in and planted the mice and spoiled food. It recorded everything. In fact, I was at the police station delivering the evidence to Chief Alvares the day you discovered her body in her bakery. I was standing right there in front of him when he got the call. I couldn't believe it."

"Did you see Lisa after we saw you in her shop a few days before she died?" Hayley asked.

Helen shook her head. "No, I knew it was probably best to keep my distance. And after I got the call from the health department acting on an anonymous tip, I knew it had to have been her who called them. But I still didn't want to confront her or engage her in any way after that, because I finally realized what a vindictive person she was, and what she was actually capable of doing to exact her revenge."

Hayley studied Helen, who was acting calm, cool, and collected.

Helen noticed Hayley staring at her. "I know what you're thinking. You want me to say Lisa was a conniving, despicable, poor excuse for a human being, and the world is a better place without her, and that I refuse to shed one tear over the fact that she's gone for good. Is that what you want me to say?

Because that would give you sufficient cause to keep me on your list of suspects. But I won't do that. I am grateful to Lisa. Without her, none of this would have ever been possible. And now I am a successful businesswoman. I owe it all to her."

"We believe you," Hayley felt the need to say, even though she was not entirely one hundred percent convinced Helen was being sincere.

"Look, let me save you a lot of time investigating me. I did not kill Lisa. I'm simply not capable of it. I can't even pronounce the name of the poison that killed her."

After running Bruce's credit card and handing it back to him along with the big paper bag of goodies he had purchased, Helen's smile returned. "Now, let's please put all this ugly chatter aside and talk business. Now that Lisa's out of the picture, is her cousin Liddy looking for a new wedding cake baker? I know a spectacularly talented one who might be available!"

"You?" Bruce guessed, already fully aware of the answer.

"Yes! I promise I will do a bang-up job. She won't regret it. And as for references, all Liddy has to do is check out all of the glowing testimonials on my Yelp page before she makes a final decision," Helen said, driving the sales pitch home.

"Will do," Hayley said.

She didn't want to reveal to Helen that Liddy had already made her final decision about who was going to design and bake her wedding cake and it was Hayley and Gemma. Because if there was

even the slightest chance Helen did get rid of Lisa,
Hayley feared she wouldn't hesitate bumping off
Hayley and Gemma in order to get the job baking
Liddy's cake. Although Helen put on a good show,
there was still a nagging suspicion in the back of
Hayley's mind that it was all an act. Behind the fake
smile and fawning compliments and protestations
of innocence quite possibly lurked the mind of a
cold-blooded killer.

   Helen Fennow was right about one thing.

   She was staying on Hayley's list of possible suspects.

Chapter 18

"I was hoping to see Gemma and Dustin tonight," Randy said as he hungrily devoured a plateful of Hayley's newest concoction: a chicken Parmesan casserole, a delectable, rich, savory dish smothered in two of his favorite foods—mozzarella cheese and crushed garlic croutons.

"I'm afraid we don't rate high on their priority list anymore. They're both only here until after the wedding, then Gemma heads back to New York and Dustin starts his new semester at CalArts in California in the fall, so they only have a limited amount of time to spend with their friends this summer," Hayley said as she watched both Randy and Sergio gobble up their dinners, effusive in their compliments in between bites.

"Why haven't you made this for us before?" Sergio asked, stabbing a piece of chicken before scraping some tomato sauce onto his fork and stuffing it in his mouth.

"I just discovered the recipe online. I wish I

could take credit for it, but it's not mine," Hayley said before grabbing their now-empty plates and carrying them into the kitchen to refill them with another serving.

"I'm sorry Bruce couldn't join us tonight either," Randy yelled from the dining room as Hayley used a spatula to cut two more pieces from the casserole dish.

"He's working late. He's hoping to get here in time for coffee and dessert. Mostly because he wants to hear if Sergio has had any breakthroughs in the Lisa Crawford case," Hayley answered, returning to the dining room and setting the plates down in front of Randy and Sergio, who both immediately grabbed their forks and started inhaling their second helpings.

"Not because he loves us like brothers and wants to spend more quality time with us?" Randy asked with his mouth full.

"Well, that too," Hayley laughed before turning serious and glancing at Sergio. "So, has there been any progress?"

"A little," Sergio said, nodding. "I examined Lisa's business records and appointment books today and found a list of names jotted down in her calendar on the day she was poisoned."

"But Lisa claimed she never bothered writing down appointments, which was why she never seemed to be expecting us whenever Liddy and I would stop by her shop," Hayley said.

"Well, she was lying," Sergio said matter-of-factly.

"Of course she was," Hayley sighed. "So what did you find?"

Hayley started to grow impatient while waiting for Sergio to finish chewing on a piece of chicken. Why couldn't people in her orbit talk and eat at the same time?

"Most of them were local customers, names I recognized; no one who would ever raise a red flower," Sergio finally said after swallowing.

There was a long pause.

Randy tenderly put a hand on Sergio's arm and quietly whispered in his ear. "Flag. It's raise a red flag."

Sergio didn't argue and just nodded.

The Brazilian, who sometimes mixed up his words—English being his second language, after all—was getting better at just accepting the corrections without comment.

"Red flag," he said. "None of them had any other connection to Lisa other than the obvious one of being interested in hiring her services. One name did stand out, however . . ."

Sergio scooped a big piece of chicken drowning in melted cheese on his fork and opened his mouth to suck it in when Hayley's hand suddenly shot out and grabbed his wrist before he could reach his mouth.

"Wait, the suspense is killing me! I cannot wait until you chew and swallow that piece of chicken! I will not allow you to put that in your mouth until you tell me the name!"

Sergio eyed Hayley like she was a crazy person, but then just shrugged and said, "Tony Capshaw."

"Who is Tony Capshaw?" Hayley asked, puzzled.

"Whips me," Sergio said.

Another long pause.

Curious as to exactly what he meant, Hayley asked, "I beg your pardon?"

Randy leaned in again, whispering in his husband's ear. "Beats me." Then he turned and smiled at Hayley. "He means 'beats me,' as in he has no idea. He was not suggesting anything else, I promise you."

Hayley stifled a chuckle.

"Can I please eat my chicken now, Hayley?" Sergio asked.

Hayley realized she was still squeezing the poor man's wrist, keeping him from feasting on his last piece of chicken Parmesan casserole. She released her grip, and without wasting a second, Sergio stuffed it in his mouth and happily chewed on it, savoring every morsel.

"So Tony Capshaw was the only name you didn't recognize," Hayley said.

Sergio nodded, setting his fork down and picking up his napkin to wipe his mouth. "Yes. But that's not unusual. Thousands of tourists pour into Bar Harbor every summer, and many of them throw parties and picnics and barbecues or have special occasions like birthdays and anniversaries while they're here and need to hire a baker. But why Tony Capshaw stood out was because he was Lisa's last appointment of the day."

"So he was there right before I found Lisa dead in the back of the bakery?"

"Yes. Which is why it's very important that I locate this guy and find out what he knows. Could be nothing, or maybe he might remember something that could prove useful to the investigation," Sergio said. "Now, what's for dessert? And do we have to wait for Bruce to get here?"

"Milk chocolate banana pudding, and no, I'll get you some right away," Hayley said, standing up again and collecting all the plates, her mind churning over and over with the name Tony Capshaw. She was even more determined than Chief Sergio to figure out who this mystery man was and if he had any connection to Lisa Crawford's murder.

Chapter 19

Randy placed six different possible signature wedding cocktails on top of the bar at Drinks Like a Fish for Hayley, Liddy, Mona, and Sabrina to taste in order to decide which one was best to serve at the wedding reception. In the final contention were a grapefruit ginger spiced rum punch, a rum orange swizzle, a bourbon peach sweet tea, a blackberry whiskey lemonade, and finally, a raspberry Limoncello Prosecco.

"I'm leaning toward the Prosecco," Sabrina said after taking a sip. "It's so light and refreshing."

"Forget it," Mona growled. "If I'm going to sit through twenty minutes of Liddy's sickeningly sweet wedding vows, I'm going to need some hard liquor. I vote for the whiskey lemonade."

After throwing Mona a side eye, Liddy sipped every alcoholic concoction one more time. She considered each one carefully, then turned to Hayley. "I can't decide. Which one do you like?"

"The bourbon peach sweet tea is delectable. I'm not a huge rum fan, so I'm ready to knock out the first two, but Mona may have a point . . ."

Liddy glared at Hayley, who quickly continued, "Not about your wedding vows! I'm sure they will be moving and emotional and just the right length of time. But everyone knows I love a good whiskey cocktail, so I think the lemonade is a great choice!"

Liddy turned back to Sabrina. "Sabrina? Do you agree?"

"I agree you're all alcoholics. I already told you I prefer the Prosecco, but clearly I'm outvoted."

Liddy grimaced. "I just can't decide. Randy, which one do you think I should choose?"

"These cocktails are like my children. I love each and every one exactly the same."

"Just serve them all and let's be done with this stupid taste test," Mona yelled. "Enough with these fancy drinks. Randy, get me a beer."

"Coming right up," he said, dashing off to find a clean mug.

"Maybe Mona's right. Maybe I should just serve them all," Liddy sighed.

"You can't have six signature wedding cocktails, Liddy. You really should settle on just one," Hayley said.

"I've settled on one," Sabrina said with lust in her eyes. "And he's right over there!"

They all turned to see Mona's dreamy young assistant AJ playing a game of darts with a buddy in the back of the bar. He was wearing a plaid shirt with the sleeves cut off, which showed off his taut muscles, and a pair of tight jeans that accentuated his perfectly formed butt. A Boston Red Sox cap was pulled down far enough to shadow his handsome face.

Smitten, Sabrina slid off her bar stool and sashayed over to AJ, pretending she was heading to the restroom, but stopping on the way, blocking him from throwing his dart at the board. She feigned surprise at running into him. He smiled and stuck his hand out to shake hers, but she waved it away and threw her arms around his neck, hugging him, smashing her breasts against his chest. The poor kid didn't know quite how to react so he just patiently patted her back with his hand. When she finally let him go, she continued to stand between him and the dartboard, chattering incessantly, long enough that his buddy got tired of waiting and ambled up to the bar for another bottle of Budweiser.

Randy returned with a mug of beer and set it down in front of Mona, who scooped it up and took a big swig just as Liddy remarked, "Look at Sabrina shamelessly flirting with that boy. I mean, really, he's half her age! What kind of woman *does* that?"

Mona did a spit-take, spraying beer all over the front of Randy's shirt.

"Thanks, Mona," Randy sighed, grabbing a towel

and wiping his shirt off as he headed for the kitchen.

"What's the matter with you?" Liddy asked.

Hayley, who was sitting on the stool next to Mona, kicked her lightly on the leg with her shoe, silently begging her not to start anything.

Mona, who was obviously dying to remind Liddy that Sonny, the man she was about to marry, was also nearly half her age, for once decided to keep her remarks to herself. She just wiped her mouth with the sleeve of her sweatshirt and shrugged. "Nothing."

Unfortunately, at the end of the bar, a local drunk by the name of Butch Haggerty, who was in Sonny's class at Bucksport High School before they both moved to Bar Harbor, was on his fourth or fifth bourbon straight up and had no compunction about joining their conversation. "Come on, Liddy, you know you like 'em young too. I mean, look at Sonny. What is he, twenty, thirty years younger than you?"

Liddy sat up straight on her bar stool, nostrils flaring, and howled, "Hardly! There's barely an age difference between us!"

Poor Mona had just taken another sip of her beer and couldn't help herself. She spit it out again. Randy, who had just emerged from the kitchen in a fresh shirt, tossed a white rag at Mona so she could clean up the mess she had just made on the bar, which, to her credit, she did.

Hayley prayed boozy Butch would mercifully

withdraw from the conversation as it became obvious he was angering Liddy, but her prayers sadly were not answered. He just plowed ahead, slurring, "Don't get me wrong. I love dating older women. I get to meet a lot of them on my postal route."

Butch was a mailman and also fancied himself a ladies' man. However, with his long, stringy, unwashed hair, glassy eyes, and gaunt frame, she wondered just how much action he really got with any woman, let alone an older woman.

"Thank you for your valuable input, Butch," Liddy sneered as she swiveled around on her stool, making sure her back was to him in an attempt to give him a hint to stop horning in on their private conversation.

"Hey, I didn't mean to eavesdrop," he muttered.

"Then don't," Liddy said curtly.

He didn't heed her suggestion. "I'm just saying cougars make the best girlfriends because, for one thing . . ."

"Oh no, here we go," Hayley whispered to Mona.

". . . they are experienced in the sack and can teach an eager young man a few things under the covers, if you know what I mean . . ." Butch said, holding up a finger. "And two . . ."

"He's not going to stop," Hayley said, shaking her head.

". . . they usually pay for dinner," he slurred, holding up two fingers. "And three . . ."

He paused, trying hard to think, raised a third

finger, and continued. ". . . they have a lot of years of experience in the bedroom . . ."

"You already said that!" Mona barked.

"I did? Wait, and three . . ." He tried hard, but it was apparent nothing immediately popped into his mind, and he finally put his fingers down. "Maybe there were only two."

Liddy had heard enough. "Please do not compare my Sonny to your disgusting exploits!"

Butch guffawed, nearly toppling over from his bar stool. "Come on, Sonny is much worse than I am! He's been chasing after older broads for years, ever since we were in high school in Bucksport when he flirted with our geometry teacher, Mrs. Halperin."

"I'm sure it was just a phase. He was in high school with raging teenage hormones like every other boy his age," Liddy argued.

"No, seriously, he's always been like that," Butch said, trying to focus on her with his bleary eyes. "When he moved here and opened his law practice, he was all over that sweets lady who just kicked the bucket too."

Except for Cody Johnson singing on the jukebox, the bar fell completely silent.

Liddy fixed her eyes on Butch, who still had no idea how potentially devastating the news he had just delivered was, as casually as dropping a letter in one of the mailboxes on his postal route.

"You don't mean . . . ?" Liddy asked quietly, her

hands suddenly shaking, the ice cubes clattering against the side of her cocktail glass.

"Yeah, the one that was poisoned. Lisa what's-her-name . . ."

No one knew what to say at that moment, so Mona, in her own attempt to defuse the quickly escalating, stressful, nerve-wracking situation, simply offered, "I really think you should go with the blackberry whiskey lemonade."

Chapter 20

Before Hayley could stop her, Liddy blew past Sonny's startled secretary, who barely had time to croak out, "He's in a meeting," before she burst through the large oak door into Sonny's office. Hayley could see Sonny jump up from his desk as a startled couple in their late sixties jerked their heads around to see what kind of tornado was at that moment tearing into the room.

"Hi, babe, what are you doing here?" Sonny muttered, knowing full well that whatever had brought Liddy here was nothing good.

"Hello, Ed, hello, Janice, I'm sorry to interrupt your meeting with Sonny!" Liddy screamed at the top of her lungs, and not because poor old Ed was equipped with a hearing aid.

Ed and Janice exchanged a worried look, not sure what to do. Janice finally decided to speak. "Nice to see you, Liddy. We're just here because Ed and I are suing the company that manufactured his pacemaker. It's giving him trouble—"

"I'm so sorry to hear that!" Liddy roared so loudly that Ed instinctively covered his ears with his hands.

His doting wife gently put a comforting hand on Ed's arm. "We're just trying to keep his stress levels low until we can figure out—"

"That's probably a wise decision!" Liddy shrieked, completely unaware that she was still yelling at the top of her lungs.

"Liddy, maybe we should wait outside until Sonny is finished talking with Ed and Janice," Hayley quietly suggested as she hovered in the doorway with Sonny's curious secretary, Pat—or Penny; Hayley couldn't remember her name, except that it began with a P—who peered over her shoulder into the room watching the scene unfold.

"Yes, I think that's a good idea. Patrice can you make a pot of coffee?" Sonny said, his eyes darting from Liddy to Hayley, searching for some kind of indication of what this was all about.

Patrice.

Yes. Of course.

"That won't be necessary, Patrice. I'm not staying. I just dropped by to tell Sonny the wedding is off!" Liddy dramatically declared.

A silence fell over the room as Liddy took a break from her incessant shouting to let her announcement fully sink in.

"What?" Sonny asked, confused.

"Yes, I'm breaking up with you. We're done. Finished. Kaput."

"Why?" Janice gasped, now ignoring her husband,

who was rubbing his chest as if he feared he was about to have a heart attack from all the stress and the tension and pressure that had suddenly filled the room.

Liddy turned to Janice. "He dated my cousin behind my back!"

Incensed, Janice spun around and glared at Sonny. "What? How could you?"

"Where did you hear that?" Sonny asked, utterly perplexed.

"At Drinks Like a Fish. Butch Haggerty told me!" Liddy wailed, her eyes now moist with tears as she once again relived the humiliating moment.

"That's crazy! Butch Haggerty is a clueless lush with a big mouth!" Sonny cried. "What would he know about me?"

Liddy stepped forward, eyes narrowing. "So you're denying you dated Lisa?"

Sonny plopped down in his chair and ran a shaky hand through his wavy hair, his mind obviously racing as he considered how to honestly but carefully answer Liddy's question.

"It's a simple yes-or-no question, Sonny," Janice sniffed, sitting upright, now firmly planted on Liddy's side.

"Well, yes. I mean, no. I'm not denying it. We went out a couple of times," Sonny quietly admitted.

"Sonny, how *could* you?" Janice huffed, shaking her head.

Ed stood up. His face was pale, and he was still

rubbing his chest. "I don't feel well. I think I'm going to go outside and lie down for a minute."

Ed stumbled past Hayley and out of the office, and then sprawled out on the couch in the waiting room. Janice, however, didn't budge. She wanted to see where this was going.

"Lisa and I went out on a couple of dates years ago. It didn't take me long to figure out she was basically a crazy person, completely unstable. So I stopped calling her. But let me be clear about one thing, Liddy"—Sonny noticed Janice, her arms folded and an accusing look on her face— "and Janice . . . it was months before I even met you!"

He was still looking at Janice. "Liddy, I mean."

"Oh . . ." Janice groaned, then turned to Liddy, whose face was still flushed and furious. "That's technically not cheating, Liddy."

"But you never told me about it!" Liddy wailed.

"I was embarrassed!" Sonny cried.

"Remember the night we got drunk on wine at my place and we both listed all the people in town we've dated in the past? Do you remember that, Sonny?"

"Yes," Sonny said, chastised, his head bowed like a scolded puppy.

"You conveniently left out Lisa's name!"

"I knew you'd get upset, and we were having such a fun night," he whispered.

"Of all the women in town, of all the women in the world . . . how could you have dated that stupid, awful ogre Lisa?" Liddy hollered, throwing her hands up in the air.

"It's not nice to speak ill of the dead," Janice admonished.

"Plus, she left you a lot of money," Hayley added.

Liddy ignored both of them and kept her eyes fixed on Sonny. "Did you *sleep* with her?"

Janice cranked her head around to get a good look at Sonny's reaction to Liddy's very direct question.

Hayley couldn't help but try to read his face too.

They both were *dying* to know.

Sonny looked down at the floor, shuffled his feet, and slowly nodded. "Once, yes, if I'm being honest."

"That's the problem with you, Sonny. I always get the feeling you're not being honest with me, that you're constantly hiding things from me. How do you expect me to marry you when I feel uneasy and suspicious of everything that comes out of your mouth?"

"Can we just put a pin in this until I finish up with Ed and Janice?" Sonny begged. "And then I promise we can sit down and deal with this before things get way out of hand?"

"No, Sonny. It's too late. You haven't shown any interest in this wedding, and you're obviously keeping secrets from me. I'm sorry, but we're through. This time for real!"

Sonny jumped back up and came around his desk to stop her from leaving. "Babe, please . . ."

But Liddy had already stormed past Hayley and out of the office.

Hayley put a hand up in front of Sonny, who was about to chase after her. "No, let her go and calm down, Sonny. I'll talk to her."

Then suddenly, Liddy popped her head back in the office. "You might want to call a doctor. Ed's not looking too good."

And then she was gone again, leaving a shattered Sonny behind.

Chapter 21

Gemma pulled a tray of bacon-wrapped Peppadew poppers out of the oven and set it down on the stove top to let them cool.

"Those look delicious," Liddy commented from the kitchen table before downing the rest of her Cosmo that Hayley had specially made for her hoping it would relax her.

"Martha Stewart swears by them. The best part is they're stuffed with cream cheese," Gemma said, joining them at the kitchen table. "They'll be ready to eat in ten minutes."

"I'm so proud of my daughter," Hayley remarked. "She's going to be a world-famous chef some day."

"I was just hoping to be a part of designing Liddy's wedding cake, but I guess that's off the table now," Gemma said.

"You're damn right it is!" Liddy roared. "I'm not going to marry a man who clearly does not deserve me just so you can gain professional experience as a baker!"

"I know, I'm sorry. I didn't mean to make this about me," Gemma said. "I was just really looking forward to working with Mom."

Hayley smiled and reached out and touched her daughter's hand. "When did you get so sweet? It feels like yesterday you were a moody, morose teenager who hated everything that came out of my mouth."

Gemma chuckled. "I grew up."

Hayley turned to Liddy. "So are you sure you want to cancel the wedding? Maybe tomorrow morning, after a good night's sleep, you might feel differently."

"I've never been more sure of anything in my life! There's no point in carrying on with this charade any longer. Sonny and I are not meant to be together, and that's that," Liddy huffed.

Hayley shrugged, accepting the fact that there was probably no talking her out of her decision.

The wedding was off.

Again.

"What's that?" Gemma asked, sitting up straight in her chair.

"What's what?" Hayley asked.

"That . . . that sound . . ." Gemma said.

Liddy looked around the kitchen. "I don't hear anything."

Gemma stood up. "Someone's playing music."

"Is it Dustin upstairs?" Hayley asked.

"No, he's not here. He and his friend Spanky

went to see a movie in Bangor," Gemma said, crossing to the kitchen window. "Where is it coming from?"

Gemma parted the kitchen window curtain and gasped. "Omigod, it's Sonny!"

Liddy suddenly jumped up from her chair and scurried over to the window. "Sonny? What on earth is he doing here?"

Hayley joined them as well, and the three women peered out the kitchen window at Sonny, wearing a long trench coat and standing in the driveway with one of those old boom boxes raised in the air, blasting Peter Gabriel's 1980s classic "In Your Eyes."

"He's re-creating the scene from *Say Anything*!" Hayley cooed.

"Say what?" Liddy asked.

"Oh, come on, *Say Anything*! The movie! It's a classic! John Cusack tried to win back the love of his life by showing up at her house with a boom box and playing a love song to express his feelings for her!" Hayley said, clapping her hands. "This is so romantic."

"I never saw it," Liddy said.

"Of course you did. We rented the DVD when we were in high school one Saturday night! We loved it! How can you not remember it?"

"I remember it, and I'm half your age," Gemma said.

"You are not half my age!" Liddy barked.

"Yes, I am, I'm twenty-one, and you were born in—"

Hayley begged Gemma with her eyes to stop

talking, and her daughter finally got the hint. "No, you're right, I forgot you were still in your thirties."

They returned their attention to Sonny, who was still outside gamely doing his best John Cusack impression.

Liddy shook her head and walked back to the kitchen table and picked up her cell phone. "I'm calling the police. He's disturbing the peace."

"Liddy, no! Don't do that! Go outside and talk to him," Hayley said.

"I absolutely will not! I never want to see or speak with Sonny Lipton ever again!"

Gemma put a hand over her heart as she stared out the window. "He looks so cute, like a puppy dog who knows he's misbehaved. I'll marry him!"

"You have a boyfriend in New York," Hayley reminded her before snatching Liddy's cell phone out of her hand. "You are *not* calling the police."

"Fine, then let him stay out there all night if he wants," Liddy said, throwing her hands up in the air and marching out of the kitchen into the living room. They heard her turn on the TV to a Turner Classic Movie and raise the volume up until Humphrey Bogart's voice was drowning out Peter Gabriel's singing outside in the driveway.

"What should we do?" Gemma asked her mother.

"Why don't we go out there and give him some of your bacon-wrapped Peppadew poppers before we send him home?" Hayley said as she opened the cupboard to get a plate.

"You're right," Gemma said. "No one should beg on an empty stomach."

Chapter 22

"Liddy, it's kind of bad around here today," Hayley said as the phone on her desk rang and rang and her boss Sal blustered about reporters missing their deadlines in the back bull pen of the *Island Times* office.

"Hayley, the news comes and goes. This is my life we're talking about," Liddy wailed, hugging herself, sniffing to keep from crying, as she stood in front of Hayley's desk.

"Okay, hang on, let me just take this one call," Hayley said, scooping up the phone receiver.

It was a reporter on the scene of a kitchen fire at a local restaurant that was under control but causing smoke damage at neighboring businesses.

"Hayley, where the hell is Jim? He should be getting photos of this!"

"Yes, Hank, I know, Jim's on his way. Just hold on."

The photographer had been getting a root canal at the dentist, but when he got a text about the restaurant fire, he had apparently discarded his paper bib, and with a mouthful of Novocain, dashed out to his car to race to the scene.

Sal roared into the front office just as the reporter told Hayley, "Never mind! Jim just got here!"

And then he hung up.

"Where the hell is Jim? I just got a text from Hank that he's MIA!" Sal snarled.

"He's there! He's on the scene!" Hayley cried. "It's handled!"

Sal tried calming down. He grabbed the coffeepot and poured himself a cup. "I'm going to need something stronger than this damn coffee before this day's over!"

"Hello, Sal," Liddy said, smiling.

He grunted a reply before brushing past her and stalking back to his office.

Hayley looked at Liddy apologetically. "I'm sorry, Liddy, I just can't come with you today."

"Then I'll wait," she said, plopping herself down in a metal chair near the coffee station.

"It'll be another couple of hours before I can get away," Hayley warned.

"That's fine. It's not a problem. I just can't do this alone."

Hayley understood why Liddy desperately needed moral support. Today was the day she was scheduled to pick up her wedding dress at a bridal shop in Ellsworth, where they had been painstakingly making alterations in order to meet her exact specifications. Now that the whole wedding had been called off, there was no need for the dress anymore. But since it had already been bought and paid for and could not be returned, like it or not, somebody had to drive up there and get it. Liddy was just too emotionally fragile to do it by herself, so she was pressuring Hayley to accompany her.

The fire story died down about twenty minutes later, and after a burglary call that eventually turned out to be a false alarm, the only pressing story the *Island Times* had to stay on top of was a town council meeting scheduled to begin at five o'clock.

Liddy sat quietly, a tight smile on her face, staring at Hayley, waiting for her to finally call it a day so they could make the quick twenty-minute drive to Ellsworth. Liddy's presence was making Hayley extremely uncomfortable. It was hard doing her job with someone constantly eyeballing her, so by four thirty, with only a half hour left before quitting time, Hayley sighed, stood up, and headed back to Sal's office.

She found him sitting behind his desk watching a cat video on YouTube. That made the prospect of her leaving a little early suddenly more attainable.

"Sal, Liddy's been sitting in the front office for a while now . . ."

"I know. What the hell is this, Bring Your Friend to Work Day?"

"It's just that she's going through a tough time right now . . ."

"Yeah, my wife told me. So what does that have to do with me?"

"Well, it doesn't really, but she needs to go pick

up her wedding dress and she wants me to go with her . . ."

"Why? The wedding's been called off! What does she need the dress for?"

Hayley sighed and explained the whole non-refundable issue because it had been custom tailored and how it would be a waste of money to just leave it at the tailor's.

Sal thought about this and shrugged. "Fine, but you better be here a half hour early tomorrow morning to make up for it."

"Yes, I promise. Thank you, Sal."

Sal grunted and then went back to watching his video. As Hayley slipped out, she heard him giggling at the cat's hilarious antics on his computer screen.

Hayley scooted back to the front office and waved at Liddy to get up and follow her out the door before Sal changed his mind. Hayley grabbed her bag and the two slipped out of the office. Hayley quickly texted Bruce to let him know she would be back in town by six to have dinner with him at her house.

As Liddy pressed the remote in her hand to unlock the doors on her Mercedes, Hayley quietly asked, "Have you thought about what you're going to do with the dress?"

Liddy nodded. "Probably put it on eBay and say something like 'Never Before Worn Designer Wedding Gown! Cheap!' Whatever gets rid of it."

"That dress is so beautiful, I'm sure it will make some young bride very happy," Hayley said.

Liddy slid behind the wheel and Hayley buckled up in the passenger's seat. Liddy reached over and pressed the engine button and the car roared to life, but instead of putting the car in drive and pulling out of her parking space, Liddy just sat there silently staring out the window.

Hayley watched her a few seconds, and then gently placed her hand on Liddy's arm. "It's all going to be okay. You will get through this."

"I know . . . But it's so hard . . ."

Liddy suddenly burst into tears, dropping her head and covering her face with her hands. Hayley tenderly rubbed Liddy's back, trying to comfort her, patiently waiting for her to stop crying.

After ten minutes, Hayley checked the clock on the dashboard. Liddy was still wailing and rubbing her eyes. She knew she had to say something, but didn't want to be insensitive. However, the clock was ticking, and she knew the bridal shop locked their doors at five o'clock.

"Liddy . . ." she whispered.

"I know, they're going to close soon. We should get going."

Liddy put the car in drive and squealed away from the curb, nearly sideswiping a plumber's truck that was passing by at the same time. The driver blared his horn, and Liddy acknowledged him with a half wave before wiping her tears with the sleeve of her blouse and zooming off down the street.

Once they were on Route 3 out of town, heading toward the Trenton Bridge on their way to Ellsworth, Liddy pressed her heel down on the accelerator, and Hayley noticed the speedometer clocking in at fifty in a thirty-five-mile-an-hour zone.

"Liddy, you might want to slow down," Hayley warned.

"We have to get there on time, Hayley. I have to do this today, because I will have a full-on nervous breakdown if I have to go through with this again tomorrow!"

"I know, but if we get pulled over for speeding, we'll never make it in time."

"Your brother is married to the police chief. I'm sure we can talk our way out of a ticket."

Liddy swerved the Mercedes around a bend and down a hill, picking up speed as they barreled along the bumpy road that was in desperate need of a fresh paving.

"Liddy!"

Liddy sighed, and pressed down on the brakes.

The car kept racing along at full speed.

She pressed her foot down on the brakes again, harder this time.

Liddy gasped.

Hayley turned to her. "What is it?"

"Something's wrong!" Liddy cried.

"What do you mean?"

"The brakes aren't working!"

"*What?*"

"I'm pumping the brakes, but we're not slowing down!"

Hayley glanced over to see Liddy's foot pressed to the floor.

Liddy screamed as they reached the bottom of the hill, now whizzing along at sixty-five miles an hour.

"What are we going to do?" Liddy screamed.

"Keep your eyes on the road!"

A tanker truck rounded the corner ahead of them.

"Keep the wheel steady!" Hayley yelled.

The giant tanker truck seemed to be taking up most of the road, and they both took a sharp inhale of breath before zooming past it. They both exhaled.

Suddenly the steering wheel rattled violently and Liddy screeched, "Hayley!"

She was losing control of the car.

Liddy's Mercedes veered into the opposite lane of traffic.

Another vehicle, this one a pickup truck, careened straight at them.

Liddy yanked the wheel hard to the right, and the Mercedes jerked back just as the pickup truck, horn blasting, whisked past them.

But there was no chance to steady the vehicle, and with tires skidding, the Mercedes suddenly flew off the road, sailing through the air and smashing into a telephone pole.

The last thing Hayley remembered was screaming and covering her face with her hands as glass shattered all around her, and then everything went black.

Island Food & Cocktails
BY HAYLEY POWELL

My old high school friend Beth Leighton-Mays recently showed up in town from her current home in California to attend the upcoming nuptials of my BFF Liddy Crawford, who you all know is marrying one of our local attorneys, Sonny Lipton.

I invited Beth to stop by my house her first night in town for a taste test of a couple wedding appetizers that my daughter Gemma has been preparing for the reception.

It was fun catching up with Beth as we hungrily scarfed down Gemma's delicious treats. Beth brought a lovely bottle of white wine, so I whipped us up some citrus wine spritzers, and suffice it to say, they complemented the appetizers perfectly.

We both agreed that Gemma's baked crab poppers were the absolute showstopper, and between the two of us, we eagerly devoured the entire tray even before Gemma had a chance to pop the second batch in the oven.

About ten years ago, Beth met her now-husband Danny (not to be confused with my own ex-husband Danny) when he was a volunteer summer policeman. They were first introduced at a party I hosted, and they immediately hit it off. Well, never one to dillydally, Beth asked him out on a date before he even had the chance to crack open his first bottle of Corona, and soon the relationship took off like a three-year-old Thoroughbred at the Kentucky Derby. Needless to say, a wedding soon followed.

It was to be held in the fall at the end of September before the temperature dropped too much on the front lawn of the Bar Harbor Inn, overlooking the vast dark blue ocean and the outer islands, with a perfect view of all the fancy yachts and working fishing boats drifting in and out of the harbor. It boasts one of the most breathtaking views of our impossibly picturesque Frenchman's Bay.

After the ceremony, the wedding party would simply file inside the inn for the reception in a lovely room with its own outdoor space so everyone could step outside for some fresh air with their champagne and hors d'oeuvres in between the dancing and the wedding toasts.

Beth and Danny were determined to keep the wedding ceremony small by just inviting close friends and family. Beth chose her sister to be her maid of honor, and Danny asked his brother to be his best man. However, the reception was going to be opened up to a much larger crowd, so pretty much half the town would be waiting for them to arrive after they said their "I do's" to celebrate.

Beth was incredibly nervous the night before her wedding, and she called me, Liddy, and Mona, begging us to join her for a quick cocktail, hoping it would calm her nerves before the big day in the morning. We all jumped at the invitation in the event that Beth got a case of cold feet. We could all be there to talk her out of any thoughts she might have of becoming a "runaway bride."

We met at Geddy's, which was situated across the street from the Bar Harbor Inn on Main Street, so it would be easy for Beth to just walk back after we said good night, since both families were treating themselves to rooms there for the night.

Beth announced that she wanted to be sharp and clear-eyed for the wedding ceremony and that she would only have one cocktail just "to take the edge off." Three cocktails later, Beth was relaxed and happy, and she couldn't stop talking about how wonderful her groom-to-be Danny was, and how nervous and excited she was to move to Belfast, Maine, after the wedding, since Danny had just accepted a job at the local police department there in his hometown. I glanced at Liddy and Mona, both with big smiles on their faces, because we all knew we had done our job—keeping the bride-to-be chatty and content before her big day.

Finally, Beth called it a night and floated back to the inn on a cloud, anxious for all the possibilities ahead as a woman married to the man of her dreams. The three of us decided to stay for a nightcap. By now, the bar had filled up with a lively crowd, a live band took to the small stage, and pretty soon we found ourselves on the dance floor, shimmying and shaking until we were all exhausted and ready to go home to collapse into bed. Liddy made a beeline for the ladies' room while Mona and I headed back to our table to gather up our bags and pay the check. Well, not thirty seconds later, Liddy dashed back toward us, breathless, eyes bugging out of her head. She could hardly speak and her face was pale, as if she had just seen a ghost. All she could do in the moment was frantically point toward the back of the bar near the restrooms. Mona and I turned, and when I saw him, I gasped. I couldn't believe it. Beth's fiancé had a petite blond girl, not more than twenty-one, pinned up against the wall, grinding her with his pelvis. The blonde giggled and grinned, and she reached up and clasped her hands around his neck. She pulled his head down until their lips were touching, and they shared a passionate kiss.

The three of us just stood there in frozen silence, our mouths hanging open, in utter disbelief.

After what seemed like an eternity, I finally heard Mona yell, "Oh, hell no, this is not happening!" And then she took off in a flash, marching over to an unsuspecting Danny. Liddy and I knew this was not going to end well, so we both lunged after Mona, because we didn't want her beating the groom to a pulp the night before his wedding.

By the time we reached her, she was already laying into Danny, shaking her fist at him, threatening to smash in his face. The blonde panicked and skedaddled past us, not wanting any part of

this possibly violent confrontation. I almost felt
sorry for Danny, who just stood there in shock.
Every time the poor guy opened his mouth to
speak, Mona shut him down, refusing to allow him
to insult her with any of his lame excuses. Mona
was so loud, the band decided to take a fifteen-
minute break so everyone in the bar could gather
around and listen to her tirade. A lot of four-letter
names were used, followed by a litany of threats
detailing how Mona would cause Danny serious bodily harm if he in any way hurt our dear,
beloved Beth.

Finally, after ten minutes, Mona ran out of
steam and in a steely, cold voice, informed Danny,
"You are one lucky son of a you know what that
Beth is a dear friend of mine and that I don't want
to see her heart broken, so we are not going to tell
her about this little incident so long as you clean
up your act and start acting like a devoted husband
who is going to make his wife the happiest woman
for the rest of her life. Otherwise, mister man, you
and me are going to have big, big problems. Am I
making myself clear?"

At this point, Danny had no intention of antag-
onizing this wild-eyed woman any further, so he
just nodded, not saying a word. Mona threw him
one more murderous look and then whipped around
and marched out the door, stopping only to
confront the cowering blonde, who was trying her
best to be invisible at the bar.

"By the way, he's taken!" Mona growled. And

then she slammed out the door with Liddy and me running to catch up to her.

The next day, as we settled in our seats on the lawn of the Bar Harbor Inn for the wedding, Mona still hadn't calmed down. It was a perfectly beautiful, sunny day for a wedding, except for the storm clouds in Mona's eyes as she sat silently, staring straight ahead out toward the vast ocean. I sat between Mona and Liddy and was feeling immensely guilty about withholding such important information from Beth, but Liddy had convinced me that it was probably for the best that we just stay out of it.

Suddenly, Liddy clutched my arm and squeezed it so hard I had to catch myself from yelling out loud. She signaled me with her eyes to the groom's side of the aisle, and when I saw her I couldn't believe it—the petite blonde Danny had been kissing the night before was seated right there with Danny's parents!

"Whatever you do, don't tell Mona," I whispered.

"Don't tell Mona what?" Mona bellowed before her eyes fixated on the blonde, who had yet to notice the three of us. "Oh, hell no!"

At that moment, the string quartet launched into the "Wedding March," and it took every ounce of self-control for Mona not to leap over the other guests and strangle the pretty young blonde home wrecker.

And then I saw Beth, looking absolutely gorgeous

in a lace wedding gown and escorted by her father, slowly make her way down the aisle, passing the blonde, walking toward her fiancé and their now-questionable future together.

That's when I saw him.

And I burst out laughing.

I quickly slammed my lips shut, ignoring the quizzical stares from both the bride and groom's family and friends.

Liddy and Mona finally noticed him too.

The groom's best man.

Down front next to Danny and the minister.

Danny's brother.

Or should I say, his identical *twin* brother.

As all three of us realized this had all been a simple case of mistaken identity, we shrank in our seats. The petite blonde actually turned out to be Danny's brother's wife! Well, needless to say, the three of us got an incurable case of the giggles, which lasted until the minister mercifully said, "I now pronounce you husband and wife," and the whole thing was over.

Later, at the reception, we were all introduced, and thankfully a good laugh was had by all. In fact, Mona and Dean, Danny's brother, became fast friends, and to this day, they still see each other at least once a year when Dean comes by every summer to buy lobsters at Mona's shop. They love telling the other customers how their friendship started.

Now I know you've all been dying to get to the

end of this story so you can start making your own delectable batch of baked crab poppers that you can enjoy with a citrus wine spritzer, so I wouldn't dream of keeping you any longer!

CITRUS WINE SPRITZERS

Ice

Thin slices of lemon and lime

1 bottle of your favorite white wine (I love a pinot grigio)

12 ounces lemon-flavored sparkling water or seltzer

Fill each glass with ice. Add one slice of lemon and one slice of lime. Add 4 ounces of wine and 2 ounces of sparkling water. Enjoy!

BAKED CRAB POPPERS

1 cup plain Panko bread crumbs, divided

1 cup canned corn

½ cup finely diced red bell pepper

¼ cup chopped green onion

16 ounces fresh crabmeat (you can use lump crab too)

¾ cup real mayonnaise, divided

1 egg, lightly beaten

½ teaspoon kosher salt

1 teaspoon ground black pepper

¼ teaspoon cayenne pepper (more to taste)

1 lemon, juiced

Heat your oven to 425°F. Coat a 24-count mini muffin pan with cooking spray. (You may need to spray an additional pan depending on the size you make.)

Sprinkle the bottoms of the tins with half of the Panko bread crumbs.

In a bowl, combine your corn, red bell pepper, onions, crabmeat, half of the mayo, egg, salt, and black pepper. Mix gently so as not to break up the crabmeat too much, but combine well.

Spoon your mixture evenly to fill the cups in the pans. Sprinkle the rest of the Panko over the mixture.

Bake in your preheated oven for 10 minutes or until golden brown. Remove and cool poppers for about 10 minutes and then remove to cooling rack to finish cooling.

While cooling, combine the rest of the mayonnaise, the cayenne pepper, and the juice from the lemon in a small bowl and brush over the tops of the baked crabmeat poppers.

Trust me, you'll be making more before you even polish off your first batch!

Chapter 23

By the time Hayley had crawled out of the heaping pile of crunched-up metal, two police cars and an ambulance were already pulling up at the scene. Liddy was still fastened in the driver's seat, and Hayley feared she might be seriously injured, but when the handsome young paramedic named Jay was lifting her out of her totaled Mercedes, she heard Liddy remark, "You're looking awfully handsome these days, Jay."

Hayley knew she would be all right.

Sergio raced down the embankment from the road, kicking up dirt in his haste, followed by his two loyal deputies, Donnie and Earl. He grabbed Hayley by the arm to help keep her steady in case she was feeling woozy and might lose her balance, but Hayley felt perfectly fine and just patted Sergio on the hand, indicating she thankfully could walk without assistance.

"What happened?" Sergio asked, his face full of concern.

"The brakes just gave out coming down the hill, and Liddy lost control of the vehicle," Hayley said, watching as Liddy continued flirting shamelessly with Jay the paramedic as he insisted on her lying down on the gurney that he and his fellow medic had carried down to the scene of the crash.

"We need to get you both to the hospital," Sergio said.

"That won't be necessary, Sergio, we're not hurt," Hayley argued, as she touched a small cut on her forehead from a piece of broken glass. "We're just a little banged up, that's all."

"Well, I'm not taking any chances. I want a doctor to check you both out," Sergio said, handing Hayley off to the other paramedic, the one not as dashing and good-looking as Jay, who escorted her up the grassy embankment to the ambulance, where Liddy waited for her in the back.

Hayley barely had a chance to sit down across from Liddy and Jay, who was busy taking her vitals as she grinned from ear to ear and winked at Hayley when the door slammed shut and they were speeding off back toward town, siren wailing.

There was a flurry of activity when they pulled up outside the emergency room and the hospital staff converged upon the ambulance. Hayley felt all of this was an extreme overreaction, since both she and Liddy appeared perfectly fine, but Sergio insisted on making sure that neither of them had suffered a head injury, which might take its deadly toll a few hours later if not quickly identified and diagnosed.

When the back doors to the ambulance were flung open, Hayley offered to walk herself inside, but the nurse was having none of it and insisted she plop down in a wheelchair. Hayley reluctantly complied, and then she was whisked inside, right behind Liddy, who was lying prone on a gurney, smiling up at Jay, clutching his hand. He awkwardly smiled back down at her.

After being thoroughly examined, X-rayed, and questioned by a couple of different doctors on duty, Hayley and Liddy were soon ensconced in a semi-private room with two beds, where they were told to lie still and rest until the doctors had a chance to study all of the X-rays.

Hayley was impatient and annoyed by the whole situation. She just wanted to go home and have dinner with Bruce. Liddy, on the other hand, was enjoying the drama of it all, reveling in all of the attention.

"What happened to Jay?" Liddy asked, perplexed, looking around, expecting him to show up with a fistful of flowers and a get well card.

"His job was finished once he dropped us off at the hospital," Hayley patiently explained.

"Well, it would have been nice of him to come by the room to check on me and see how I'm doing."

Hayley decided not to comment on that.

Suddenly Bruce tore into the room, his face stricken. At the sight of Hayley alive and well, he exhaled a huge sigh of relief. "Thank God you're okay!"

He raced to Hayley's bedside and practically

threw himself on top of her, wrapping his arms around her and squeezing her tight.

"Bruce . . . I'm fine . . . I just can't breathe . . ."

Realizing he was smothering her, he released his grip and stood upright. "You wouldn't believe the rumors swirling around town about you two . . ."

"What rumors?" Liddy asked, sitting up in her bed, intrigued.

"Once the accident came over the police scanner and the town gossips heard your names, they went into overdrive exaggerating the seriousness of the accident."

"Oh no . . ." Hayley moaned.

"Well, to be fair, it *was* serious! My Mercedes got wrapped around a telephone pole! It's completely totaled!" Liddy cried.

"Yes, but the important thing is, *we're* fine!" Hayley reminded her. "Just a few cuts and bruises."

"I know, but I loved that car," Liddy murmured, frowning.

Bruce hugged Hayley again. "I was so scared when I heard the news. I couldn't bear the thought of losing you."

Hayley was surprised by the sincerity of his tone. Bruce had such a reputation for sarcasm and deadpan humor, watching him now filled with such raw emotion, his eyes welled up with tears, was quite frankly startling, and yet, it gave Hayley a warm feeling inside.

Bruce really did care for her.

Out of the corner of her eye, Hayley caught Liddy

lying in bed across the room, forlornly watching them.

Bruce gently kissed the bandaged cut on Hayley's forehead.

Liddy grimaced and then turned over in the bed, unable to take it anymore. It was clear she was thinking about Sonny and how it had all gone wrong. And now, in her hour of need, he wasn't here for her like Bruce was for Hayley.

But then, almost as if on cue, suddenly they heard shouting coming from down the hall.

"Where is she? Where is she?"

Some nurses were trying to speak calmly to the hysterical man, but were drowned out by his bellowing voice. "Where's Liddy? I need to see her right now!"

Liddy turned back over and bolted upright in bed again. "Is that . . . ?"

Sonny blew into the room, eyes wild, face full of panic. He saw Hayley first and gasped, fearing she had made it through the accident, but Liddy tragically had not.

His eyes finally settled on Liddy in the bed across from Hayley's. She was busy adjusting her baby blue paper hospital gown to show more cleavage.

Sonny burst into tears. "Liddy!"

He scampered over to the bed and snatched up her hand and placed it over his heart. "They said . . . they said . . ."

He couldn't get the words out, he was so overcome with emotion.

Tears streamed down his cheeks.

"They said what?" Liddy asked, clenching his hand tightly.

"They said you were in a coma, on life support . . ."

"Who?" Liddy demanded to know.

"Some old biddies at the Shop 'n Save. I stopped in to buy a bottle of wine because it's been one of those days, and I overheard them talking about the accident . . . and how you had been nearly crushed by a telephone pole . . . and I . . . I . . ."

"I'm fine, Sonny. Just some bruises on my arms and legs and a small cut on my cheek, thankfully not on my good side."

Liddy gasped as Sonny got down on one knee, clutched both of her hands in his, and whispered, "I'm never letting you out of my sight for as long as I live. Please, sweetheart, I've been a fool, taking you for granted like that, not making you my number one priority. That whole dating Lisa episode is in the past, long dead and buried . . . I mean, no disrespect to poor Lisa, who is actually dead . . . But if you give me one more chance, just one, I promise I will never disappoint you again, never, ever, as long as I live!"

He stared lovingly at her, his eyes full of hope, his bottom lip quivering.

Hayley and Bruce watched the scene unfolding across the semiprivate hospital room like they were watching a Nicholas Sparks movie. All that was missing was a box of popcorn that they could share between them.

Liddy, always one to milk a moment, waited just long enough to make Sonny squirm, and then, she dramatically broke into a wide, loving smile. "I've always been a sucker for a man who's not afraid to cry."

The wedding was back on.

Again.

Hayley crossed her heart and prayed there would be no more hiccups on the way to the altar.

Sometimes prayers are answered.

And sometimes they're not.

Chapter 24

Pete Lyle wiped the grease off his hands with a sullied gray rag, his droopy eyes settling on Hayley and Sergio, who stood expectantly in his garage next to the giant pile of crushed metal that was once Liddy's Mercedes.

"What did you find?" Sergio asked.

"The brake line was cut," Pete said with a detached drawl, as if the severity of his conclusion was completely lost on him.

"You're saying someone deliberately sabotaged Liddy's car? Who would do that?" Hayley blurted out, stupefied.

Pete shrugged. "Beats me. Although if you give me some more time, I could probably come up with a pretty long list."

There was a bitterness to Pete's tone, and Hayley wondered why, until it finally dawned on her that he and Liddy had a checkered history. Of course, it went all the way back to high school, when Pete asked Liddy to the prom and she flatly refused the invitation. She had her eye on the quarterback of the football team, Chad Simpson, and Pete, who was rather shy and withdrawn, usually found sitting in the back of the classroom, wasn't even on her radar. As Hayley recalled, Pete was so crushed by Liddy's outright rejection, he stayed home on prom night and never forgave her. That was over twenty years ago now. But Pete, as Hayley was learning, really knew how to hold on to a grudge.

"Come on, Pete, Liddy may have her enemies, but I don't think any of them would be so nasty as to intentionally endanger her life . . . and mine, by the way!" Hayley said.

Pete shrugged again. "You never know, the way she treats people. I can sure see someone having had enough of all her foolishness and cruelty and just snapping."

He was obviously talking about himself.

Sergio glanced at Hayley, confused, with a look that said, *Should I be arresting him right now?*

Hayley stepped forward, closer to Pete, who was now staring at the grease-stained rag in his hand. "Pete, I know you had a beef with Liddy back in high school, but that was so long ago . . ."

"She changed the course of my life, Hayley," Pete said, eyes fixed on the floor. "I was a confident kid, made good grades . . ."

Okay, that one was a stretch. Hayley remembered having Pete in her chemistry class where he was briefly her lab partner, and when he wasn't skipping school, he could barely tell the difference between a beaker and a test tube.

"Then, when Liddy so callously broke my heart in senior year, without a second thought, and I saw her in the cafeteria laughing about it with all her girlfriends, my life took a sudden turn. I lost my confidence. I felt really bad about myself, and it took its toll on everything in my life . . . I wanted to be a NASCAR driver, but thanks to Liddy and her heartlessness, I didn't dare pursue it, because I was afraid of further rejection and people laughing at me, so I went to work in my uncle's garage, and here I am today . . ."

"But you own the garage now," Sergio offered, trying tactfully to be helpful.

"Big whoop. I'm not living my dream. I'm a two-bit mechanic, divorced from a crazy shrew who takes every penny of profit I make because of a bad alimony deal her fancy lawyer conned me into signing."

Sonny Lipton had represented Pete's ex-wife in the divorce settlement, which suddenly made Pete look even more suspicious in Hayley's mind.

"Pete, you can't seriously blame Liddy for all that's happened to you since high school . . ." Hayley said.

Pete spit a glob of saliva out of his mouth and onto the floor and then wiped his mouth with the sleeve of his gray coveralls. "I sure can. She's like the devil, as far as I'm concerned. Anyone who tries to take her out has my respect, if I'm being honest."

"You're being very honest with us, Pete," Sergio said, a stern look on his face. "Maybe too honest. Have you ever worked on Liddy's car before today?"

Pete snickered. "Hell, no. I don't want her business. And if you're trying to nail me down as the bad guy here, why would I tell you someone cut the brake line if I was the one who did it?"

He had a point.

"Besides, I've been out of town the last few days. Me and a couple of buddies flew to Arizona to see Kevin Harvick compete in the TicketGuardian 500 at ISM Raceway."

Hayley didn't even pretend to know what he was talking about.

"I just got back this morning when I got your call to have a look at Liddy's car," he said. "I can give you the phone numbers of my buddies, if you think I'm lying, who can corroborate my alibi."

"That would be helpful, Pete, thank you," Sergio said, all business.

Pete Lyle certainly had a clear motive to see Liddy perish in a fiery crash. He was still wounded from her rejection in high school, and the man she was about to marry screwed him over financially. What better revenge than to seriously injure or even kill the woman Sonny was about to marry? However, if his alibi did check out, then he was in the clear.

Still, Hayley was more driven than ever to find out who was behind this, and if it was in any way connected to Lisa's poisoning. Because after all, Hayley too had nearly lost her life in that car crash, so in addition to protecting her best friend, she was out to protect herself as well.

"We'll be in touch, Pete. Don't leave town for

another NASCAR rally until I have a chance to speak to your friends, okay?" Sergio warned.

Pete just shrugged, nonplussed.

Once they were outside, Hayley had her phone to her ear and was calling Liddy.

"Hi, what's up? Sonny and I are at the florist picking out arrangements," Liddy cooed, having already forgotten she had just been in a near-fatal car accident. "Oh, honey, aren't those tulips gorgeous?"

"Yes," Hayley could hear Sonny obediently agree.

Hayley took a deep breath. "Liddy, pay attention. I have some news . . ."

Chapter 25

"Oh, Gemma, you have outdone yourself! This is absolutely scrumptious," Liddy cooed as she sampled a piece of cake, freshly baked, while sitting at the table in Hayley's kitchen.

"I'm so relieved you like it," Gemma sighed. "I was afraid it would be too dry."

"Not at all, it's very moist, and the frosting is perfection!" Liddy said, scooping some up with her small silver dessert fork and popping it into her mouth. "You were so smart putting Gemma in charge, Hayley! She's so gifted!"

Hayley patiently waited for Liddy to finish eating the cake before she attempted to get their conversation back on track. "Okay, now that the taste test is over, can we get back to discussing the postponement of the wedding?"

"There is absolutely nothing to discuss, Hayley. Sonny and I talked it over, and we have decided to move ahead with the wedding as planned."

"But somebody intentionally fiddled with the

brakes on your car, Liddy! Your life is in danger!"
Hayley cried.

"And our beloved Sergio is on the case. In the
meantime, I have a gazillion things to get done
before the big day," Liddy said, setting her dessert
fork down and standing up from the table. She
marched over to Gemma, who was standing by the
oven across the kitchen, and planted a big kiss on
her right cheek. "Thank you so much, Gemma. Your
cake is exactly the type of traditional cake I always
dreamed of having for my wedding reception."

"You're welcome," Gemma said, smiling. "I was
so nervous. I know this is a big opportunity, so I
really didn't want to blow it. Mom's been so busy
I decided to take matters into my own hands and
see what I came up with."

"Am I the only one who is the least bit concerned
about nearly getting killed in a car crash?" Hayley
yelled.

"For your information, Hayley, I am very concerned too, but if I dwell on it, then I will scare
myself silly and probably never dare leave my
house, which is definitely *not* an option with so
much left to do for the wedding," Liddy argued.

"Gemma, help me out here . . ." Hayley begged.

"I'm just happy she likes my cake," Gemma said,
grinning from ear to ear.

"Of course I do! You actually listened to me
about what kind of cake I wanted, unlike stupid,
awful ogre Lisa . . . may she rest in peace!"

"But Lisa *did* listen to you, Liddy," Hayley

sighed. "She finally relented and baked the cake you requested, the angel food cake with buttercream frosting, and then someone poisoned it!"

"So? That's Lisa's problem, not mine," Liddy sniffed, still not getting it.

"Oh . . ." Gemma groaned, finally realizing.

Liddy spun around after stuffing one more forkful of cake in her mouth. "What? What am I missing?"

"I think what Mom's trying to say is, whoever poisoned the cake may have known Lisa specifically made it for *you* . . ."

Liddy's eyes darted back and forth between Hayley and Gemma, slowly comprehending what they were trying to tell her. "Are you saying you believe someone poisoned that cake expecting I would be the one who ate it?"

Hayley threw her hands up in the air, relieved that she was finally getting through to her. "Yes!"

Liddy swallowed the cake in her mouth and stared at them for a few seconds and then, with a look of steely determination, wiped her hands on a dish towel and headed for the door. "Sonny and I have a meeting with Reverend Staples to go over our vows. I better get going."

Hayley raced to stop her. "Liddy, please, listen to reason. You need to call off the wedding, at least until we figure out what's going on here."

Liddy spun around, her face flushed, her fists clenched, and said quietly, "Never. I have been waiting for this day my whole life, and honestly there were times when I thought this day was *never* going to happen. But I found the man I want to spend the rest of my life with, and the wheels are finally in motion, so I have no intention of putting on the brakes at this late stage—"

"Someone *cut* your brakes!" Hayley cried.

"That was a metaphor, Hayley," Liddy sighed. "I've already called off this wedding once—"

"Twice," Gemma interjected.

"Twice." Liddy winced, correcting herself. "I'm not going to do it again."

"Even if it means you're a target for murder?" Hayley challenged.

"That's a risk I'm just going to have to take," Liddy said, spinning on her heels and marching out the back door, down the side porch steps, and to her car.

Hayley watched her get into her loaner from the insurance company, a sleek black Audi, back out of the driveway, and peel away.

"I have such a bad feeling about this," Hayley whispered.

Gemma put a comforting hand on her mother's shoulder. "You can't force her to go into hiding, Mom."

"I know . . ." Hayley said, her stomach flip-flopping.

Every intuition was screaming at her that Liddy's life was in imminent peril.

And yet, if Liddy refused to listen to her sage advice or adhere to her severe warnings, there was very little she could do to stop her from plowing ahead, attempts on her life be damned.

"So what are you going to do?" Gemma asked.

"What I always do when I'm worried," Hayley said, grabbing the large knife off the counter and cutting herself a big piece of Gemma's delicious, moist wedding cake. "Stress eat."

Chapter 26

The following day before work, Hayley met Mona for breakfast at Jordan's Restaurant, which was known for its mouthwatering blueberry pancakes. It was eight in the morning, and Mona had already been out on her boat hauling traps for hours, so this was essentially her lunch break, even though Hayley had yet to even start her day at the *Island Times*.

Mona always ordered a king's breakfast after working up an appetite on her lobster boat, and today was no different. She scarfed down scrambled eggs, bacon, hash browns, a short stack of pancakes, and a side of sausage, washing it all down with enough cups of coffee to fill at least two pots.

Hayley brought her up to speed on how worried she was about Liddy and her suspicions that she was now the target of someone, still to be revealed, who was out to do her bodily harm.

"It could be just about anyone," Mona cracked. "Liddy's got enough haters to fill a phone directory."

"I know she's not the most popular person in town," Hayley said, taking a sip of orange juice. "But it's hard to believe anyone would hold such a grudge against her, or that he or she would go to such lengths to try and kill her."

"Believe me, I've thought about it a few times," Mona said, upending a bottle of maple syrup and drowning what remained of her blueberry pancakes.

"Mona, be serious," Hayley admonished, sprinkling a small paper cup of brown sugar on top of her oatmeal with strawberries and bananas, a temporary attempt to eat healthier in the morning.

Mona clearly didn't get the memo, as she stopped the waitress and ordered another short stack before turning back to Hayley.

"So if you're right, and there is someone out to get Liddy, who the hell could it be?" Mona asked, slathering butter on her piece of white toast and stuffing it in her mouth.

"I don't know. I'm at a loss . . ." Hayley said, her voice trailing off.

"Could be someone Liddy pissed off on one of her shopping trips to New York or fancy European vacations—somebody we don't know, a complete stranger, like the woman who came into my shop the other day."

Hayley slid a spoonful of oatmeal into her mouth and then swallowed quickly. She set her spoon down on the table. "What woman?"

"Some lady. She came in to buy some lobsters. Said she was a tourist and was planning a cookout with her family. She mentioned to me that she knew Liddy."

"What did she look like?"

"I don't know. Kind of pretty, I guess, but not in an overly made-up way like Liddy. She was natural-looking, brunette, around our age, maybe a few years older."

"Did you get her name?"

"No, I didn't ask and she didn't tell me."

"Did she use a credit card?"

"Nope. She paid cash."

"Well, what else did she say? Did she tell you how she knew Liddy?"

"Nope. She just said they were old friends, and that she hadn't seen her in a long time, and thought she might look her up while she was here in town on vacation just to say hello."

"Then what?"

Mona chewed on a piece of bacon, trying to remember. "I took her to the tank to pick out some lobsters, and that's when she started hinting around, trying to find out where Liddy lived. She told me she was thinking about just showing up on her doorstep and surprising her."

"Did you give her Liddy's address?"

"I didn't have the chance. When I told her I just happened to be a close friend of Liddy's, and that I could call her up right there on the spot and get her over to the shop for a reunion, the woman got this panicked look in her eye, like she was afraid I was actually going to do it."

"I wonder who it could be," Hayley said, her mind racing.

Mona shrugged. "Beats me."

"Then what?"

"Well, once I suggested calling Liddy, she got real nervous and made up some lame excuse about being late for a whale watching tour and ran out of the shop without buying any lobsters!"

"Why didn't you mention this before?"

"Because I don't have time to think about Liddy and all her hyped-up drama, that's why!"

"Do you remember anything else about her?"

"No, Hayley! I'm too busy running a business to spend my day trying to investigate some weird lady from Rhode Island!"

"Rhode Island?"

"Yeah, that's where she was from. I saw her license plate as she was screeching away in her Volvo. She raced off so fast she left a skid mark on my driveway!"

"Did you—?"

Mona put up a hand to stop her. "No, I didn't get the license number, just that she was from the Ocean State! Now stop interrogating me so I can eat my breakfast in peace!"

The waitress dropped off Mona's second short stack, and after gulping down the rest of her coffee, she dug in, leaving Hayley sitting across from her, reeling over the fact that there was a stranger in town from Rhode Island who claimed to know Liddy, but had no clue where she lived.

Hayley considered the fact that the woman's

inquiry might be completely innocent, but then after mulling that over for a few seconds, she discarded it, fearing this mystery woman suddenly popping up in town was too much of a coincidence. This was possibly something far more sinister.

Chapter 27

That night, over Hayley's vociferous objections, Liddy's bachelorette party went ahead as planned. In the end, after all of Sabrina's expensive suggestions and Mona's offer to host the whole thing in her backyard, Randy's bar Drinks Like a Fish was the chosen venue. About twenty women, a mix of friends and clients of Liddy's, showed up ready to party.

Randy's wedding gift to Liddy was providing an open bar for the ladies until midnight, and most of them took full advantage of it. There was lots of boisterous laughter and high-pitched shrieking as the evening wore on, along with embarrassing stories told about Liddy from high school, college, and from her life as one of Bar Harbor's premier real estate agents.

Hayley, who deliberately remained sober for the whole night, sat at the end of the bar on a stool and kept a watchful eye over the festivities. She still couldn't shake the sense of dread that had been consuming her ever since the car accident.

Randy appeared and set a glass of Diet Coke down in front of her. "You sure you don't want something stronger? It's just going to keep getting louder and louder."

Hayley shook her head. "No, I want to stay alert, just in case."

"I don't think anything's going to happen here. If there is some kind of crazed stalker out to get Liddy, I'm sure he's not going to strike in such a public setting."

"I'm not sure of anything anymore," Hayley said, taking a sip of her soda.

Hayley glanced toward the back of the bar, where the women had turned an open area near the dart-board into a makeshift dance floor and were grind-ing and swiveling their hips to an old Mariah Carey '90s dance hit playing on the jukebox. Liddy was right in the middle, clapping her hands and sway-ing from side to side, laughing uproariously as her friends made a circle around her so she could show off her dance moves and rejoice in being the center of attention.

Hayley turned back to Randy. "That moment when Liddy realized the brakes on her car weren't working and lost control—I've never been so scared in my life. I thought we were goners. I keep playing it over and over in my mind."

Randy shook his head. "I just can't imagine who would deliberately do something like that."

Mona strolled into the bar and took a spot on the stool next to Hayley's. "Bottle of Bud, Randy, if you don't mind."

"Coming right up," Randy said as he scooted off to fetch the beer.

"You're late," Hayley said, eyeing Mona.

"I wasn't even going to come. I hate bachelorette parties. Too many silly, loud, obnoxious women who drink too much and act way younger than their age. Gives me a damn headache. But I figured I'd never hear the end of it from Liddy if I didn't at least show my face."

"Liddy will appreciate you being here," Hayley said. "And it's the least you can do since you're now refusing to be a bridesmaid at her wedding."

"Like I told her, I'm not going to embarrass myself by wearing a dress that makes me look like I belong in a nursery rhyme. I'm better off sitting in the church pew like everybody else. I may even wear a skirt."

"I won't hold my breath," Hayley said.

Mona looked toward the back of the bar, where Liddy was now dirty dancing with Tilly McVety, a petite, bubbly nurse from the Bar Harbor Hospital, who was obviously a lightweight, because she was only on her second cocktail and was already stumbling into tables and the jukebox as she tried to dance. Meanwhile, Sabrina, who was already tipsy by the time she arrived at the bar for the party, was desperately trying to form a conga line—to no avail, because the other women were too drunk to notice her.

"Trust me, I'd rather be at home watching *Wheel of Fortune*, but I had to come anyway. The stripper needed a lift," Mona said.

Hayley jerked her head back in Mona's direction. "What stripper?"

Suddenly the front door to the bar slammed open, and a police officer charged through the door. His blue uniform was skintight, and he wore dark sunglasses even though the sun had set hours ago. On his feet were a pair of shiny black boots, and there was a silver badge pinned to his muscular chest.

Randy slipped out from behind the bar and unplugged the jukebox, bringing the music to an abrupt stop, which finally got the women to stop dancing and look around, confused.

"All right, ladies, you're all under arrest!" the cop yelled.

The giggly party girls all snapped to attention at the sight of the hunky young police officer who had suddenly appeared in the bar.

Hayley stared at him for a moment.

He looked so familiar.

"What are you arresting us for?" Liddy asked tentatively, genuinely nervous.

"Indecent exposure," he drawled.

"What are you talking about? We're all fully dressed," Sabrina argued, looking around at all the other women gathered around.

"Not you, babe . . . *me*," he said, removing his glasses.

Hayley gasped.

It was AJ, Mona's hot and hunky summer helper from her lobster shop.

At the sight of AJ, Liddy and Sabrina both squealed with delight.

AJ pulled out his phone, and with his Bluetooth, linked it to Randy's speaker system. Suddenly an electro house dance mix blasted through the speakers, and before anyone could react further, AJ was up on top of the bar, unbuttoning his shirt to reveal his bronzed, chiseled chest.

The women surged forward, pushing and shoving, eager for a closer look. Once the blue shirt was discarded so they could see his muscular biceps, one sporting his American flag tattoo, he slowly removed his black leather boots and tossed them out to the crowd. Tilly caught one in her arms and excitedly clutched it to her chest as she jumped up and down.

Hayley spun around to Mona and tried yelling above the deafening sound of the music. "Did *you* hire him?"

Mona shook her head. "Nope! Wasn't me. It was Sabrina. She came by my shop the other day to pick up some more lobsters and hung around chatting with AJ. He mentioned that he was looking to make some extra cash for a few college courses he's planning on taking in the fall at the University of Maine in Orono, so Sabrina offered to pay him a couple hundred bucks just to show up here tonight and strut his stuff for an hour or so."

Hayley nodded, then looked up at AJ, who was now in front of her shimmying out of his pants.

The women screamed at the top of their lungs as if they were at that historic Beatles concert on *The Ed Sullivan Show* way back in 1964.

Mona covered her ears with her hands. "Come on, girls, settle down, the kid's not *that* good-looking!"

"I suspect it's not just AJ's rocking body, but also the six Jell-O shots they all did earlier," Hayley said.

AJ, now with only a white jockstrap covering his private parts, finally jumped down off the bar to the floor and swaggered up to Liddy. He took her by the chin with his hand and guided her over to a chair, where he gently pushed her down into the seat.

Liddy clapped her hands, eager to find out what was going to happen next. AJ straddled her and then began giving her a full-on lap dance as the other women howled with laughter and jumped up and down with glee.

Sabrina shoved her way to the front and center in order to get a better look at the young man's goods. Her eyes were wild with desire. She reached into her purse and snatched a twenty-dollar bill before rushing over and stuffing it in the waistband of his jockstrap. A few other women followed suit, so by the time AJ was grinding his hips deep into Liddy's lap, he had about a hundred dollars.

Randy returned with Mona's bottle of beer and

just stood there gripping it in his hand because he was so drawn to the hot young stud's riveting performance.

"It looks like he's done this before," Randy remarked, grinning.

Hayley nodded. "It sure does."

Exasperated, Mona grabbed the beer from Randy.

"Do you mind? I'm thirsty!" Mona wailed as she took a big swig.

As the women's excitement reached a fever pitch, Hayley was surprised to see another man in a police uniform appear in the doorway.

It was Sergio.

Randy zipped out from behind the bar again to give his husband a kiss on the cheek. "Are you going to strip for us too?"

Sergio was not amused. "No. I'm answering a noise complaint."

"Are we that loud?" Hayley yelled over the music.

"Let me put it this way. The complaint came from two blocks away," he growled.

Mercifully, AJ's show ended shortly thereafter and the party broke up, especially since it was a work night, and most of the women knew they would be nursing hangovers at their jobs tomorrow morning.

It was time to go home.

Sergio let his husband off with a warning as long as he promised to keep the volume down until closing. Once the party girls had all dispersed and Sonny had shown up to make sure his bride-to-be got home safely, the only ones left in the bar were

Hayley, Mona, Sabrina, and AJ. Randy was in the kitchen cleaning up.

"Come on, AJ, we have to be up in a few hours to haul traps. Let me drop you off so I can get home for some shut-eye," Mona said.

Sabrina, who was still rather drunk, slurred, "Don't be such a buzzkill, Mona, the night is young . . ."

"It's nearly one in the morning . . ." Hayley said, checking her watch. "And there is no way I'm allowing you to drive home tonight. Come on, I'll take you."

"You don't have to do that," Sabrina said, eyeing AJ lasciviously. "AJ's going to give me a ride."

All eyes turned to AJ, who smiled shyly.

"But you came with me," Mona said.

"I can drive her home in her car," AJ suggested with a wolfish grin.

"And then how will *you* get home?" Mona asked.

"There's no reason we need to decide that now, Mona . . ." Sabrina said, stumbling over to AJ and collapsing in his arms. "Besides, he's welcome to stay over at my place . . . for as long as he wants . . ."

"Good night," AJ said, half dragging, half carrying Sabrina out of the bar.

Hayley and Mona exchanged a look.

"He better be on time tomorrow or his sorry butt's fired," Mona snapped.

"Well, that's what I call a scandalous turn of events," Hayley said, shaking her head.

Hayley had to hand it to Sabrina.

She had set a plan in motion from the moment she first laid eyes on the handsome young man at Mona's lobster shop, and through her tenacity and aggressiveness, she was on the cusp of successfully accomplishing her single-minded mission.

Getting hot stud AJ with the American flag tattoo into her bed.

Chapter 28

After dropping the bride-to-be off at her house, Hayley drove home. The clock on her dashboard read 12:52 A.M. She was tired from the long night and anxious to curl up in her bed for a solid six hours of sleep before she had to be up and ready for work at the *Island Times*.

As she approached her house, Hayley spotted a car parked in front of her house. At first she didn't recognize it, but as she swung into her driveway, she realized it was Bruce's blue Camry. She could see his shadowy figure in the driver's seat, his face illuminated by the light from his phone as he scrolled through for text messages or headlines on his news apps.

By the time she pulled to a stop and got out of her Kia, Hayley heard him slam his car door shut. She glanced around and saw him shuffling toward her and instantly noticed a strange look on his face, very serious and full of apprehension.

"It's nearly one in the morning, Bruce. What are you doing here?"

"I've been waiting for you to come home," he said in a quiet voice.

"For how long?"

"I got here around ten, maybe ten thirty . . ."

"What? I told you I was going to Liddy's bachelorette party at Randy's bar tonight and I wouldn't be home until very late."

"I know. It gave me some time to clear my head and get my thoughts straight," he said, eyes downcast.

"About what?"

"Can we go inside?"

"Sure," Hayley said, suddenly worried where this conversation was going to go. It was unlike Bruce to be so mysterious.

Hayley spun around and headed up the porch steps, rummaging through her bag for her house key.

Bruce followed close behind her, so close she could feel his hot breath on the back of her neck.

Inside, Hayley started to panic.

What was so important that he was willing to wait outside her house for almost three hours to talk to her?

Was he going to break up with her?

Did he have some really bad news to deliver?

She could hardly take the suspense.

Once inside the back door that led to the kitchen, Hayley had to take the time to greet her dog, Leroy, who was jumping up and down, excited she was finally home. Her cat, Blueberry, sat in the hallway, glaring at her, annoyed over being left alone for so long with a hyperactive, annoying dog.

Bruce stood patiently waiting for all the hoopla to die down.

After feeding her pets, Hayley finally managed to turn and face Bruce, who now had a stoic, almost unreadable look on his face.

"So, what's up?" she asked.

"Let's go sit down in the living room," he said gravely.

Bad news.

It had to be bad news.

No one ever had to sit down to hear good news.

Bruce brushed past her and led her into the living room where they both sat down on the couch.

Bruce took her hand and squeezed it gently.

Hayley held her breath, preparing herself for what was about to come.

He stared at her, but she couldn't tell what he was thinking, and that was driving her absolutely crazy.

"What, Bruce? Just come out with it! Is it Gemma or Dustin? Where are they?"

He looked genuinely perplexed. "I don't know. I assume they're both upstairs in their rooms asleep."

"Then what?"

He squeezed her hand again. "I've been a mess since the accident."

"Why? There's no need to be. I'm fine."

"I know, and I thank God for that, but there was

this period of time, like twenty minutes or so, right after I heard about the accident on the police scanner and the dispatcher said your name, when I didn't know whether you were alive or dead . . . And so, like I always do, I just assumed the worst . . ."

"Bruce . . ."

His eyes welled up with tears. "I thought I had lost you . . ."

He broke down crying.

Hayley leaned in and hugged him. He rested his head on her shoulder as he let it all out. Hayley had no idea how to react, except to be there and comfort him and pat him tenderly on the back. This was a side of Bruce she had never seen in all the years she had known him, including the nearly two years they had been dating.

"As I raced to the hospital, I could barely breathe, I was so distraught, and later, after I saw you, and I knew you were going to be okay, I . . . well, I . . ."

Hayley moved her hand up to the back of his head and pulled him closer into a warm embrace.

Bruce fought to stop crying, but he was too emotional. He wept on Hayley's shoulder a few more minutes before he was finally able to collect himself and continue. "After I saw you in the hospital, and this huge wave of relief washed over me, I knew . . . I knew my feelings for you ran much deeper than I ever thought possible . . ."

Hayley slowly leaned back, and in one of those rare moments in her life, was rendered utterly speechless. She had never believed that Bruce Linney, of all the men in the world, would *ever* be capable of baring his soul.

"That night, after I left you, I kept thinking, what if something *did* happen to you? What if one day you were just ripped away from me? I just couldn't handle it . . ."

"Bruce, I don't know what to say . . ."

"You don't have to say anything. I just had to get it off my chest. It was crushing me."

He sniffed a couple of times. His eyes were finally dry of tears, so he wiped his face with the sleeve of his flannel shirt and then looked up at Hayley.

She could tell he was feeling extremely vulnerable.

For her part, Hayley was both touched and freaked out by Bruce's raw admission. But as she gazed into his eyes, not sure how to respond, suddenly she found herself saying, "I feel exactly the same way."

Bruce exhaled, a smile slowly creeping across his face.

It was exactly what he had waited three hours outside her house in his car to hear.

They embraced again and shared a dizzyingly passionate kiss, and then Bruce stood up, took her by the hand, and led her quietly upstairs.

Chapter 29

Hayley was up early the next morning and was on her way to work when she decided to swing into the Big Apple gas station and grab a cup of coffee and one of those plastic-wrapped cheese Danishes, since her own fridge was empty. So much for trying healthier breakfast options.

When she flew out of the store, struggling to rip open the plastic covering her Danish, she spotted Sergio at one of the pumps, filling the gas tank of his police cruiser.

"Morning," he said with a nod.

"Hey, sorry about the noise complaint last night," Hayley said sheepishly.

"No problem. Liddy only gets married once . . . we hope," he said, chuckling. "Listen, I was going to mention this last night when I was at the bar, but you looked like you had your hands full."

"What is it?" Hayley asked, finally prying open the plastic wrapper and taking a bite of her stale Danish.

"I had Lisa's ex-boyfriend Timmy Blanchard come into the station for more questioning late yesterday afternoon."

Hayley stopped at her car. "And?"

"And he admitted to stopping by Lisa's shop unannounced on the day of the murder to try and get the money she owed him back . . ."

Hayley chewed on her Danish and sipped her coffee. This was news she was already aware of, but she nodded, hanging on Sergio's every word.

"When he arrived, he saw someone leaving the bakery."

"Who?"

"He didn't know the guy, but he gave me a description. About six feet, nice build, good-looking, blond hair, maybe early to midtwenties . . ."

Hayley suspected who it might be, but then Sergio confirmed it.

"Tommy said he was wearing a tank top and there was a tattoo of the American flag on his left bicep."

Mona's dreamy summer employee AJ, who was also moonlighting as a stripper at bachelorette parties.

"Do you have any idea where I might be able to find him?" Sergio asked.

Hayley thought carefully before she answered. She had seen Sabrina leave the bar with him the night before, and if her hunch was right, AJ was probably still at her rental house, if he hadn't slipped away in the middle of the night after fooling around with Sabrina. But she certainly didn't want Sergio rolling up in front of Sabrina's rental in a squad car, alerting all the neighbors, who would undoubtedly gawk through their windows and see the young stud emerging, no doubt shirtless, to be questioned by the police chief. It would get too many tongues wagging for sure. No, and she also was not one hundred percent certain that was where he would be found, so to avoid any unnecessary gossip, she decided to check out her hunch on her own.

"I might," she said to Sergio. "I'll give you a ring in about a half hour."

"Okay, I'll be in my office waiting for your call."

Sergio finished filling his tank, replaced the pump, got his printed receipt, then ducked inside his cruiser and drove away.

Hayley scarfed down the rest of her Danish, tossed the plastic wrap into a garbage bin, jumped into her Kia, and drove straight over to Sabrina's rental just outside of town, downing the rest of her coffee on the way.

When she arrived, it was quiet. She didn't see any activity through the front windows. Hayley got out of her car and walked along the pebble path to the front door. Sabrina had certainly splurged on herself by renting a beautiful home with an impressive view of Frenchman's Bay during her stay in Bar Harbor.

Hayley rang the bell and waited.

There was no answer.

She rang the bell again.

Finally, after five minutes and three more rings, she heard some stirring inside, and after a few moments, the door flew open. Sabrina stood in the archway, wearing a pink silk robe with a Japanese print design and matching furry slippers. Her face was drawn and wiped free of makeup, and her eyes were bleary and watery—the signs of a massive hangover. Her hair was tousled and sticking out in all kinds of directions.

"Hayley?" She yawned, pulling her robe closed tightly with her hands. "What are you doing here? What time is it?"

"It's seven thirty. I'm sorry, Sabrina, I know it's early and you got home very late last night, but it's kind of important . . ."

"What's the matter?"

"I have to know, did you come home alone last night?"

Sabrina blinked at Hayley, not sure why she needed to know this, but before she had a chance to open her mouth and answer, Hayley spotted AJ, in nothing but a pair of boxer shorts, scratching the top of his head and yawning as he padded to the kitchen.

"You got a coffeemaker? I want to have a cup before I head over to Mona's and get reamed for being so late," he said.

Sabrina turned her head around. "It's on the left side of the counter, next to the toaster."

"Got it," he called back from the kitchen.

Sabrina turned back around and, with a Cheshire cat smile and blushing face, said matter-of-factly, "No, Hayley, I did not."

Island Food & Cocktails
BY HAYLEY POWELL

There is something about the beauty of
Mount Desert Island, where Bar Harbor is located,
and especially our picture-perfect Acadia National
Park that draws people from all over the United
States every year. But not just for vacation. Couples
flock here every summer to get engaged or married.
Romance is definitely in the air when it comes to
this world-famous scenic hot spot.

From Memorial Day all the way through to
Labor Day, on top of a mountain or on a sandy
beach, or along a rocky overlook at the ocean's
edge, you're bound to see a hopeful young couple,
clearly in love, exchanging vows. Weddings are
so commonplace on the island, cars barely slow
down anymore when they see a ceremony in
progress.

However, one engagement that occurred last
summer stands out above them all.

I was at work on a sweltering July afternoon
during an unusually scorching heat wave when I
received a phone call from a friendly and earnest
young man named Calvin, who told me that he
and his girlfriend, Priscilla, would be visiting

Bar Harbor in a couple of weeks to fulfill her lifelong dream of taking a whale watching tour. The island has several companies offering excursions for nature enthusiasts to view humpback, fin, minke, and right whales frolic, breach, and blow in their natural habitat.

What Priscilla didn't know, however, was that both their families, who were also coming to the island for a long preplanned vacation, were going to secretly join them on the tour and come out of hiding so they would all be there to bear witness as Calvin got down on one knee and proposed to Priscilla with the beauty of large migratory whales as a backdrop.

I was so touched by the lengths to which Calvin was willing to go to arrange such a memorable proposal, I excitedly offered to help in any way I could.

Calvin's dilemma was that in all the planning, arranging the flights and hotels for both families, booking the tour, tipping off the boat crew, and buying the perfect ring, he had completely forgotten to hire a photographer to record the moment for posterity. He thought since I worked at a newspaper that employs a number of professional photographers, I might have a referral for him. Well, our local shutterbugs are always looking for a way to make some extra cash in the summer, so I told Calvin I would happily assist him in finding one. I promised to get back to him in a day or two.

Well, before I had even hung up the phone, our crime reporter, Bruce Linney, who also liked to brag about what a talented photographer he was, generously volunteered his services. I was skeptical at first about Bruce's talent because, after all, he was only *telling* me he was talented, but there was no photographic evidence, since I had never seen one picture he had taken. But when Bruce suggested the added bonus of the two of us splitting the money if I accompanied him on the whale watching tour and helped him carry the equipment and serve as his assistant, I decided to give him the benefit of the doubt.

Luckily, Calvin quickly signed off on us, and we had our first official photography assignment.

I was so excited to help Calvin create the perfect proposal, but I was even more anxious to go on the whale watching tour and get an up close look at those amazing and breathtaking whales.

Well, about two days before the tour, Calvin swung by the *Island Times* office to introduce himself and fill me and Bruce in on all the details of how his plan would go down.

He wanted Bruce to discreetly take pictures of him and Priscilla at the start of the boat tour so they would have a record of the day from start to finish for the album he would eventually have made. Then, when we were far out at sea, he would covertly signal Bruce and both families to come forward just before he got down on his knee and popped the question, surrounded by their loved ones.

After that, Bruce could freely come out of hiding and snap away, capturing Priscilla's anticipated joyous reaction.

It sounded like a solid plan.

On the day of the whale watching tour, everything went according to plan. We pulled out of the dock with the couple's families hiding on one end of the large catamaran boat and the happy couple up front, holding hands. The boat was sprinkled with unsuspecting tourists. And the weather was on our side, so it was the perfect day for both a whale watching tour and a surprise proposal.

Bruce effortlessly blended into the crowd of tourists, pretending to take pictures of the scenery while surreptitiously grabbing some shots of the young couple like a veteran Hollywood paparazzo. Priscilla was blissfully happy and didn't suspect a thing.

Per Calvin's instructions, once they spotted the first couple of whales, that would be signal for the families to make their move and head to the bow of the boat for the proposal.

Well, my heart was beating fast and I was a nervous wreck, anticipating the moment, as the boat's captain announced over the loudspeaker that we should be seeing some whales ahead. Just about that time, I noticed some fog rolling in, and the water suddenly became a bit more choppy than usual. However, there was still some good visibility on the water.

The captain's voice crackled over the loudspeaker. "If everyone would look to your left, you will see a mother humpback and her calf alongside the boat."

The tourists ran to the left side of the boat, phones and cameras flashing.

Calvin caught my eye and nodded.

It was time for the families to make their grand entrance.

I raced to the back and waved the large group forward. We all stumbled and swayed as the boat rocked back and forth, harder and harder with each rising wave. The fog grew thicker, and the humpback whale and her baby disappeared behind it. Up front, the families gathered around, clasping hands, mostly to keep from falling over in the rocking boat that was now pitching violently from side to side.

Priscilla still had her back to us.

Bruce took his position and started snapping pictures. Priscilla's parents welled up with tears. The emotion of the moment was overwhelming.

Calvin smiled from ear to ear and approached Priscilla, but had to grab the railing to keep from falling down. He dropped to one knee and reached into his jacket pocket.

Out came the ring box.

"Priscilla?" He whispered softly.

She turned around. She looked down at Calvin and gasped. She shook her head back and forth, not believing this was happening, still oblivious to all the family members surrounding them.

That's when I suddenly noticed her face had a slightly green hue and she put a hand over her mouth.

"Priscilla, will you—?"

She didn't wait for him to finish. She took off running as fast as she could to the side of the boat, where she flung herself at the railing and hurled. The poor girl was hopelessly seasick.

Calvin leapt into action and ran to her aid, but before he reached her, he tripped over a tourist's bag that had been set down on the deck of the boat, and while trying to regain his balance, flung his hand out to grab anything for support. Unfortunately it was the hand holding the ring box, which flew open. The ring itself was ejected and sailed into the air as all the boat's passengers watched in frozen horror as the ring zipped across the rail and dropped into the deep, dark water below—just like the old woman throwing the Heart of the Ocean diamond necklace overboard at the end of *Titanic*.

No one spoke for a minute. That is, no one except for Bruce, who was still snapping away with his camera, and who rudely asked Priscilla to turn more toward him, callously ignoring the fact that she was still green and vomiting.

Calvin, in a true testament to his character, just burst out laughing and tried again to get down on his knee and finally propose to Priscilla. It took a few more tries, because Priscilla had to stop him twice to go throw up over the side of the boat again, but he finally got through it, and yes, she happily accepted. Five more family members got seasick too before they mercifully found themselves back on dry land. They had all missed the fine print on the whale watching tour brochure strongly advising they pick up Dramamine at the local drugstore.

Well, as locals used to the choppy waters of the Atlantic, both Bruce and I were spared from getting sick, and in fact, were hungry after we wrapped our first photo assignment, so we treated ourselves to some yummy chicken skewers (not surprisingly, we were not in the mood for fish) and a Madras cocktail at a nearby eatery to celebrate a job well done.

MADRAS COCKTAIL

1½ ounces vodka
4 ounces cranberry juice
1 ounce orange juice
Ice
Lime wedge for garnish

In a highball glass, combine your vodka, cranberry juice, and orange juice. Add ice and garnish with the lime wedge.

This is definitely one of my favorite cocktails to sip when I really need to relax!

HONEY GARLIC CHICKEN SKEWERS

I love chicken skewers! They are such a simple but reliable dish. I couldn't be happier that my friend Liddy is including them on her own wedding reception appetizer menu.

½ cup honey
2 tablespoons soy sauce
2 tablespoons vinegar
½ teaspoon ground ginger
½ teaspoon garlic powder
1 tablespoon cornstarch
8 skewers
2 chicken breasts cut into eight 1-inch strips

Preheat your oven to 400°F.

In a bowl, whisk your honey, soy sauce, vinegar, ginger, and garlic powder until combined.

Add your cornstarch to thicken. Soak the skewers in water for about 10 minutes, then put the strips on the skewers by poking through one side and coming back through the other until the strip is securely on the skewer.

Set aside a little sauce for basting the chicken while it is cooking, then marinate the chicken skewers in the sauce for at least two hours.

Place your marinated chicken on a parchment paper–lined baking sheet and bake in oven for 14 minutes. Baste each side once or twice while baking.

When done, remove from oven and dig in!

Chapter 30

Hayley pushed past Sabrina and followed AJ into the kitchen, where she found him rummaging through the cupboards for a coffee mug.

"AJ, why didn't you ever say anything about seeing Lisa Crawford at her bakery on the same day she was poisoned?"

AJ turned around and stared blankly at Hayley.

He seemed to think for a moment about how he should answer, and then just shrugged. "Because nobody asked."

"I'm asking you now," Hayley said evenly.

Sabrina scurried into the kitchen and nearly hurled herself between Hayley and her newfound boy toy. "There's no need to be so confrontational, Hayley. AJ's just tired. He didn't get much sleep last night."

AJ smirked, obviously remembering exactly what had just transpired between him and his obviously adept hostess in the bedroom.

"It's okay, Sabrina. I've got nothing to hide," AJ

said, yawning and scratching his head again. "I went to see that lady at her shop because I was looking to buy a cake for my sister."

"Your *sister*?" Hayley asked.

"Yeah, she lives up in Brewer. She's getting married this summer, and now that I'm making a little money working for Mona, I thought I'd do a good deed and spring for her wedding cake. I dropped by the bakery, the lady showed me a few pictures of different cakes, I told her I'd think about it, and then I left. End of story."

"See, there is a perfectly reasonable explanation, Hayley," Sabrina said, folding her arms, annoyed that Hayley had so rudely interrupted her romantic morning tryst with her boy wonder.

"I just don't understand why you never said anything. The whole town has been buzzing about Lisa's murder, and you were one of the last people to see her alive."

"Because what happened to the cake lady has nothing to do with me," AJ said, his eyes narrowing. "And I don't appreciate you trying to drag me into it."

"I totally understand, dear," Sabrina gushed, rushing to his defense. "Why get all caught up in some nasty business when you are one hundred percent innocent?" Sabrina cried, desperate to convince herself, if not Hayley.

AJ glared at Hayley, who was trying to gauge whether or not he was being truthful.

Finally, he turned around to Sabrina, who was hovering behind him. "Where are my jeans?"

"On the floor in the bedroom, I think," Sabrina whispered, blushing again.

"Could you go get them for me, please?" he said before turning back to Hayley.

"Yes, of course," Sabrina said, scooting out of the kitchen, leaving Hayley and AJ standing across from each other, eyes locked in a staredown.

It only took Sabrina a few moments to retrieve the jeans and return to the kitchen, where she handed them to AJ. He pulled a phone from the back pocket, punched in a four-digit code to unlock it, and then made a call.

"Hey, sis, it's me. I got some lady here who doesn't believe I have a sister in Brewer who's getting married and that as the loving brother I am, I'm springing for your wedding cake," AJ said, sneering. "Hold on."

He held out the phone to Hayley.

"She wants to talk to you."

Hayley sighed and took the phone. "Yes, this is Hayley Powell."

"Hello, Hayley," the woman said in a cheery voice. "This is AJ's sister Adele, like the singer, but not. I have a terrible singing voice! Lord knows I can't hold a note."

"Nice to meet you, Adele," Hayley said.

"Adele Capshaw, soon to be Adele Capshaw-Bennett—Bennett's the name of my fiancé, but I'm not giving up my maiden name, because I want to maintain my own identity. I'm a card-carrying feminist!"

"Girl power!" Hayley said without raising her fist.

"You got it! Anyway, I just want to confirm to you that I have the sweetest brother in the whole wide world. My fiancé is sadly between jobs and his family up here in Brewer is dirt-poor, so we can't afford much of a wedding, but we're trying to do the best we can. And my darling brother AJ has offered to pay for a nice wedding cake. He's so appreciative that his boss Mona is giving him the extra hours to raise the money."

"Yes, Mona is a good friend of mine," Hayley said.

"She's an angel sent directly from heaven, in my humble opinion!"

Adele had obviously never met Mona in person.

"Anyway, I heard the tragic news about that poor woman who he was going to hire to make the cake, so now he's going to have to find another bakery to do the job. I heard there's another good one in Bar Harbor, which he was planning to go check out on his next day off."

"Yes, I know that one. Good choice."

"He tells me he really likes living in Bar Harbor. There is a lot to do there in the summer. He's met a lot of really nice and interesting people."

"Yes, he's been keeping himself very busy," Hayley said, watching Sabrina jump as AJ playfully pinched her on the butt as he headed back into the kitchen; thoughts of him stripping on top of a bar the previous evening flashed through her mind. "Well, it's been nice chatting with you, Adele. Congratulations on your wedding."

"Thank you, Hayley," Adele said. "Take care of my little brother."

"Don't worry about that. He's getting a lot of TLC down here. Bye, now."

She handed the phone back to AJ.

"Satisfied?" Sabrina said, snuggling up next to AJ, who was now pouring grounds in the top of the coffeemaker.

Hayley half nodded.

AJ's sister had indeed confirmed his story.

But she was not completely at ease around this well-muscled lothario.

There was something off about him.

Just because he had a sweet-sounding sister who was singing his praises didn't make him any less suspicious.

And despite the raves he was getting from his fawning cougar of the moment Sabrina Merryweather, Hayley had a strong feeling the young buck was still hiding something.

And she was determined to find out exactly what it was.

Chapter 31

On her way back to the office, Hayley received an ominous text from Bruce that he needed to speak with her right away. Bruce hated texting and rarely communicated with her that way because, as he explained, he spent his entire day typing his crime column on a computer, so the last thing he wanted to do was type messages with his stubby fingers on his tiny phone. So the fact that he was now texting meant that whatever he needed to discuss with her was probably important.

When Hayley arrived at the office and tossed her bag underneath her desk, she stopped long enough to pour herself coffee in a Styrofoam cup before heading into the back bull pen to Bruce's office, just past her boss Sal's office, which was empty. Sal had been battling a summer cold and wasn't expected in today, so there was a relaxed atmosphere in the office as the other reporters hung out, chatting and laughing over the latest gossip in town.

Hayley found Bruce behind his desk, hands

folded, waiting for her. He had a grim look on his face, which both surprised and worried her. She instinctively closed the door behind her as she entered so they could have some privacy and took a deep breath. "What is it?"

Bruce cleared his throat. "Have a seat."

Hayley pulled a chair in front of the desk and sat down. She could feel a knot in the pit of her stomach, but she didn't say anything further.

She instinctively knew this had nothing to do with how Bruce felt about her.

This was something else entirely.

She waited for Bruce to talk.

"Some information has come to light that you need to know about."

"Okay."

"After your car accident, when you and Liddy were rushed to the hospital to get checked out, just to make sure you both were fine and didn't have any serious injuries . . ."

"Yes," Hayley whispered, clasping her hands together on her lap, expectantly.

". . . Sonny and I spent some time together in the waiting room."

This surprised her. She hadn't expected this to be about Sonny.

But she just kept her lips sealed and nodded.

"Sonny kept getting a bunch of calls while we were there, and he kept racing out of the waiting room to take them, like he was afraid I might over-hear his conversation. After he got the third call, I decided to go grab a candy bar from the vending machine, and I found him in the hallway, looking very anxious. When he saw me, he spun around so his back was to me and he brought his voice down to a whisper so I couldn't hear what he was saying. I didn't think much of it at the time. I mean, I figured whatever he was up to was none of my business, so I just let it go."

"Liddy has mentioned his secretive behavior recently," Hayley said.

"I know. And, well, you know me, the investigative reporter in me got curious, and the more I thought about it, the more it bugged me. What the hell is this guy hiding?"

"So what did you find out?"

Bruce paused, carefully considering how to proceed.

This vexed Hayley even more.

Based on Bruce's expression, whatever was coming was significant—far more serious than your average case of a groom getting cold feet.

"Sonny has been taking a lot of trips out of town the past few years," Bruce said.

"I know. Liddy told me he has been doing some part-time work for his old firm in Boston, where he worked as an associate after law school. He's been spending a lot of time working on two cases, one in Revere, and one in Woonsocket, Rhode Island, if I remember correctly."

"I know, but his story doesn't pass muster."

"Why not?"

"Because Sonny's old law firm in Boston shut down in two thousand twelve. Three partners retired, and the other two younger partners took most of the clients and started their own firm."

"Maybe Sonny was working with the new firm."

"He's not. I called and checked. He's been lying."

"But why?"

"Here's the tough part . . ."

Hayley braced herself for what was coming and how it might devastate Liddy.

"I stopped by Sonny's office under the guise of needing legal advice on some family property that was left to me and my brothers by my uncle Shane, which his ex-wife is contesting, and I was going to casually ask him about his time in Boston, but before I even opened my mouth, his cell phone, which was sitting on his desk right in front of me, started ringing. Before he had a chance to scoop it up, I saw the name of the person who was calling . . . Nancy Malone."

"Never heard of her."

"Neither had I. But I went on Facebook and looked up every Nancy Malone I could find in the New England area, and one turned up in Revere, Massachusetts, just outside of Boston."

"That could be a complete coincidence."

"That's what I thought. I saw on her page that she has a brother, so I sent a message and a friend request claiming to be a buddy of his, and she accepted. Once she did that, I had access to all her photos."

Hayley breathed slowly, remaining calm. "And?"

"I found this," Bruce said solemnly.

He tapped the Facebook app on his phone,

scrolled through a bit, and then, with a grimace on his face, handed his phone to Hayley.

Hayley stared at the photo. It was a picture of a pretty blond woman, late twenties or early thirties, in a bikini top, snuggling next to a shirtless Sonny on a beach with a crystal blue ocean in the background.

"Maybe she and Sonny dated in the past, before he even met Liddy."

"I wanted to believe that too. But she posted this photo to her page three months ago while she was on vacation with her boyfriend, Sonny, in Key West."

Hayley gasped.

Hayley distinctly remembered Sonny had to go out of town three months ago for a week, because she had to listen to Liddy complain about it the entire time he was gone. He claimed he was working on a case but had been suspiciously vague on the details.

There was no way to sugarcoat this.

Sonny Lipton was cheating on Liddy with another woman.

Chapter 32

"Patrice, could you shut the door and give us some privacy?" Sonny squeaked as he stood behind his desk, loosening his tie so he could breathe easier.

Patrice, who hadn't heard what Hayley had said after marching past her desk and barging into Sonny's office unannounced, scooted to the door, gave her boss a curious look, and then slowly closed the door, hoping she might catch a piece of their conversation that might illuminate what was so important that she couldn't hear about it.

But no such luck. Sonny waited until he heard the door click before he said anything to Hayley. When he was absolutely sure they were alone, he said in a hushed whisper, "Who the hell is Nancy Malone?"

Hayley smirked. She knew Sonny well enough to know he was lying. If it wasn't the beads of sweat streaming down his forehead even though it was a relatively cool sixty-eight degrees outside, it was his bottom lip that quivered nervously.

"Don't lie to me, Sonny. I know she's your girl-friend."

Sonny made his way around his desk, his arms clasped together almost as if he was about to drop down to his knees and start praying. "Please tell me you haven't mentioned this to Liddy!"

"Not yet," Hayley said, eyes narrowing, disgusted with him. "Sonny, how could you?"

"I swear to you, Hayley, I dated Nancy a couple of years ago, during the period Liddy and I were taking a break!"

"Stop lying! She posted a picture of you two to-gether in Key West just a few months ago!"

"She may have posted it recently but it was taken long before that. We met while I was in Boston shortly after you, Liddy, and Mona got back from your girls' weekend in Salmon Cove. We were tech-nically no longer together, so I started seeing Nancy when I would make trips down to Massachusetts while working for my old law firm."

"Your old law firm closed down in two thousand twelve, Sonny."

Sonny's face went pale. "How did you know . . . ?"

Hayley folded her arms, expectantly waiting to see just how he planned on wiggling out of this one.

"You're right. It did. But a couple of the partners started their own firm and offered me a few free-lance assignments."

"Bruce called the new firm, and they claim you are not working for them."

"That's because they don't want the other partners knowing I'm there doing some consulting. They had to deny it. There are a lot of politics involved, and it's kind of a complicated situation."

Hayley glared at him skeptically. "You're right about one thing, Sonny. This is a very complicated situation."

"Look, it's true. Stop making everything look so suspicious."

"I'm not doing anything of the kind, Sonny. You're doing an admirable job of that yourself."

"Nancy and I did go on a trip to Key West . . . almost two years ago . . . she wanted to get serious, but I was still in love with Liddy. Then, when Liddy and I got back together, I ended it. Full stop!"

Hayley studied his face, trying to surmise if he was telling the truth or not.

"Nancy didn't take it well. She kept calling me all the time. I was afraid she was going to turn into some kind of stalker and try reaching out to Liddy, but after I pretended to lose my phone and changed my number, we finally lost contact."

"So why would she post that old photo of you two on her Facebook page?"

"I don't know. Maybe she's trying to find me again, and thought if someone recognized me, they might be able to tell her where I am. You see, after I broke up with her, I let it be known I was taking a job at a law firm in Chicago, hoping she'd believe it and not track me down here in Bar Harbor."

"Why didn't you tell Liddy any of this?"

Sonny smirked, surprised she even had to ask. "Have you met Liddy?"

"Okay, I understand. But if this Nancy Malone is unstable and trying to reconnect with you, then you *have* to tell Liddy."

"I will, I will . . ."

"Sonny . . ."

"She's just been so overwhelmed with the wedding plans. Come on—you've been spending a lot of time with her, you know she's on edge about everything! My God, Hayley, she's already canceled the wedding twice. I'm afraid if something sets her off again, I'll lose her for good this time."

"You can't keep something like this from her."

"I know, but just give me a little time to figure out a gentle way to tell her . . . Please, Hayley . . . I honestly don't believe that Nancy Malone is a threat. That picture may have just been one of those Throwback Thursday posts that are on everyone's feeds, showing a memory from two years ago . . . But I would have no way of knowing that, because after I dumped her, I unfriended her and cut off all ties!"

"Somebody tampered with the brakes on Liddy's car!"

"It couldn't be Nancy! She would never do something like that!"

"Sonny, I'm going to give you the benefit of the doubt here . . ."

"Thank you . . ."

"For now. But Liddy is my best friend, and if you

do anything, and I mean anything, to hurt her in any way, I will come for you."

Sonny threw his hands up in front of him. "I understand . . ."

"You know I will, Sonny . . ."

"Yes, Hayley, I promise. I love Liddy and I am committed to marrying her and making her happy for the rest of her life. That's the God's honest truth!"

She wanted to believe him, and she had a feeling he genuinely cared for his bride-to-be, but something was still wrong about this situation, as if there was still a missing piece of the puzzle she had yet to find.

And yet, she decided to trust him.

At least for now.

Which, in hindsight, would prove to be a monumental mistake.

Chapter 33

The next couple of days were uneventful. Hayley spent her free time with Liddy attending to last-minute wedding details. Liddy was relatively calm as the big day approached, and Sonny was by her side at all times when he was not in his office, making sure he behaved in a devoted manner to illustrate his undying love and eager support and firm commitment to marrying her. He did everything he had promised Hayley he would do. He was an attentive, loyal fiancé.

Until the night of the rehearsal dinner.

Hayley left the *Island Times* office around five o'clock to rush home and change clothes in order to get to the Congregational church for a quick run-through of the ceremony with the entire wedding party before the rehearsal dinner. The dinner was scheduled for seven o'clock at the Looking Glass Restaurant, a relaxed space with tasty American fare situated on a hilltop inside the Wonderview Inn, which boasted a deck with bay views. It was the perfect location for a laid-back meal and a few cocktails for the bride and groom's families and friends before the big day.

Hayley was fussing with her hair in the bathroom and still had to get dressed when her cell phone rang.

It was Liddy.

Hayley answered the call. "What's up?"

"Sonny's a no-show!" Liddy wailed.

"Calm down, Liddy. I'm sure there's a reasonable explanation."

"I'm standing here, all dressed and made up, ready to go to my wedding rehearsal and dinner, and Sonny's not here. He was supposed to pick me up at my house twenty minutes ago!"

"Maybe he just got stuck at the office."

"I called the office. His secretary Patrice said he left right at five to go home and change, so why isn't he here already? Well, we both know why! He's changed his mind! It's my worst fear becoming a reality! He's a runaway groom who is probably halfway to the state line by now!"

"Stop being so paranoid, Liddy!"

"You and I both know that Sonny has given me every reason to be paranoid, Hayley!"

She was certainly right about that.

But Sonny had sounded so sincere when Hayley confronted him in his office a couple of days earlier, and she was having a tough time buying that he would stand Liddy up now so late in the game.

"Have you tried calling his cell phone?"

"Of course, but it keeps going directly to voice mail."

"Okay, let's not panic."

"That's easy for you to say. You're not the jilted bride!"

"Let me see if I can find him. You stay put. I'll call you right back."

Hayley hung up and tried to contemplate her next move.

She decided to drive directly over to Sonny's house to see if he was hiding out there. If not, there might be some kind of clue to his whereabouts on the premises.

Hayley quickly slipped on the floral minidress and white sandals that she had selected for the rehearsal and dinner, grabbed her purse, and ran out the door. Gemma and Bruce were going to meet her directly at the Wonderview at seven, since neither of them was involved in the actual rehearsal and they had just been invited to the dinner. Dustin was going to take pictures of the rehearsal since a professional photographer had been hired to take the photos on the actual wedding day, and he had left the house earlier to set up his equipment in the church.

She was halfway to Sonny's house when her cell phone rang.

It was Dustin.

She grabbed her phone off the passenger's seat, slid it into the hands-free phone holder attached to the car's air vent, and pressed the answer button.

"Hi, honey . . ."

"Mom, where's Liddy? She's not at the church yet."

"I know. She's still at home."

"Well, when's she going to get here? Sonny's getting nervous."

"Sonny? He's at the church?"

"Yes, and he's starting to sweat, because he's afraid Liddy might be a runaway bride!"

"What? Put him on!"

Hayley heard some rustling sounds and muted voices as Dustin handed his phone over to Sonny.

"Hayley?"

"Sonny, what the hell are you doing at the church?"

"Waiting for Liddy. She hasn't shown up yet. and I'm afraid she might be getting pre-wedding jitters! Hayley, I don't think I could take it if she ditched me at the altar! Have you spoken to her? Has she told you what's going on?"

"She's at home, Sonny! Waiting for you to pick her up!"

There was a long silence on the other end of the phone.

"Sonny . . . Sonny . . . are you still there?"

"Oh God . . ."

"You forgot, didn't you, Sonny?"

"We talked about it weeks ago, about me swinging by to get her because she said she'd be too nervous to drive, and I guess I never wrote it down in my calendar, because, you know, I've had so much on my mind lately . . ."

"After all you've put her through, Sonny, how could you forget this one very important detail?"

"I know, I know, I'm a major screwup!"

"And why haven't you been answering your phone?"

"I left my charger at home this morning, and my phone died right after I arrived at the church . . ."

Hayley shook her head. "This is not good, Sonny . . ."

"Hayley, call her and tell her to stay put! I'm on my way! I can probably be there in fifteen, twenty minutes . . ."

"No! I'm closer to her house than you are! I'll pick her up. You stay at the church and stall for time. Knowing Reverend Staples, he's probably booked a funeral back-to-back with the wedding rehearsal."

"Thank you, Hayley. Thank you so much. I can't tell you what a good friend you are—"

She didn't have time to listen to him.

She ended the call and swung her car into a U-turn at the next traffic stop, reversing direction toward Liddy's house.

Hayley placed a call to Liddy.

"Hello?"

"He's at the church waiting for you, Liddy."

"*What?*"

"There is no time to explain. Bottom line is, I'm picking you up. I'll be there in a few minutes. Wait for me outside. We're going to be late enough as it is."

"Okay, I'm heading outside now."

She heard some rummaging and a door open and then, quite suddenly, she heard a scream.

Hayley's heart nearly leapt into her throat.

"Liddy?"

There were sounds of a struggle.

And then another scream, this time more frightened and desperate.

Hayley slammed her foot down on the accelerator, and her car shot forward like a bullet as she raced thirty miles over the speed limit.

Liddy was in trouble.

It took an agonizing four minutes to reach Liddy's neighborhood and another precious forty seconds to careen down her dirt driveway, pebbles flying in all directions, one ricocheting off Hayley's windshield before she reached Liddy's house, which was hidden from the road.

What she saw on the front lawn almost caused her to crash her car into a tree, but she then slammed on the brakes, her Kia screeching to an abrupt stop.

There was a man, or woman, dressed all in black, a gray ski mask pulled down over his or her face, on top of Liddy, straddling her. Liddy was sprawled out on the grass. The assailant's hands were wrapped around Liddy's neck, choking her. Hayley could see Liddy's face was bright red, her tongue hanging out the side of her mouth as she was slowly losing the struggle.

Hayley shoved the car door open and yelled at the top of her lungs. "Get away from her!"

The assailant had been in a trancelike state, oblivious to the car even arriving on the scene. But

Hayley's war cry as she sprinted to her friend's rescue snapped the attacker back into the moment, and before Hayley could reach them, the assailant released the grip on Liddy's neck, popped back up on his or her feet, and fled toward the back of the house and into the woods.

Hayley crouched down and gently put a hand behind Liddy's back, carefully sitting her up. Liddy gasped for air, and then submitted to a coughing fit as she hugged Hayley tightly.

It took a few moments before she was breathing normally again, and then she broke down and cried.

"It's okay, Liddy, I'm here. You're safe now . . ."

"He nearly choked me to death . . . I thought I was a goner . . ."

Hayley rocked Liddy back and forth in her arms as she contemplated whether or not the attacker had indeed been a man.

Or was it a woman?

"Why would anyone want to do that to me?" Liddy spouted, giant tears streaming down her cheeks.

Hayley knew of at least one person.

Nancy Malone.

And she was now guilt-ridden for not speaking out sooner, because her pact with Sonny to remain silent had perhaps just nearly cost Liddy her life.

Chapter 34

"You cannot breathe a word of this to Sonny!"

"Liddy, what are you talking about?" Hayley cried, taking her by the arm and lifting her up off the grass.

"Not until after the wedding!"

"But you were attacked! He has to know!"

Liddy grabbed Hayley by the shoulders after steadying herself on her feet and locked eyes with her. "If we tell Sonny, then he's going to want to call the police, and then there will be a big investigation, and someone, my mother no doubt, will suggest we postpone the wedding until the cops find some answers! And I'm not going to allow that to happen! I have come too far at this point to risk stopping the train now!"

Hayley tried explaining about Sonny's ex-girlfriend Nancy Malone, and how she could be in town targeting Liddy, which might explain the masked assailant who had just tried strangling her on her front lawn. But no matter how disturbing this news was to the bride-to-be, Liddy remained steadfast in her determination to get to the altar and marry Sonny, dangerous ex-girlfriends be damned!

"Liddy, I can't let you ignore what just happened to you. I have to call Sergio and report it so they can catch the creep."

"Hayley, I'm begging you, don't do this. I was the one who was attacked, not you, and if I want to wait until after my wedding to tell people, specifically the police, that's *my* choice!"

"I just don't think you're thinking rationally right now."

"I've never been more clear-eyed and focused about anything in my entire life. I'm going to marry Sonny Lipton tomorrow, and no crazy-eyed ex-girlfriend is going to prevent me from doing that! Do you hear me?"

There was no reasoning with her.

She had always been aggressively stubborn, and in her heightened emotional state, she was more bullheaded than ever.

"Now, listen, we'll go to the church and rehearse with the rest of the wedding party, and then we will join everyone else at the Wonderview for dinner. We won't mention what happened here to anyone, and then, first thing in the morning, before I get my makeup and hair done and squeeze into the dress, I will stop by the police station with you, my matron of honor, and my mother and report the incident to Sergio. That way, he can start the process of investigating while I'm at the church getting married to Sonny and it'll be too late for anyone to suggest postponing."

Hayley sighed. "Fine. If you insist on putting yourself at risk like this, there's not a whole lot I can do to stop you."

"Thank you, Hayley, you're a dear friend."

"What kind of friend will I be if I wake up tomorrow morning and find out you're dead?"

"Was verbalizing that thought really necessary?"

"Sorry, sometimes I can't help thinking out loud."

Liddy raised her head high, exposing her neck. "Do you see any marks on my neck?"

"Yes, there is definitely going to be some bruising," Hayley said.

"Well, come on, we need to find something to cover it. I'm sure I have a scarf or something inside!" Liddy cried, grabbing Hayley by the hand and pulling her inside the house.

Liddy quickly changed into a blouse with a high collar to hide the rapidly reddening choke marks on her neck. She tossed her previous outfit, which was now grass-stained from her tussle on the lawn with the marauding assailant, into the washing machine. Then, Liddy and Hayley hurried outside, jumped into Hayley's car, and broke speed records in order to get to the church.

The wedding party, including Liddy's very annoyed mother, who hated anyone being the least bit tardy, exchanged quick hellos as Reverend Staples checked his watch, irritated they were so far behind schedule.

Sonny descended upon Liddy with a barrage of

apologies and excuses, but she just smiled and hugged him and said she was not angry at him for failing to pick her up.

Hayley's mind raced as she marched down the aisle ahead of Liddy, worrying that Nancy Malone, or whomever had attacked Liddy, was lying in wait outside the church to strike again.

But the rest of the ceremony rehearsal went off without a hitch, with one exception. Liddy's dog, Poppyseed, who was the ring bearer with a baby blue pillow tied to his back that had the ring box nestled in it, wasn't behaving and kept barking at Reverend Staples, whom he had never liked. Dustin, who was assigned the position of official dog handler as well as rehearsal photographer, had to keep him on a leash. He dragged Poppyseed back so he didn't lunge at the skittish reverend, who had a fear of dogs after getting bitten by one at Bible school when he was a boy.

By the time the rehearsal finally wrapped up and they were all sipping champagne and dining on halibut and seared asparagus at the Looking Glass Restaurant overlooking beautiful Frenchman's Bay, the mood was so festive, Hayley almost managed to put thoughts of the brutal assault on Liddy's front lawn out of her mind.

Almost.

When Sonny insisted on driving Liddy home after the dinner, Hayley followed closely behind them in her own car to make sure she arrived safely. And then, after Sonny kissed Liddy good night on the doorstep and headed home, Hayley sat outside her house for most of the night on a stakeout to make sure no one tried to break into the house and have at her again.

The following morning, when she was stirred awake by a noisy garbage truck lifting plastic bins up on the main road with its giant metal claws, Hayley rubbed her eyes, stretched her aching bones from sitting all night in a car seat, and checked the clock on her dashboard.

It was seven thirty in the morning.

Liddy's wedding day.

The ceremony was scheduled for late afternoon, with an early evening reception.

Hayley meticulously scanned the area.

There were few houses in the wooded area outside of town where Liddy lived, and no signs of movement except for a squirrel that dashed across Liddy's front lawn, right over the spot where she had nearly been strangled. Hayley watched the squirrel scamper up a tree, freeze halfway, look around, and then continue climbing up the bark.

Through Liddy's kitchen window, Hayley could see Liddy wearing a pink robe, her hair in curlers, sipping a cup of coffee.

She was so engrossed in watching Liddy, relieved that she had made it through the night alive, that she didn't even hear the car pulling up behind her. Only when a car door slammed did she jolt up in her seat, and when someone's knuckles rapped on her driver's side window, she let out a surprised yelp.

"Hayley, what are you doing sitting out here?"

The voice was muffled through the car window but she recognized it immediately.

It was Liddy's mother.

Celeste was immaculately dressed in a smart green dress, though Hayley suspected this was not her wedding attire, because it was too early for that yet. Her hair was coiffured and elegantly styled, her face painted to perfection and accentuated with a bright pink lipstick and a smooth rouge to give her a healthy, rosy complexion.

Hayley pressed the button to roll down the window. "Good morning, Celeste."

"Is that the same outfit you wore last night?"

Of course Celeste would notice something like that. It explained a great deal about the fractious nature of her relationship with her daughter.

"Yes, I never made it home last night."

"Why on earth not?"

"I've been out here all night watching the house."

Celeste, who had been hunched over talking to Hayley through the open window, stood upright. "What's going on, Hayley?"

Hayley knew they couldn't hide the truth anymore, especially from Liddy's nosy mother, so she spilled everything.

Celeste's eyes widened and she gasped, covering her mouth with her hand, and as Hayley wrapped up the improbable story with the final detail that Liddy had insisted they keep mum until there was a ring on her finger and Reverend Staples had

finished his "By the powers invested in me . . ."
speech, Celeste was already halfway across the lawn,
screaming at her daughter to let her inside.

When a surprised Liddy opened the door and
saw the wild-eyed look on her mother's face and
Hayley trailing behind her in the same wrinkled
clothes she had worn the night before, she knew
the jig was up.

Fifteen minutes later, the three of them were sitting in Chief Alvares's office, going over the details
of what had transpired the day before.

Sergio typed up all the details on his computer
as Liddy recounted the horrific attack with Hayley
sitting beside her holding her hand for moral support and her mother, a bundle of nerves, pacing
back and forth in the tiny office.

"You really should have reported this sooner,
Liddy. I may have been able to arrest a suspect by
now," Sergio said with an admonishing look.

"I know, I'm sorry, but I'm reporting it now,"
Liddy said, touching her hair, which was still in
curlers.

Sergio glanced at Hayley, disappointed that she
was a part of this plot to keep him in the dark. She
wanted to explain herself, but felt it was probably
best just to keep her mouth shut at this point.

Celeste had no compunction about not staying
quiet. "You need to go out and find this Nancy
Malone and arrest her right away, Chief, before she
has a chance to come at my baby girl again!"

"I'll locate her as quickly as I can, but we cannot
be certain she was the one who—"

Celeste cut him off. "Of course it's her! She'll obviously do anything to ruin my daughter's happiness, including choking the life out of her on her own front lawn! You have to find her *today*! What if she shows up at the church and crashes the wedding?!"

Sergio nodded patiently. "I'll do my best to track her down."

"The wedding is only a few hours away! We can't afford any more surprises!" Celeste screamed.

Liddy nodded in agreement, her hair curlers bobbing up and down, a look of grim determination frozen on her face.

Celeste stepped over and took her daughter's arm. "Maybe we should think about—"

Liddy shook her head. "We are not postponing the wedding, Mother, and that's final!"

Liddy Crawford was going to get married today.

Even if it killed her.

Chapter 35

As Hayley struggled to slip on the gaudy, over-the-top Little Bo Peep matron of honor dress that Liddy had ultimately chosen for her to wear for the wedding, she checked the clock in her bathroom. It was already one thirty.

She had spent the morning after their visit to the police station running errands for the bride, which, to be fair, was the official job of the matron of honor. But that left precious little time to get herself ready in time for the ceremony. Instead of trying to put on her makeup and style her wild, unruly hair in the midst of all the chaos at Liddy's house, she slipped away to come home and get ready in peace.

Liddy and her mother Celeste were already horribly tense from the news that a jealous ex-girlfriend's of Sonny was on the loose and possibly homicidal. That was enough to spoil any woman's wedding day, but Liddy tried her best to remain calm and vigilant, despite her mother repeatedly reminding her to stay alert in case Crazy Nancy struck again.

Hayley finished spraying her hair and, with no time left to paint her nails, resorted at the last minute to some pink press-ons she found in the drawer. Checking herself out in the mirror, she concluded she was at least presentable if not a vision of pure loveliness. At least she wouldn't steal focus from the bride, which was the most important thing.

As Hayley dashed down the stairs, hiking up her dress so she wouldn't trip and fall and wind up sprawled out unconscious in the foyer, a knock at the front door startled her.

Leroy, who was snoozing on the couch, snapped to attention and let loose with a few yelps as he leapt to the floor and scampered toward the door, playing guard dog to full effect. "Playing" was the operative word, because at the sign of any real threat there was no doubt in Hayley's mind he would retreat upstairs to hide under her bed.

Hayley flung open the door, and Leroy's barking abruptly stopped, replaced by excited panting at the sight of Sergio, who had changed out of his police uniform and was now wearing a nice gray suit and yellow tie.

"Oh, good, I'm glad you're here," Hayley said. "You can give me a ride to the church. I'm not sure I can fit behind the wheel of my own car in this dress! I'll probably need the whole backseat!"

"You better sit down for this one," Sergio said ominously.

"Oh no . . ." Hayley groaned. "What now?"

"I found Nancy Malone."

"Is she here in Bar Harbor?"

Sergio shook his head. "No, she's in Boston."

"Boston? Are you sure? She could be lying."

Sergio reached into his back pocket and pulled out his cell phone. He opened the YouTube app, pressed play on a video, and handed the phone to Hayley.

Hayley stared at the video, which had just been posted the previous evening. It was definitely Nancy Malone—the same Nancy Malone from the Facebook photo of herself with Sonny in Key West. Pretty, bubbly, and around thirty years old. She was bopping up and down to some rock music with about five girlfriends.

"That's her last night at a Pearl Jam concert in Fenway Park," Sergio said.

Hayley wasn't ready to give up. "Maybe the video is somehow doctored. You know people can do that."

Sergio pressed his finger down and scrolled through the video about seven minutes in, when Pearl Jam's lead singer, Eddie Vedder, reached down into the mosh pit and lifted Nancy up onto the stage, where she dirty danced with the rock star for the next three minutes, bumping and grinding and gyrating and squealing with delight.

"I'd say she's got about ten thousand witnesses who saw her there," Sergio said.

Hayley handed the phone back to Sergio. "Okay, so she's definitely in the clear."

"When I got her on the phone, she claimed she had never even heard of a Liddy Crawford, and honestly, she sounded pretty darn convincing."

"So I assume she has no contact with Sonny anymore," Hayley concluded.

"No, she didn't say that. She talks to him quite regularly."

"How could his ex-girlfriend not know he's engaged to Liddy, especially if they're still friendly and talking all the time?"

"Because she's not his ex-girlfriend," Sergio said solemnly.

"They're still together? So that bastard lied! He's still involved with her!"

Sergio nodded. "Except she's not his current girlfriend either."

"Then what is she?"

Sergio took a deep breath. "Okay, I'm going to quote her directly now. Are you ready?"

Hayley scrunched up her face, confused, her stomach flip-flopping. "Why wouldn't I be? Why? What is it? What did she say?"

"She said, and I quote, 'I have never heard of this Liddy Crawford, and I can assure you my husband, Sonny, hasn't either,' end quote."

It was like a gut punch.

Hayley reeled back, grabbing the banister at the bottom of the staircase to steady herself. "*Husband?*"

"That's what she said."

"Are you sure she was talking about the same Sonny Lipton?"

"You saw the Facebook photo. What are the odds of one person knowing two lawyers named Sonny Lipton?"

"Did you tell her that Sonny is marrying Liddy?"

"I did. She didn't believe me."

"But how could she be married to a man who lives five hours away in Bar Harbor? They couldn't possibly spend much time together."

"Because, according to her, Sonny travels a lot for his job, and she holds down their house in Revere when he has to drive up to Maine to work on cases. The same false story he gave Liddy about having to drive down to Boston to do legal work for his old firm. According to Nancy, she's actually quite happy with the arrangement and the freedom it gives her, as long as they love each other and he's a decent provider."

Hayley's head was spinning as she struggled to process this startling, incomprehensible revelation.

"I don't believe it. Sonny's already *married*?"

"Looks that way."

"I'll kill him," Hayley whispered.

"You won't get the chance once Liddy finds out. She'll do the job for you."

Liddy.

What about poor Liddy?

This was going to destroy her.

"I'm on my way to the church now. Should I break the news?" Sergio asked.

"No! Let me do it! It will be better coming from me."

"Okay, but just promise me you'll do it before she says 'I do,'" Sergio said.

"Of course."

Suddenly Sergio's phone buzzed. He exited the YouTube app and read a text. "It's Donnie. There's been an accident on the Trenton Bridge. Looks like I'm going to miss the wedding anyway."

"Go, I'll handle this. Thank you, Sergio."

Sergio shot out the door to his car.

Hayley sat down on the bottom step of her staircase and grabbed the top of her head with both hands. She had a pounding headache. The thought of crushing her best friend on her wedding day was almost too much to bear.

And it was about to get a whole lot worse.

Island Food & Cocktails
BY HAYLEY POWELL

Ever since my brother, Randy, started serving food at his local bar, Drinks Like a Fish, he has enlisted me to be his go-to guinea pig whenever he wants to add a new item to his menu. Sure enough, I had heard rumblings that he was kitchen-testing a brand-new appetizer all week, so I was not surprised when I received the call at work to swing by the bar after quitting time for an impromptu taste test.

I had planned to do some grocery shopping, and my house was in desperate need of a thorough cleaning, so I tried to beg off at first, but Randy was insistent. And when he threw in an added incentive of a refreshing pomegranate Cosmo on the house, I instantly caved. I adored his pomegranate Cosmos!

And boy, was I a happy camper when I showed up, because not only was the Cosmo sitting on top of the bar waiting for me at my usual stool, but the aromatic smell of bacon wafted in from the kitchen. I was already hooked. As most readers of my column already know, I love any recipe that has bacon as an ingredient!

Well, it turned out Randy had been playing around with a recipe tailor-made for my taste buds—a bacon, Asiago cheese, and caramelized onion dip. Needless to say, it was absolutely to die for! I would definitely be serving this dip up at the Fourth of July post-parade party that I was planning to hold in my backyard this year.

While I was wolfing down Randy's delicious dip in between sips of my Cosmo, a group of five twentysomething, giggling, and, dare I add, tipsy women, all obviously part of a bridal party, came stumbling into the bar. They were all dressed in figure-hugging tank tops that were bedazzled with sparkly fake jewels, each one designating their position in the wedding party—bride, maid of honor, bridesmaid, you get the gaudy picture.

My first thought was, "Thank goodness Liddy didn't make us wear tank tops like that at her bachelorette party the other night! There was no way I could pull off something like that even back when I was in my twenties!"

One of the attractive blondes—there were three, I think, along with one brunette and a flaming redhead—anyway, one of the blondes wore the obligatory cheap-looking tiara. I guessed she was the bride, though I didn't really have to, since the word "Bride" was clearly emblazoned in pink sparkles all over her figure-hugging white tank top. She sat at one end of the table, next to pretty blonde number two, who was wearing a light pink tank top that loudly labeled her "Maid of Honor." The other three drunken girls—the remaining blonde, the brunette, and our wild, curly-haired redhead—sat opposite them on the other end of the table, all sporting dark pink tank tops that told us in bright glittery letters that they were the "Bridesmaids."

It looked like a Barbie explosion, and it took every ounce of my self-control for me not to ask them if a Barbie Pink Beach Cruiser was parked outside, or if the groom's name happened to be Ken. But I had only downed one Cosmo so far, so I managed to refrain myself.

As the girls downed more booze and got progressively louder, I started getting a headache and was almost ready to call it a night. But then Randy served up a second bowl of his delectable dip, so I kept my butt firmly planted on that bar stool, at least until we finished it off with some crackers.

The Bridal Barbies were on their fourth round of margaritas, ordering them so fast Randy's right-hand bartender, Michelle, could barely keep up with them. As Randy and I polished off the dip and gossiped about the latest town scandals, suddenly an earsplitting shriek nearly busted my eardrum. Unsurprisingly, it came from the table of rowdy girls.

The maid of honor jumped to her feet so fast she knocked over the chair she was sitting in and it tipped over onto the floor. Aghast, she started screaming at the top of her lungs at the bride, but her voice was so loud and shrill we couldn't make out what she was saying. Randy managed to identify a few key words and told me he thought she said something like, "No, I did not," as though she was denying some kind of accusation. The bride angrily shot up out of her chair then too and got right up in the maid of honor's face and wailed, with tears streaming down her cheeks, "Yes, you did!"

The third blonde, the brunette, and yes, our standout redhead, all sat frozen in their seats, watching the train wreck as if in slow motion, not sure what to do.

Now the bride and maid of honor were trying to shout over each other, and the rest of the bar patrons, made up of a few fishermen and a college-age couple who looked like they were on a first date, stared slack-jawed at the commotion, riveted to what was going to happen next.

In the background, playing on the jukebox, was Taylor Swift crooning "Love Story"—not quite appropriate for the current situation.

Shaking her hands and sobbing, the bride bawled, "How could you do this to me? I trusted you! I don't even know how I can ever forgive you for a betrayal like this!"

Our maid of honor, who by now knew she had royally screwed up, lowered her voice, trying to explain, "I am so, so sorry. Please don't hate me! I swear, if I could take it all back I would . . ."

Then, in the blink of an eye, the bride threw herself across the table, grabbing her maid of honor by the hair, and they tumbled to the floor, margarita glasses shattering all around them. From then on, it looked like one of those 1980s Gorgeous Ladies of Wrestling matches, with hair pulling, fist punching, and nail scratching. The three bridesmaids then all piled on, trying to pull the bride and maid of honor apart, but to no avail.

Next to me, Randy sighed and pushed his chair back, mumbling under his breath, "Here we go again." This wasn't his first time at the rodeo with high-strung bridal parties. As he moved to break up the brawl, he turned his head back toward me and shouted, "I've seen this so many times before. The maid of honor drinks too much and starts feeling guilty and confesses to once sleeping with the groom!"

Apparently, over the yelling and screaming, the bride overheard Randy and suddenly released her maid of honor from a headlock. "*What* did you say?"

The bridal party all fell silent.

Randy shrugged. "Believe me, this happens in my bar all the time."

You could hear a pin drop as Taylor Swift finished her song and the rest of the patrons watched in quiet anticipation.

The bride gasped. "Pippa most certainly did not *sleep* with my fiancé! She would never, ever do that to me!"

Pippa, the maid of honor, nodded vigorously. "Of course not! I would *never*!"

Randy stared at them, confused and exasperated. "Then what? What else could possibly upset you so much that you would attack your own maid of honor and smash up my bar? Which you *will* pay for, by the way!"

The bride sniffed, gathering the courage to admit what horrible transgression her former best friend was guilty of, as if just saying it out loud would stir up the trauma all over again. She pointed a finger at the maid of honor. "She . . . She . . . Oh God, I can't even . . ."

"Just say it!" Randy demanded.

"She said I looked fat in my wedding dress!"

And then a fresh flood of tears poured down her face as she collapsed in her chair, the bridesmaids swarming around her, offering comfort.

The entire bar erupted in raucous laughter. There might have been slightly more empathy for the devastated bride if she didn't look like she wore a size two.

The bride was visibly irritated at the lack of sympathy she felt she clearly deserved, and so she quickly ordered Randy to ring up the bill for the drinks and damage and then stormed out of the bar, followed by her gaggle of sycophants, who offered soothing words, and a maid of honor whining about how sorry she was and begging the bride for her forgiveness.

I will tell you one thing—I sure would have loved to have been a fly on the wall at that wedding.

After I helped Randy sweep up the broken glass and upright a few chairs, Taylor Swift went back to singing another song, the patrons finished their drinks, and Randy and I eagerly began work on a third bowl of his delicious dip.

POMEGRANATE COSMO

Ice
2 ounces citron vodka
1 ounce Cointreau
2 ounces pomegranate juice
Squeeze of fresh lemon juice

Add all of your ingredients to an ice-filled cocktail shaker and shake really well to make sure it is nice and cold. Strain into a chilled martini glass and serve.

RANDY'S ASIAGO, BACON, AND CARAMELIZED ONION DIP

2 tablespoons olive oil
6 to 7 cups chopped onion
4 bacon strips, cooked and crumbled
4 ounces shredded Asiago cheese, divided
4 tablespoons chopped chives, divided
2/3 cup real mayonnaise
2/3 cup sour cream
½ teaspoon kosher salt
½ teaspoon ground black pepper

Preheat your oven to 425°F.

Add the two tablespoons of olive oil to a large skillet and heat over medium high heat. Add your onion to the skillet and cook for about 5 minutes, then bring your heat down to low and sauté the onions, stirring occasionally, until golden brown—about 20 minutes. Remove from heat and cool slightly.

Add your crumbled bacon, half of your Asiago cheese, half of your chives, and the rest of the ingredients, stirring to combine.

Spray a one-quart baking dish with cooking spray and put your onion mixture into the baking dish. Sprinkle the top with the rest of the Asiago cheese.

Bake in the oven for 20 minutes or until bubbly. Remove and sprinkle with the remaining chives.

Serve with your favorite crackers and enjoy!

Chapter 36

Hayley found some Advil in the medicine cabinet of her bathroom, popped two pills into her mouth, and then chased them down with a cup of water.

She stared at herself in the mirror.

Despite the makeup and styled hair, she looked drawn and tired.

It was undoubtedly the stress of having to break her best friend's heart on her wedding day.

She straightened up and steeled herself, mentally preparing for the awesome responsibility that she was about to carry out.

If one of Liddy's wishes were to come true, it would be that this day she had been planning for, ever since she was a little girl would be remembered for years to come.

Always be careful what you wish for.

Hayley grabbed her phone. She still didn't want to drive herself to the church in her bulky dress, which already looked wrinkled. Since Dustin was already there wrangling Poppyseed the ring bearer, and Gemma was at the reception hall putting the finishing touches on the wedding cake, she knew who was left to recruit as her personal driver.

She picked up her phone, brought up her contact list, and pressed the screen. After a few rings, he answered.

"I was just going to call you," Bruce said in a more serious tone than Hayley had expected.

"Where are you?"

"At the office."

"What are you doing there on a Saturday?"

"I've been researching a story, and I got a little delayed."

"Please tell me you're already in your suit for the wedding."

"Sorry, I still have to swing by my place first and get dressed, but I have a good excuse. Something that has come up . . ."

Hayley wasn't sure she could take any more bad news.

"At least tell me it has nothing to do with Liddy and Sonny . . ."

"It has to do with Liddy and Sonny . . ."

Hayley had to hand it to Bruce. He was a damn good reporter when it came to investigating a story. He was only one step behind Sergio.

Hayley sighed. "I already know, Bruce . . ."

"You do?"

"Sergio was just here. He told me all about Sonny's other wife."

There was a long pause on the other end of the call.

"I'm sorry . . ." he said quietly.

"I don't know how I'm going to tell Liddy."

"Well, you better do it fast. She's supposed to walk down the aisle in less than an hour . . ."

"How did you find out?" Hayley asked.

"I did a little digging, called a few of my journalist contacts in the Boston area, and located a guy who knew Sonny. He's a fellow lawyer. He and Sonny used to blow off steam together in a bar in the Back Bay once a week. Sonny kept pretty mum about his private life, but he once said he couldn't meet for drinks because he was going on a trip with his wife."

"Key West?"

"No, a Royal Caribbean cruise to the Virgin Islands."

"He certainly gets around, doesn't he? Poor Liddy had to beg him to take her to a crafts fair in Northeast Harbor last month."

"The guy had been surprised to hear he was married, because Sonny had never mentioned a wife before. Sonny told him they had to live apart because of his job."

"Yes. She lives in Revere. That's only fifteen minutes outside the center of Boston."

"Sonny said she lived in Woonsocket," Bruce said.

"Rhode Island? But that can't be . . ."

"It's true. I found her there. A Mary Beth Lipton."

"No, Bruce, her name is Nancy Malone . . ."

"I'm telling you, Hayley, I'm one hundred percent

right about this. I double-checked my information. Three times, in fact. It's all true. Sonny is married to Mary Beth Lipton. She is in her midforties and works at a chemical lab just outside Woonsocket. Her maiden name is Capshaw. Her family's been there for generations. She has a son in his early twenties named Anthony from a previous relationship just after college. They met at a Red Sox game four years ago . . ."

Hayley felt her heart skip a beat. "There's more than one . . ."

"What?"

"He's already married to two women and he's about to marry a third . . ."

"Are you saying our Sonny Boy is a genuine, card-carrying polygamist?" Bruce asked, obviously having trouble believing it himself. "But why?"

"Who knows why someone's a polygamist? If there is one thing we know about Sonny, it's that he loves women! I guess one just isn't enough! Maybe he's addicted to marrying them!" Hayley said.

"Oh my God," Bruce cried. "He could be like one of those creepy religious sect lunatics who hide out in the woods with nine or ten wives!"

"This is so much worse than I just thought two minutes ago . . ." Hayley's voice trailed off.

Liddy's whole life was about to be upended. She was already in an emotionally fragile state. This could smash it into a million pieces. Hayley cared deeply for her, was willing to do anything to protect her, but she feared Liddy might not survive a betrayal on such a dramatic and inconceivable scale.

"Bruce, don't bother picking me up, I'll drive myself. Just meet me at the church. And don't breathe a word about this to Liddy. Let me do it. This should come from her best friend so I can offer the kind of support she's going to need."

"Okay, I promise. But I don't have to go home and change anymore, right? I mean, there's no way this wedding is going to happen now, right?"

"Yes, Bruce, just meet me there!"

She ended the call and rushed down the stairs and out the back door to her car, which was parked in the driveway.

Once she managed to stuff herself behind the wheel, the enormous and cumbersome fabric of her dress bunched up around her threatening to completely engulf her, she turned the ignition key and fired up the engine. Suddenly her hand froze on the gear before she could push it in reverse and back out of the driveway.

A name was stuck in her head.

Capshaw.

Where had she heard that name before?

Capshaw.

Hayley gasped.

AJ.

Mona's summer help and Sabrina's current boy toy.

His last name was Capshaw.

His sister in Brewer, the one getting married, casually mentioned it on the phone. She was keeping her maiden name to maintain her own identity.

Which meant AJ's last name was Capshaw.

Lisa had said she was meeting with a Tony Capshaw in her appointment book.

Sonny's wife, Mary Beth, had a son in his early twenties, according to Bruce.

His name was Anthony.

Maybe AJ was short for his first and middle name.

Anthony James or Anthony John.

Tony!

If that was true, then AJ was Sonny's stepson.

But Bruce never mentioned that Mary Beth had a daughter too.

So who was Adele, with whom she spoke on the phone?

What if it was Mary Beth herself?

AJ's cheery sister Adele on the phone; the strange tourist from Rhode Island asking questions about Liddy; the attacker who tried to strangle Liddy on the front lawn; all of them could have been the same person—Mary Beth Lipton.

And according to Bruce, Mary Beth worked at a chemical lab. She could have easily gotten her hands on the poison that killed Lisa.

Hayley's mind continued to race, desperately trying to put all the pieces of the puzzle together.

Sonny was never present when AJ was around. Perhaps AJ made sure he kept his distance from Sonny, so he wouldn't have the chance to recognize him.

AJ had shown up in town, a penniless college kid claiming to need extra money. He was young and strong, the perfect fit for a job at Mona's lobster shop.

But what if his reasons for coming to Bar Harbor were far more nefarious?

AJ and his mother, Mary Beth, if they had somehow found out about Sonny's polygamous ways and then discovered he was about to marry a successful real estate agent, well that would certainly be a strong motive for them to try and stop the wedding from ever happening!

Hayley's mission was no longer about finding Liddy and gently breaking the bad news about Sonny before she walked down the aisle and married him.

No, she had to warn her right now that her life was in imminent danger!

Chapter 37

Hayley took her hand off the gearshift and quickly called Liddy.

After three rings, a cheery voice sang, "Liddy's phone!"

It was Celeste.

"Celeste, it's Hayley. I need to speak to Liddy right now!"

"I'm afraid that's impossible, dear. We are desperately behind schedule. Liddy hasn't even put on her wedding dress yet, and we're due at the church in ten minutes. We don't want poor Sonny to think he's been left at the altar."

"Celeste, this an emergency, please, just put Liddy on—"

Celeste didn't give her a chance to finish. "I'm sorry, but without the matron of honor here helping us, it's all hands on deck, and I'm dealing with a number of emergencies myself, like the bridal bouquet not being what we ordered . . ."

"Celeste, please, just tell Liddy—"

She heard a click, and the line went dead.

Celeste, after managing to get a personal dig in about how Hayley wasn't helping Liddy in her time of need, like a good matron of honor is supposed to, had just hung up on her.

Hayley slammed her phone against the steering wheel and cried, "No!"

She frantically tried calling Liddy's phone again, but this time, the call went directly to voice mail.

She was starting to hyperventilate as panic overcame her. If she couldn't get anyone on the phone to warn them about AJ and Mary Beth, Liddy might wind up dead.

Hayley sat in her car, white-knuckled as she gripped her steering wheel with one hand while clutching her phone in the other. She tried calming herself down, taking in deep breaths, until she was clear-eyed and focused again.

She could do this.

She would find another way to warn Liddy.

Sabrina.

Sabrina must be with her at the moment, helping her into her dress.

Hayley called Sabrina's number.

"Hi, this is Sabrina, I can't take your call right now—"

Hayley ended the call without leaving a message.

She sent a text to Sabrina instead. *Sabrina, this is an emergency! Liddy's life is in danger! AJ is not who he says he is. He wants to harm Liddy! Please stop her from going to the church!*

Hayley hit send.

She wasn't going to wait for a reply. She jammed her car into reverse, backed out of the driveway, and squealed away down the street, heading in the direction of Liddy's house. She kept glancing down at her phone as she drove to see if Sabrina had replied to her text yet, but saw nothing.

She was half hoping she would get pulled over for speeding so she could enlist the help of the police to back her up as she raced to keep Liddy from leaving her house. She also wanted to call 911, but she knew the local cops were tied up with the accident on the Trenton Bridge and would take too long to respond, given there were only a handful of officers on duty and all of them were probably fifteen minutes out of town at the bridge.

She prayed that Liddy and her entourage had not left for the church yet.

When Hayley swerved off the main road and plowed down the gravel path to Liddy's house, she let out a horrified gasp as she noticed that the limo Celeste had rented to take them to the church was already gone. Parked near the garage was another car, however, which she instantly recognized as Sabrina's rental. Sabrina had mentioned earlier she was not going to ride in the limo, but take her own car to the church so she could get to the reception early to make sure everything looked perfect before the newlyweds and the rest of the wedding party arrived.

Unless she had changed her mind, there was a chance Sabrina was still inside the house.

Hayley jumped out of her car. The hem of her

dress was a little too long, so it dragged across the dirt and gravel as she made a mad dash for the front door.

Suddenly a voice from behind her stopped her dead in her tracks.

"Looking for Sabrina?"

She didn't have to turn around.

She knew it was AJ.

Hayley slowly turned around to face him. He looked rather handsome in a light blue sports jacket, open white dress shirt, and black jeans.

"Where is she?" Hayley asked, keeping her voice steady.

At first she had no idea where he had suddenly come from, but then she spotted the driver's side door of Sabrina's car hanging wide open. He had been sitting in the front seat, and she hadn't even seen him because she was so panicked to find Liddy.

AJ had a strange smile on his face. It wasn't natural. He was a very good-looking young man, but this sneer just made him look off-putting and menacing.

"I volunteered to be Sabrina's chauffeur today so she wouldn't have to drive in her pretty dress. We were just on our way to the church. We left a few minutes before Liddy and her mother, but then Sabrina got a text that Liddy had left her veil behind, so we volunteered to come back and get it."

"I see . . ." Hayley said, forcing a smile, trying not to give away anything that was roiling over in her mind.

"Sabrina's inside. She'll be out in a minute."

Hayley nodded.

They stared at each other for a few seconds, until Hayley was unable to stand the building tension any longer. "I'm just going to go inside . . ."

She slowly backed away from AJ, toward the house, and was about to turn around when he suddenly pulled a gun from the back pocket of his jeans.

"What are you doing with that?"

"Sabrina was in such a rush to get the veil, she left her phone in the car, and I just happened to see your text come through. You certainly have a low opinion of me, Hayley. That I'm not who I say I am. That I want to harm Liddy."

"Am I wrong about that?"

"No, not really. You pretty much got the gist of it," he said with that smug, scornful sneer. "Now stay real quiet and get in the car."

Hayley put her hands up and walked toward her car.

"Not yours. Sabrina's. Where are your keys?"

Hayley reversed direction, back toward AJ, who snatched her car keys out of her hand and threw them into the grass near a thicket of trees. He then ordered Hayley behind the wheel. He slid in next to her from the passenger's side.

"Okay, start the car."

She sighed but complied.

Once the engine was running, she turned to AJ. "Where are we going?"

"Just drive. I'll direct you."

Hayley shifted the gear in drive and pulled away, back up the dirt driveway toward the main road.

Through the rearview mirror, she saw Sabrina running out of Liddy's house, in her beautiful cream-colored bridesmaid dress, the one so much nicer than Hayley's, clutching Liddy's veil flying behind her. She was shouting at them to come back, a confused look on her face.

As they turned onto the main road, the last thing she saw was Sabrina running for Hayley's car, but unaware that with the keys nestled in the grass near the woods, out of sight, she wasn't going anywhere.

As they continued toward town in silence, AJ's gun resting in his lap but the barrel pointed directly at Hayley, her phone began to light up with calls from Sabrina—calls she was never going to be able to answer.

Chapter 38

Hayley gripped the steering wheel with both hands, her eyes fixed on the road, not sure where they were going. AJ stared out the window, agitated and upset at the realization that everything seemed to be falling apart.

Hayley finally glanced over at him. "You came to Bar Harbor to kill Liddy, didn't you?"

He didn't answer her at first. He just kept staring at the passing trees outside the passenger's side window.

"You must have discovered some evidence back home in Rhode Island that your stepfather, Sonny, was marrying another woman, is that it?"

"No," AJ mumbled. "I had no idea about the wedding. I just thought he was cheating on my mother . . ."

"What about Nancy Malone? Did you know about *her*?"

AJ shifted in his seat, turning his body around to

face Hayley, a genuinely confused look on his face. "Who?"

"She lives in the Boston area. And she's also married to Sonny."

"Sonny's a—?"

"'Polygamist' is the official term."

AJ's mouth dropped open. It wasn't an act. He was completely blindsided about the news of Sonny's other wife.

"Liddy was going to be wife number three," Hayley said quietly. "As far as we know. There could be more."

AJ tried to speak, but no words came out.

He just gripped the gun tighter and shook his head, a pained expression on his face.

They drove in silence a few more minutes, cresting over a hill just past an entrance to Acadia National Park and then descending the other side. The car zipped around the last bend before reaching the outskirts of town.

AJ finally broke the silence. "My mother's had a rough life. My father abandoned us when I was around five. He emptied the bank account and just disappeared. We struggled for a long time, my mother working double shifts at the chemical lab just to put enough food on the table for the two of us. And then Sonny came along, a handsome, slick, smooth-talking fancy lawyer with a seductive smile and a six-figure income. He was like a miracle. A gift from God. My mother fell for him instantly, and I guess, in a way, I did too. I didn't have much of a male role model around when I was a kid, and suddenly this successful, big-time lawyer was marrying my mom and paying attention to me, attending all my ball games, buying me a bike . . ."

Hayley glanced over to see AJ nodding wistfully, remembering.

"The guy was like a superhero to me. He just swooped in and saved us. Never in my wildest dreams did I ever think I'd get to go to college, and then there was Sonny, offering to pay my tuition. He made me and Mom feel so safe and so happy . . . at least for a while . . ."

"And then you found out about Liddy . . ."

"Completely by accident. I was dating a girl at college, Chelsea, whose parents were buying a summer home up here in Bar Harbor, and they were using Liddy as their Realtor. Chelsea came here with her parents about a month ago to look at a few listings, and Liddy couldn't stop talking about her engagement to a lawyer named Sonny Lipton. I told Chelsea there was no way it could be the same guy, but after checking him out, I discovered the awful truth."

"Did you tell your mother?"

"God, no! It would've killed her. She had been so lonely and depressed after my dad left that I couldn't bear the thought of her going through that again if Sonny did the same thing to her and bolted to Maine for another woman."

"So you figured if you got Liddy out of the way, maybe you could convince Sonny to come home to

Rhode Island and be a family again," Hayley said, eyes fixed on the road ahead of them.

But then she peeked over at AJ, who was wiping a tear away from his cheek with the back of the same hand holding the gun.

Hayley worried he might accidentally pull the trigger and blow her face off, and she instinctively pressed her head against the headrest to get out of the line of fire.

The car came to a stop sign, and Hayley hit the brakes. At this point, they could go in three different directions.

"Which way?" Hayley asked.

"Keep going straight. Down Mount Desert Street."

"Where are we going?"

"You'll see," he said ominously.

Hayley continued driving.

Her phone buzzed again.

It was Sabrina, still back at Liddy's house, confused and desperate, and probably still clutching Liddy's wedding veil in her clenched fist.

AJ signaled Hayley to ignore the call.

"So what was your plan, AJ? How were you going to get rid of Liddy?"

"I hitchhiked up to Bar Harbor to get a summer job that would help pay for college expenses in the fall. It wasn't a lie. I did need the money. It was a lucky coincidence Mona was hiring at her lobster shop. I had no idea she even knew Liddy, let alone was one of her best friends. Don't you just love small towns?"

"And the plan was for you to stalk her and kill her?"

"No! I wasn't thinking like that. I was just going to talk to her and try to reason with her, explain how things actually were, and show her that Sonny already had a family that cared about him. I thought maybe she'd feel bad and do the right thing and break it off . . . but then, Sonny spotted me . . ."

"You ran into Sonny?"

"Literally. Right on the street. He saw me coming out of the bank after using the ATM where I withdrew the last of my cash to pay for the room I was renting. So I confronted him. Right then and there. Man, did he freak out."

"What did he say?"

"Nothing at first. He was just so shocked to see me standing there. Then, after a few seconds, he managed to gather his wits. He started spewing out all kinds of excuses. How it wasn't what I thought it was, how he and Liddy were just friends. But he knew I had him nailed to the wall, especially when I told him Liddy had been bragging about her upcoming wedding to my girlfriend's parents . . . That shut him up real fast."

"I'll bet it did," Hayley said, wanting to wring Sonny's neck.

"Then he just wanted to get the hell away from me. He said he was late for an appointment and couldn't talk . . . some kind of photo shoot . . ."

The wedding announcement photo.

Now Hayley knew why Sonny had unexpectedly been a no-show.

He was reeling from the reality that his stepson was in town and now fully aware of his double life. Or triple life, if you add in Nancy Malone from Revere.

There was no way he could just show up at the photo studio and act like nothing was wrong, so he blew it off and headed to Drinks Like a Fish to take the edge off and figure out what to do.

"Before he left, Sonny begged me to go back to Rhode Island. He promised me he would break it off with Liddy and come home to me and my mom, can you believe that?" AJ said, shaking his head. "For a split second, I actually believed him, so I agreed. But after he ran off, I knew he was lying. All he does is lie. So I stuck around. You know, I honestly thought Liddy was exaggerating when she told my girlfriend's parents she was engaged to Sonny. I figured she was just imagining herself marrying him, that Sonny would never divorce my mom and marry her, but then, working for Mona, I got a front-row seat to all the wedding plans, and it steamed me up real bad."

"To the point where you decided to take matters into your own hands . . ."

"Yes. I thought about going straight to Liddy and telling her everything, but I figured she would never believe me and she would still be around to marry Sonny . . . so I took a couple of days off from Mona's and drove back down to Providence to see my mom. I surprised her by showing up at the chemical lab to take her to lunch—"

"Where you stole the poison you planned to use on Liddy. Mona must have been a fountain of information. Did she tell you Liddy wanted angel food cake with buttercream frosting?"

AJ nodded.

"And when you arrived at Lisa's bakery pretending to be looking for a wedding cake for your sister Adele, who I assume doesn't even really exist, you saw the cake Lisa had already made for Liddy and set aside for her to taste."

"It was so easy. Lisa was such a chatterbox, bitching and moaning about Liddy the whole time I was there, she didn't even see me inject the poison throughout the cake with a syringe, knowing Liddy would be coming into the shop soon for a taste test."

"As well as her best friend and matron of honor who accompanied her! Me! I would've been poisoned too!"

"Collateral damage, I guess." AJ shrugged, not seeming to care all that much.

"But what you didn't know was that Lisa had already decided after baking the angel food cake that she was going to try and show off her talents as a baker. She thought the angel food cake was too bland and uninspired. She blatantly ignored what Liddy wanted and made something that she personally liked better—a chocolate walnut cake with cocoa glaze. That's what she tried to serve us!"

"How was I supposed to know that?"

"Liddy fired her on the spot, and then Lisa was left with the angel food cake with buttercream frosting, the original cake meant for Liddy. She probably didn't want it going to waste, so she ate a piece, and thanks to you, it killed her."

"I didn't mean for her to die. She was really annoying and I hated her face, but I had nothing personally against her."

"I'm sure she would be happy to hear that . . . if she was still *alive*!"

"I just wanted Liddy out of the way, and then everything got way out of hand when Lisa was the one who ate the poisoned cake . . ."

"AJ, this is nuts! You are never going to get away with this! You might as well turn yourself in!"

"Pull in here," AJ ordered.

Hayley turned down a side street which led to the back of the Abbe Museum, a local attraction that explored and celebrated the history and culture of Maine's native people, the Wabanaki tribe. The museum was filled with collections, including a large number of artifacts fashioned during prehistoric and historic times by Native Americans and by Europeans who began arriving in the area in the early seventeenth century. Stone artifacts included projectile (arrow and spear) points, bone artifices such as harpoons, hooks, combs, and a rare flute that might be as much as two thousand years old.

"Why did you bring me here? The museum isn't even open. It's been closed for renovations for the past two weeks . . ."

"Get out," AJ hissed, shoving the gun into Hayley's side.

She grappled for the car door latch and swung

it open. She considered making a run for it, but she wasn't sure what kind of aim AJ had, and so she wasn't about to risk it.

AJ was out of the passenger's side in a flash, and before she even had a chance to slam the car door shut, he was close behind her, the gun pressed firmly into the small of her back, ordering her in a low voice to head for the rear door of the museum.

AJ busted the lock open with the butt of his gun.

And then terror shot through Hayley as she realized why they were here. The Abbe Museum was located directly across the street from the Congregational church where the wedding ceremony was about to take place.

AJ was going to try and take out Liddy when she came out of the church right after Reverend Staples pronounced Sonny and Liddy husband and wife!

Chapter 39

Held at gunpoint, Hayley had no idea how she was going to warn anyone about AJ, who at the moment was busy texting someone on his phone. She assumed he was sending a message to Mary Beth while keeping his pistol trained on her.

"Calling Mommy for help?" Hayley asked.

The sarcasm in her voice was not lost on AJ, and he shot her an irritated look.

"I just let her know there's been a complication," he spat out. "She had no idea I stole the poison at her lab or that I was going to spike the wedding cake with it. She had nothing to do with it. She would have tried to stop me if she had."

"But if she's helping you now, then the cold hard fact is, AJ, your mother is an accessory. She's going to go to prison too."

"No one's going to prison," he said, more to himself than to Hayley.

"You can keep telling yourself that, but it will never make it true," Hayley said.

AJ cocked the gun. "Just shut up, okay? This will all be over soon."

Hayley kept her hands up and tried not to make a move that might spook him and cause AJ to pull the trigger.

She didn't want to die today.

"The only reason she found out about any of this was because there was an inventory at the lab and a security camera caught me swiping the vial. She begged her bosses to let her try and get it back before they called the police. She kept calling, but I didn't pick up, so she left a bunch of frantic voice mail messages begging me not to do anything rash. But it was too late. I had already injected the chemical into the cake."

"And poisoned the wrong person," Hayley added.

AJ stared off into space, regret written all over his face, but he quickly snapped out of it and continued his impassioned defense of his dear, adored mother. "She was devastated. She was afraid I had just ruined my life."

"And she was right."

AJ raised the gun. Hayley squeezed her eyes shut, expecting the worst. But he didn't fire a bullet at her.

After a few moments, when she popped her eyes back open, she found him standing a few feet away, scowling at her, silently suggesting with his narrowing eyes that she might want to just keep her mouth shut.

Hayley decided to comply.

"Mom was never going to allow me to go to

prison for murder so she raced up here to Bar
Harbor in order to help me cover my tracks . . ."

He seemed to half expect Hayley to comment,
but she refrained, keeping her eyes trained on the
gun pointing at her.

AJ shrugged and continued. "Which is why, when
you started sticking your nose into everybody's business and found out I had been in the Cake Walk
the day Lisa was poisoned, I called my mother . . ."

"It was Mary Beth pretending to be your mythical
sister Adele in order to give you a cover story as to
why you were there that day. You gave your mother
enough information so she could play along when
I spoke to her."

He paused, lost in thought, then, with a sad
smile, he said, "She loves me so much and would do
anything to protect me . . ."

Hayley couldn't help herself. It was safer to stay
quiet, but she was anxious to fill in some of the
blanks that had been bugging her. "She posed as a
tourist and showed up at Mona's shop to see you,
but it was your day off, so she pumped Mona for
information about Liddy, pretending to be an old
friend, hoping if she could find her, then she
would find you and could stop you from committing *another* murder."

AJ shrugged, his eyes downcast, angry with himself for dragging his dear mother into this whole
ugly mess.

"But unfortunately you were already off on another attempted killing spree, cutting Liddy's brake
line, and then after she survived that, attacking her

last night in her own front yard as she was on her way to her wedding rehearsal dinner. Despite your mother begging you to stop, you were hell-bent on getting the job done once and for all!"

Suddenly there was a loud bang as someone barreled through the back door of the Abbe Museum.

When AJ cranked his head to see who was coming, Hayley knew this was her only chance to save herself. She yelled at the top of her lungs, "Liddy Crawford, boy, am I glad to see you!"

AJ spun around, his eyes widened, distracted, waiting to see if Liddy was actually about to round the corner. Hayley seized the opportunity to grab his hand holding the gun and jerk it upward. The gun fired and a bullet shot into the ceiling, which caused some paint chips and dust to rain down upon them. Then, with her right shoulder, she shoved a startled AJ aside and made a run for it. By the time AJ managed to regain his senses and get control of his pistol again, she was gone.

Hayley ducked down among the display cases in the museum.

As Hayley had suspected, the person who had just entered through the back was not Liddy but Mary Beth. She heard her gruffly bark to her son, "Where is she?"

"I don't know. She was here a second ago . . . I don't know . . ."

"Well, let's find her!" Mary Beth screeched at her chastised boy before both of them set off to search the museum.

Hayley crawled on her hands and knees around

one display case and behind another to avoid being
seen by AJ, who was tiptoeing along on the other
side, clutching his pistol tightly, eyes scanning the
room for any sign of her.

"It's no use, Hayley! There is no way out of here!
You might as well come out of hiding!" Mary Beth
cried. Hayley knew she was wearing heels because
they clicked on the floor, alerting her to Mary Beth's
exact whereabouts so she was able to avoid bumping
right into her while down on her hands and knees
crawling around and behind the display cases. But
then the clicking stopped and there was silence. As
if she was playing a game with a child, Mary Beth
cooed in a singsong voice, "Come out, come out,
wherever you are!"

Hayley held her breath and didn't move a muscle.

"Just so you know, the front door is locked, your
only escape is out the back, and we're blocking the
only exit, so why don't you just come on out so we
can talk about this like rational adults," Mary Beth
said in a soft, reassuring tone.

A sweet tone Hayley didn't buy for a second.

Hayley knew if she gave away her position at any
time, she would be signing her own death warrant.

She had to figure another way out of this.

"I don't see her, Mom . . ."

"You go that way, I'll go this way. Don't worry,
son, we'll flush her out."

They separated, heading off in different directions.

Hayley raised her head just slightly over one of
the glass display cases to see AJ silently approaching
in her direction. Within seconds, he would be right

on top of her. That's when she noticed an old bow and arrow set out in a weapons exhibit just a few feet away from her. She quickly scrambled over, and as quietly as she could, picked them up. She hooked the arrow to the bowstring and drew it back, aiming so the tip of the arrow lined up with her target, just as she had learned in archery as a Girl Scout. Hayley fired. The arrow pierced the left side of AJ's chest. He howled in pain, grabbing at the shaft and screaming for his mother as he sank to his knees, sobbing.

Hayley heard the fast clicking of Mary Beth's heels running across the room to her injured son, and poked her head up to see her kneeling down and hugging him as he tentatively tugged at the arrow, gently trying to extract it from his chest.

Hayley grabbed what looked like a rare flute, and clambered to her feet. AJ's wailing and sobbing kept Mary Beth's attention long enough for Hayley to sneak up behind her and whack her in the back of the head with the flute. Mary Beth flopped over, landing face-first in the lap of her son, who was still moaning after finally removing the arrow and tossing it to the floor next to him.

Mary Beth was just stunned, not completely unconscious, but she was disoriented enough to allow Hayley to race out the back of the museum. She was still holding the flute in her hand; thankfully it didn't appear damaged after having been used as a blunt weapon, which was a good thing, since the artifact was purported to be over two thousand years old according to the placard she had read on her last visit to the museum. Hayley grabbed an old chair that had been left next to a woodpile out back and wedged it up underneath the knob of the back door to keep Mary Beth and AJ trapped inside, since the front door was already locked from the outside.

Hayley carefully set the flute down on the floor and ran next door to the candy store to call for help. The accident on the Trenton Bridge was still slowing down traffic, but the injured had been transported to the Bar Harbor Hospital, and Sergio was already on his way to the church when he got the call from Hayley that there was a serious situation, but luckily she had it under control. After explaining where to find AJ and Mary Beth, Hayley dashed across the street to the Congregational church to stop a wedding!

Chapter 40

As Hayley stumbled up the stone steps outside the church, her heart beating so fast she thought she might pass out, she was greeted at the door by Bruce, who looked uncomfortable and out of place in his jeans and a T-shirt, as everyone else around him was dressed to the nines for a wedding.

"Where have you been? I've been worried sick," Bruce said as he held the door open for her to come inside.

"I'll explain later. Did you tell Liddy about Sonny?"

"No, you told me not to."

"Where is she?"

"In the side room off the foyer."

Hayley started for the door that led into the side room, but Bruce stepped in front of her, blocking her path.

"Wait, before you go in there, you should know we have a problem . . ."

"Oh God, what now?"

"The groom is a no-show."

"What?"

"He's not here yet. We've been calling his phone, but it keeps going directly to voice mail."

Hayley peeked down the aisle of the church. Reverend Staples was making small talk with some of the wedding guests, who were starting to appear restless, and there was some murmuring about what was taking so long for the ceremony to start.

Hayley grabbed her phone and made a call.

"I'm telling you, he won't pick up," Bruce said.

"I'm not calling Sonny."

Sergio answered. "I'm here and reading Mary Beth and AJ their rights."

"Good, but we have another criminal to apprehend. Are Donnie and Earl still up at the accident on the Trenton Bridge?"

"Yes, they're just finishing up."

"Tell them to stay there and stop every car that tries to cross the bridge."

"Why, Hayley? What's going on?"

"I think Sonny knows what's going on. He could have spoken to Nancy Malone, and she may have told him that people have been asking questions about him, and he may have realized that the walls are starting to close in on him. He might be making a run for it before he's arrested for polygamy!"

"I'll get back to you."

Hayley clutched her phone and glanced again at Reverend Staples, who stood near the altar. After making eye contact, the reverend raised his hands in the air, a perplexed look on his face, wanting

Hayley to explain to him what was causing the delay.

She held up a finger for him to wait, and then turned back to Bruce. "You go stall the reverend a bit longer. I need to talk to Liddy."

Bruce nodded and headed down the aisle.

Hayley headed for the door to the side room and nearly tripped on her dress, which was now torn and smudged with dirt. As her hand touched the knob, she took a deep breath and then entered.

It was a circus in the side room.

Celeste, in a heightened state of panic, buzzed around like an annoying fly, cursing Sonny's tardiness, while Edie Staples, the reverend's wife, comforted Liddy, who valiantly tried to stay strong, but was on the verge of tears.

At the sight of Hayley, Liddy pushed Edie Staples away and charged forward. "Hayley, where the hell have you been? And where's Sabrina? She just went back to get my veil, and that was almost an hour ago."

"Sabrina is stuck back at your house. She has no way of getting here."

"What? Why? I need my friends for moral support. Sonny's not here yet, and I'm afraid something bad might have happened to him!"

Hayley's phone buzzed. It was a text from Sergio. *The boys have Sonny in custody. He was in the first car they stopped.*

Hayley locked eyes with Liddy. "I'm afraid Sonny is not coming."

Celeste finally focused in on the conversation. "Where is he?"

"On his way to jail."

"*What?*" Liddy cried.

"You better sit down," Hayley said solemnly.

Even Celeste was struck dumb after hearing the word "jail."

Hayley turned to Edie Staples. "Edie, would you mind giving us some privacy?"

Edie grimaced, having no intention of leaving the room and missing out on what promised to be a tornado of a scandal, but Celeste tersely signaled her to leave. Reluctantly, Edie sauntered out, angrily closing the door behind her—although Hayley strongly suspected she was just outside, her ear pressed against the door.

Liddy, almost afraid to hear the truth, bravely gathered herself, and quietly asked, "What did he do?"

Hayley then poured out everything. Sonny's two other wives. His vengeful stepson. How Lisa was never the intended victim. How it was Liddy who was the target all along. Hayley just kept talking, interrupted only twice by horrified gasps from Celeste as she listened and squeezed her daughter's hand so hard Liddy finally yelped in pain and yanked her hand free from her mother's tight grip.

When Hayley was finished, there was a long silence as both mother and daughter processed this incredibly wild and unbelievable tale.

And then, after having held back her emotions

through the entirety of Hayley's story, Liddy finally collapsed in a flood of tears, sobbing and sinking to the floor, almost disappearing in the piled-up fabric of her white wedding dress.

Celeste slumped over, a hand to her mouth, shaking her head.

Hayley rushed to Liddy and fought her way through all the white lace to get to her and give her a hug.

They remained on the floor, holding each other for the next five minutes. Celeste found a box of Kleenex in the little bathroom adjacent to the side room so Liddy could blow her nose and dab at the tears that were ruining her makeup.

There was a knock at the door.

Celeste opened it to find Reverend Staples, a somber look on his face. "I'm so sorry, Liddy, this is terrible. I always thought Sonny was such a good boy, and now to suddenly hear he's a rotten egg . . ."

Celeste looked at him, confused. "How do you know what—?"

Reverend Staples glanced at Edie, who had a guilt-ridden expression on her face. She had been undoubtedly eavesdropping through the door and reporting everything back to her husband.

"What should I tell the guests?" he asked, trying his best to be sincere and gentle.

Liddy crawled to her feet. "Tell them nothing. I'll do it."

And then, with a steely resolve, Liddy marched out of the side room past Reverend and Edie Staples and into the foyer, Hayley and Celeste close on her heels. She nodded at Bruce, who was still hopelessly in the dark about the latest developments, and stopped at the threshold to pet Poppyseed, who looked adorable with the blue pillow strapped to his back and the box containing the wedding rings on top. She paused to mentally prepare what she was going to say to the hundred wedding guests packed into the pews, impatiently waiting for the ceremony to finally begin.

Suddenly the door to the church burst open and Sabrina flew in, her hair a windblown, tousled mess, clutching the wedding veil. "Am I too late? I had to hitch a ride on the back of a Harley in order to get here!" She spotted Hayley. "Hayley, what the hell were you doing in my car with AJ? Why did the two of you ditch me like that?"

Hayley didn't answer her.

No one said anything.

Sabrina suddenly saw the sober faces all around her.

And for once, she was sensitive enough to know not to press it any further.

Something big was about to happen, so she gracefully stepped back and kept her mouth shut.

Liddy resolutely marched down the aisle. The organist looked relieved to finally see her and began pounding out the "Wedding March," but Liddy waved her arms in the air, yelling for her to stop. Startled, the organist lifted her fingers off the keys and just stared at the disheveled bride who finally reached the altar and spun around to address the crowd.

"We don't need to hear the 'Wedding March' because I'm not marrying anyone today!"

There were surprised gasps and more murmurs.

"I'm sorry to report that Sonny has been arrested, and though I don't want to go into the ugly details as to why at this moment, let's just say this whole ceremony would have been illegal anyway. There will be *no* wedding. I feel awful that you all took the time to come here. Everyone looks so nice, and thank you for going to the trouble of buying us gifts, which I will return, unless it's a fry cooker, because my old one broke the other day and I have a feeling I'm going to want to eat a lot of fried foods and everything else that's bad for me in the next few weeks, months, possibly years . . ."

There were some uncomfortable titters.

"But despite this sad turn of events, I don't want this day to be a total waste. We have a live band and lots of delicious food and a fully stocked open bar over at the reception hall, so if you'll grant me one request, I want you all to head over there right now and have a rip-roaring good time!"

No one in the church pews knew quite how to react. They just sat there, still stunned over the news that Sonny Lipton had been arrested.

Finally, Celeste paraded down the aisle to join her daughter, who was fighting hard to keep it together. "Come on, people! How about it? Let's party!"

The guests burst into applause and started to get up from their seats as Reverend Staples called out, half joking, "Wait, so I'm not going to get to marry *anyone* today?"

Everyone erupted in laughter and began filing down the aisle when, suddenly, out of the blue, Bruce rushed in from the foyer, stopping them. "Wait! Hold up, everybody! I have something to say!"

Hayley braced herself. What else could possibly happen now after everything they had already been through today?

Bruce stood there, his hands still raised to keep the crowd from leaving, as he seemed to be mustering up some courage, and then, after exhaling, he said, "I would hate for you people to leave this church without witnessing an actual wedding, since you all got dressed up in your fancy finery for the occasion so . . . How about it, Hayley?"

Hayley didn't react, because she thought she had heard wrong.

It was only after she started to see everyone around her smiling and giving her encouraging nods that she was able to process what Bruce had just said.

"Bruce, no . . ."

"You're turning down my proposal . . . in front of this big crowd . . . ?"

"No, I mean this isn't the time or place . . ."

"Why not? We have a bona fide minister who can legally marry us, a bunch of friends here to witness it, a reception hall ready and waiting for us to celebrate it—I don't see a downside," he said with a hopeful smile.

"But Liddy . . ." Hayley's voice trailed off.

"I think it's a marvelous idea! And I can say I planned your whole wedding for years to come," Liddy said.

Hayley turned to see ex-bridesmaid Mona sitting next to her husband, Dennis, who actually cleaned up nice when he wanted to, along with their six rowdy kids, who were surprisingly tame at this moment, all in the fourth row. Just behind them was Randy, who sat between his adored niece, Gemma, and nephew, Dustin, in the back of the church, making sure Poppyseed the ring bearer behaved and didn't try to shake off the pillow strapped to his back. They all smiled expectantly, all of them behind this whole wild and crazy notion one hundred percent.

Hayley turned back and simply stared at Bruce, slack-jawed and light-headed.

Bruce stepped closer to her. "Hayley Powell, will you marry me?"

Was this truly happening?

It seemed like such an impulsive and irresponsible idea.

Of course she needed time to think about this before just rushing in and just saying "I do."

There were a million reasons for her to stop this right here and right now.

And yet, in her heart, it seemed so perfect.

She loved Bruce.

And Bruce loved her.

She didn't need time to figure out if she wanted

to spend the rest of her life with him. She had made peace with that answer months ago.

Yes. Yes, she did.

And so, standing in the middle of the church aisle, with a hundred sets of eyes glued on her, waiting nervously to hear her answer, Hayley Powell bowed her head and whispered, "Yes."

There was thunderous applause from the crowd as they rushed back to their seats. Edie Staples was bawling as she got out of the way so her husband could slip past her and take his rightful place behind the church podium.

Bruce stepped forward with Hayley by his side.

"I'm going to kill you for this," Hayley muttered.

"I love you too," he said, grinning from ear to ear.

As they turned to face each other, Hayley could only think to say, "I never thought I'd get married in such an ugly dress."

The crowd laughed appreciatively.

But despite the fact that the matron of honor dress made her look like Little Bo Peep, Hayley suddenly now loved everything about it, because from this day forward there would be the cherished memory that would forever be attached to it.

"Wait!" Sabrina screeched, rushing down the aisle, Liddy's wedding veil flailing behind her. "You're going to need this."

She set the veil on top of Hayley's head and then sat down next to Liddy and Celeste, who were perched in the front row of pews.

Squeezing her hands in his, Bruce leaned forward and whispered in her ear, "I know this probably isn't the best timing, so tell me now if you want to stop . . . We don't have to rush this, but if you're ready, I'm ready . . ."

Hayley nodded. "I'm ready."

Bruce's face lit up as he turned to Reverend Staples. "Let's get this party started."

As Reverend Staples commenced with the ceremony, his voice seemed to disappear as Hayley stared at Bruce, still not quite believing this wasn't some nutty dream after eating too much pizza before bedtime, that this was reality, her reality, and that she was about to marry the man she loved. She couldn't stop beaming. And neither could her BFFs, her brother, her two kids, and a church full of warm, kindhearted friends, all of whom she dearly loved.

Except for Celeste.

She still couldn't stand Liddy's irritating and snobbish mother.

Only when Reverend Staples reached the part where he asked, "If anyone here has just cause why these two people should not be married . . ." did her mind snap back into the present.

Reverend Staples continued, "Speak now or forever hold your peace."

He waited for a moment, smiled at the happy couple, and then got right to the good part. "By the power vested in me by the state of Maine—"

"Wait! I do! I have just cause!" a man bellowed from the back of the church.

The crowd gasped and whipped around in their seats to see who was interrupting the ceremony.

Hayley's jaw dropped open.

She swooned, fearing she was on the cusp of fainting dead away.

Bruce gripped her hands even tighter to keep her steady as she stared at the intruder standing on the church threshold.

What was *he* doing here?

Island Food & Cocktails
BY HAYLEY POWELL

Let me preface by saying I am not one of those overly proud, gushing mothers who feel the need to drone on and on about their kids as if they are the most special people ever to grace God's green earth.

No, wait, I am. I am one of those mothers. I always have been, and so I can't help but take this opportunity to brag a little bit about my amazing daughter, Gemma.

Each day she inspires me with her poise, smarts, and kindness. I'd like to say she gets it from me, but honestly, after a fair assessment of both her parents, I have absolutely no idea where she gets it from. I'm just glad she is who she is.

I have to admit, when she dropped out of veterinarian school to pursue her dreams of becoming a master chef, I was skeptical. I silently bemoaned the fact that she was choosing a path with fierce competition, with long odds of actually becoming a success, with very little chance of ever being able to make a living. But as she always does, my daughter continues to surprise me. She was recently accepted into a top culinary school in New York and has been developing her talents to the point where she is now an impressive baker. I used to coach her in the kitchen on how to bake a cake, but now she's leaps and bounds ahead of me in that department, and our teacher-student roles have been officially reversed.

She's been home visiting this past month because my BFF Liddy is getting married, and due to unforeseen circumstances, the bride-to-be has hired my baby girl to design and bake her wedding cake for the big day, an awesome responsibility for a novice. But I have no doubt in my mind Gemma is up to the task. As matron of honor, I too have my own responsibilities, which is why I am filing this column a few days early so I'm free to focus on Liddy's wedding. By the time you read this, I'm sure Liddy and Sonny will be married, big smiles on their faces and lots of love in their hearts, ready to live happily ever after.

I plan on live-tweeting from the wedding reception, so be sure to follow my tweets as I describe how the guests react to Gemma's perfect wedding cake, because I'm sure, as a completely objective food critic and not the mother of the baker, that her efforts will be a resounding success.

Of course, it hasn't been an easy road to this moment for Gemma. She did have a few false starts on her journey to becoming a baker. To be honest, I wasn't the most encouraging cheerleader at first. As a single mother, after working a long day at the office, I would come home, tired and cranky, and would shoo the kids out of the kitchen, because it was faster getting the dinner on the table myself without any overeager kitchen helpers. But the older Gemma got, the more she insisted on learning how to cook, and so I finally relented.

During the first lesson, it quickly became clear she was a very precise and focused chef, measuring the exact amount of sugar or flour according to the recipe, whereas I have always just gone with my gut, a pinch here, a pinch there, whatever I was feeling in the moment. Gemma, on the other hand, treated baking like a science. And let's face it, any of you who went to school with me know I failed science. Again, not sure where she gets this from.

There were a few hiccups along the way, like the time she didn't wait for me to come home from work and attempted a batch of peanut butter cookies to surprise me. Unfortunately after putting the tray of cookies in the oven, she forgot about them while chatting on the phone with her best girlfriend, the smoke detector on the kitchen ceiling started screeching, her panicked brother called 911, the fire department showed up sirens blasting, the cookies were burnt like smoking lumps of coal, and, well, you get the picture.

But eventually, as she gained confidence and improved her skills, I felt comfortable leaving her in the kitchen on her own as long as she followed a few simple rules, like keeping a careful eye on the oven, making sure she turned it off when she was done, and never leaving the house at any point while she was baking. After she sighed and groaned, "Yes, Mother!" I finally took off the training wheels and left her in the kitchen with a box of cake mix while I went and had a cocktail with the girls at Drinks Like a Fish.

Once I was gone, she set about making her chocolate cake, stirring the batter while preheating the oven to the desired temperature. Once the cake was evenly poured into the cake tin, she turned around and opened the oven door, ready to slide the tin onto the rack, when black smoke billowed out, nearly choking her to death.

Unbeknownst to Gemma, the night before, with very little space in my refrigerator and a lot of left-over pizza from dinner, I had shoved the cardboard pizza box with the three remaining slices in the oven (as a rule, throwing out pizza is never an option). And unfortunately, with the oven temperature at 350, the box was about to burst into flames.

Using a pot holder, Gemma reached in and grabbed the end of the box that wasn't turning black and yanked it out of the oven, but instead of running and dumping it in the sink, she just flung it at the sink, almost inadvertently beaning my cat, Blueberry, who was sitting atop the kitchen counter, in the head! In recounting the horrible episode, Gemma said she never saw our obese cat move so fast. Unfortunately, the burning pizza box didn't quite make it. It bounced right off the counter and onto my new throw rug that was on the floor in front of the sink. You can probably guess what happened next. The rug promptly caught fire.

My baby girl had a major meltdown at this

point, screaming and crying, not sure what to do. Her brother, Dustin, who reads a lot of superhero comic books, bounded into the kitchen ready to save the day. He ran to the refrigerator, grabbed a plastic gallon container of milk, and started to douse the fire. Milk flew everywhere, drenching an already jittery and miserable Blueberry, as well as my dog, Leroy, who was nearby watching the disaster unfold.

About that time, Gemma finally got her wits back and scooped up the sink sprayer, using it like a fire hose. She sprayed a heavy stream of water on the flames while her brother, on the opposite side, splattered milk all over her face.

That's when I walked through the back door. Before I could even open my mouth to speak, Gemma dissolved into a flood of tears, begging for my forgiveness, ready to accept any punishment as long as she could have a second chance to bake again.

As we cleaned up the mess and Gemma finally baked her cake, I told my daughter the only one who needed to be punished was me, for putting a cardboard pizza box in a working oven and forgetting to tell anyone about it. I could have burned our whole house down!

In fact, the three of us laughed about it all night as we gorged on fresh pizza that we had delivered and Gemma's delicious chocolate cake fresh from the oven, which we ate with glasses of milk (only half full, since our milk supply was suddenly low).

We're a long way from that day, and I am happy

to report Gemma is flawless now when it comes to baking. So with her permission, today I'm going to share with you her recipe for the specially designed cake she baked for Liddy's wedding. Spoiler alert: It was a big success. Okay, truth be told, I wouldn't really know that yet, since we're still a few days out from the actual wedding, but I've always been an optimist! I have a good feeling that both Gemma's cake and Liddy's wedding will go down in Bar Harbor history as memorable in the best possible ways!

Before we get to the cake, any baker will tell you it's vitally important to have something to wash it down with, so I suggest we have one of my favorites, boozy iced coffee!

Boozy Iced Coffee

Ice
1 ounce Kahlúa
1 ounce vodka
1 ounce cream
6 ounces coffee

Fill tall glass with ice cubes, then add the rest of the ingredients. Mix well, sip, and enjoy!

Vanilla Cake with Raspberry Filling & Lemon Buttercream Frosting

Cake
1 cup softened butter
1½ cups sugar

4 large eggs, room temperature
3 cups cake flour, sifted
2 teaspoons baking powder
½ teaspoon salt
1 cup milk
2 teaspoons vanilla extract
One 10-ounce jar raspberry preserves

In a stand mixer, beat the butter on medium speed until creamy. Gradually add your sugar and vanilla extract, continuing to beat well. Add the eggs one at a time, beating in between. Combine the flour, baking powder, and salt and add to your butter mixture, alternating with your milk, mixing at low speed until blended. With a spatula, scrape down the sides and stir to make sure the batter is all combined.

Preheat oven to 350°F. Pour your batter into three greased and floured 9-inch round cake pans. Bake in oven for 25 minutes or until a toothpick inserted in the center comes out clean. Cool your cakes for 15 minutes, then remove from pans and let the cakes cool completely on wire racks.

When the cakes are cool, slice each cake horizontally so you end up with six layers. Place the first layer on your cake plate cut side up and spread two to three tablespoons of the raspberry preserves over the whole cake. Repeat this with the next layers, except leave the top one plain.

LEMON BUTTERCREAM FROSTING
1½ cups softened butter
1 tablespoon lemon zest
3 tablespoons fresh lemon juice
3 cups powdered sugar

Beat your butter, lemon zest, and lemon juice in your mixing bowl at medium speed until creamy. Gradually add the powdered sugar, beating until it is your desired consistency. Spread it on your cake and dig in!

Recipe Index

Appetizers:
  Baked Crab Poppers, 171
  Honey Garlic Chicken
    Skewers, 220
  Pimento Cheese Deviled
    Eggs, 77
  Randy's Asiago, Bacon,
    and Caramelized
    Onion Dip, 264
  Tomato, Basil, and
    Goat Cheese
    Bruschetta, 127

Baked Crab Poppers, 171
Beer Cocktail, 78
Boozy Iced Coffee, 312

Chocolate
  White Russian, 40
Citrus Wine Spritzers, 171

Cocktails:
  Beer Cocktail, 78
  Boozy Iced Coffee, 312
  Chocolate White
    Russian, 40
  Citrus Wine Spritzers,
    171
  Limoncello Prosecco
    Cocktail, 127
  Madras Cocktail, 220
  Pomegranate Cosmo,
    264

Coffee (boozy iced), 312
Cosmo, Pomegranate, 264

Grandma Dolly's Walnut-
  Filled Horns, 41

Honey Garlic
  Chicken Skewers, 220

Limoncello Prosecco
Cocktail, 127

Madras Cocktail, 220

Pastries:
Grandma Dolly's
Walnut-Filled
Horns, 41
Vanilla Cake with
Raspberry Filling &
Lemon Buttercream
Frosting, 312
Pimento Cheese
Deviled Eggs, 77

Pomegranate Cosmo, 264

Randy's Asiago, Bacon,
and Caramelized Onion
Dip, 264

Tomato, Basil, and Goat
Cheese Bruschetta, 127

Vanilla Cake with
Raspberry Filling &
Lemon Buttercream
Frosting, 312

White Russian,
Chocolate, 40

Wine Spritzers,
Citrus, 171